NOTRE DAME FOOTBALL

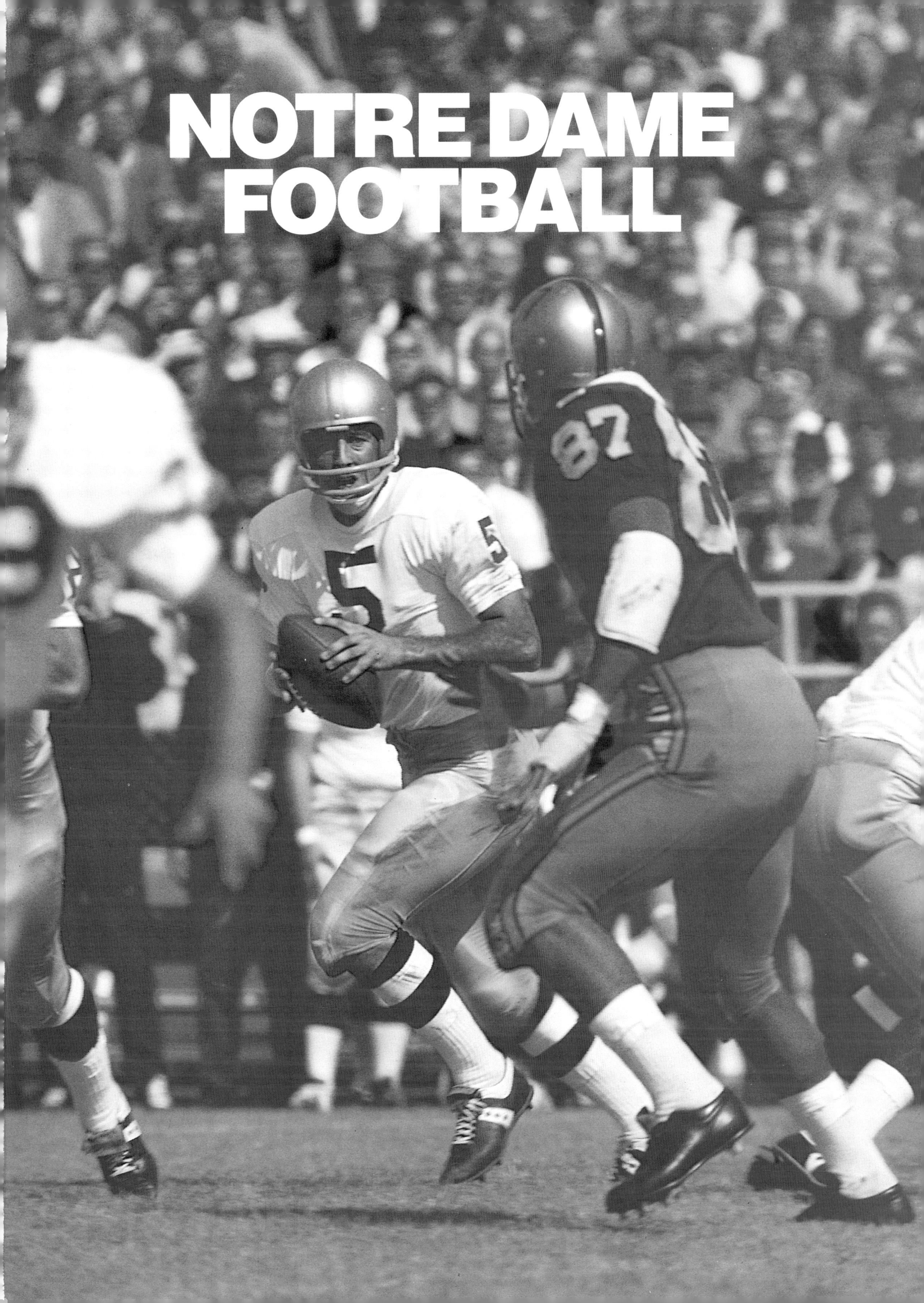

45

NOTRE DAME FOOTBALL

ROLAND LAZENBY

Bison Books

First published in 1988 by
Bison Books Ltd
176 Old Brompton Road
London SW5
England

ISBN 0 86124 458 3

Printed in Hong Kong

Page 1: *Quarterback Terry Hanratty (5) tries to avoid a Purdue attacker in 1967.*

Previous pages: *The 1986 Notre Dame team hits the field.*

Below: *Guard Marty Wendell (left) and end Bill Wightkin before the opening day of practice, 17 March 1948.*

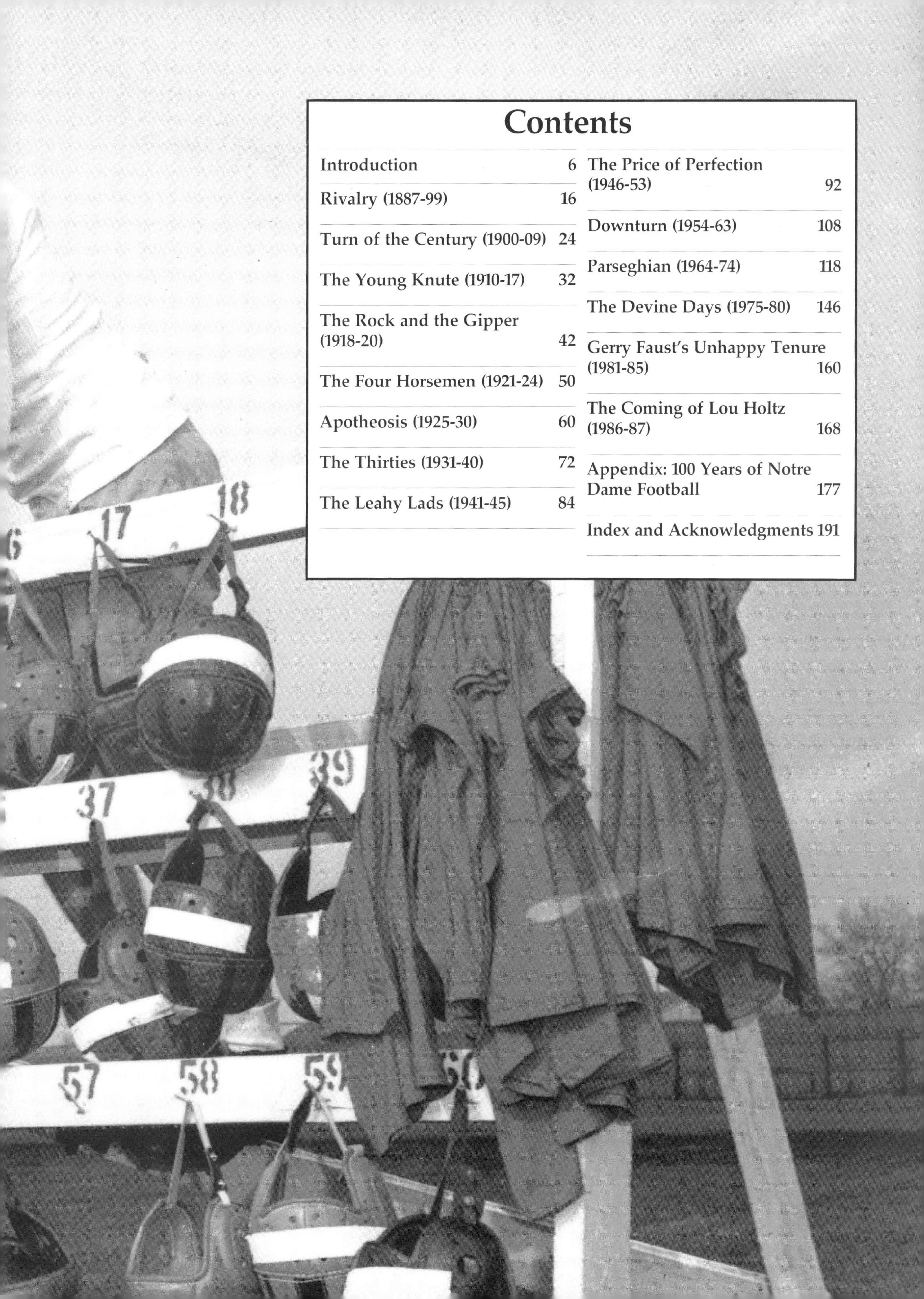

Contents

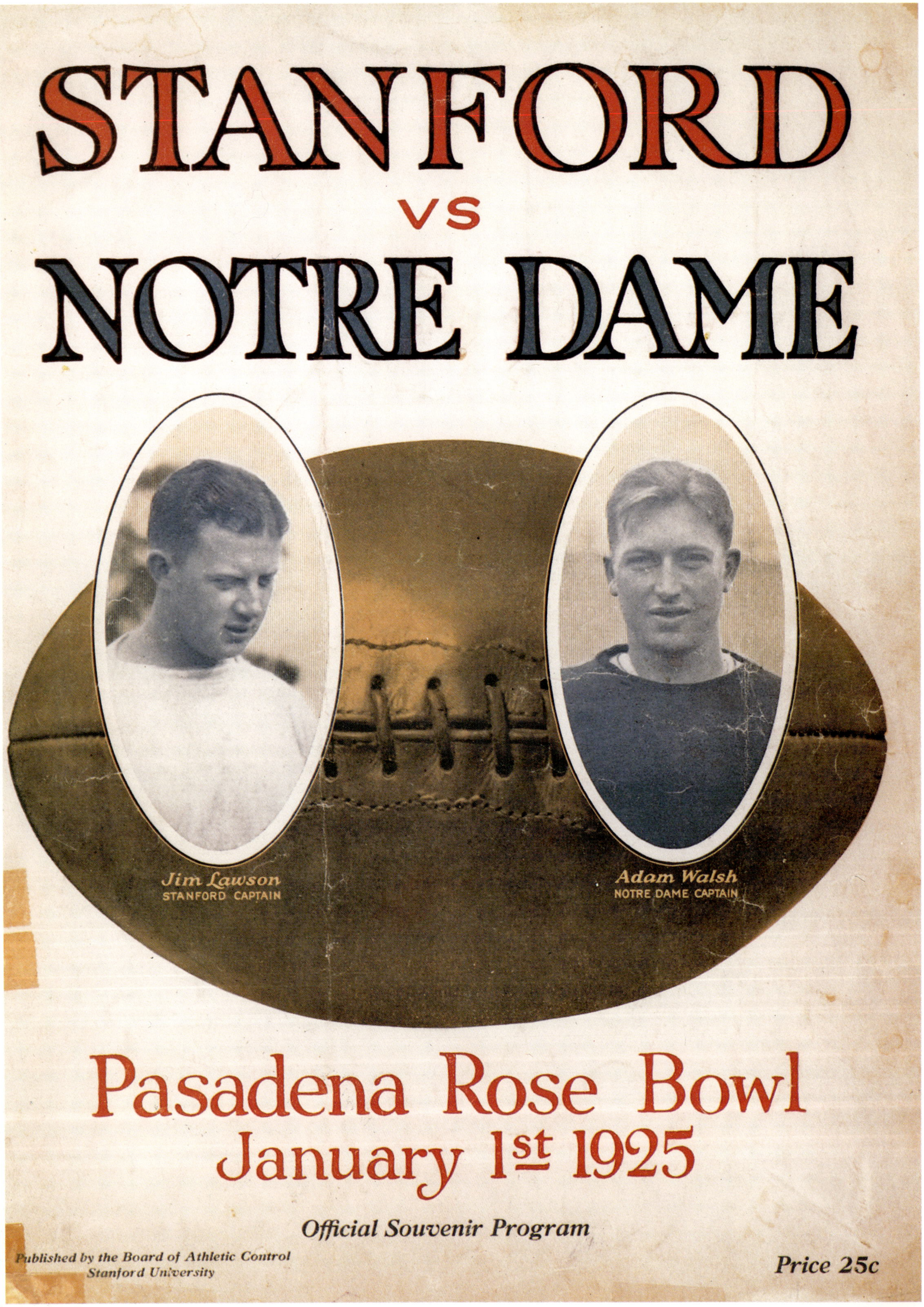
STANFORD
VS
NOTRE DAME
Jim Lawson
STANFORD CAPTAIN
Adam Walsh
NOTRE DAME CAPTAIN
Pasadena Rose Bowl
January 1st 1925
Official Souvenir Program
Published by the Board of Athletic Control
Stanford University
Price 25c

Introduction

Opposite: *The 1925 Rose Bowl program. Knute Rockne's Four Horsemen defeated Pop Warner's strong squad 27-10.*

Above: *The Reverend Edward F Sorin, who founded the University of Notre Dame in 1842. This photo was taken in 1905.*

The Rev Edward F Sorin traveled from France to the Indiana prairie in 1842 with the mission of setting up a school for frontier dwellers. Upon his arrival the young French priest and his small band of churchmen moved into an old log building, creating an outpost of enlightenment in the wilderness. They dedicated their efforts to the "Mother of God." In so doing, they set one of the cornerstones of American higher education, the founding of the University of Notre Dame.

In those days, the area that was to become South Bend held little more than a collection of fur trading outposts and Indian villages. It would be nearly half a century before the first football game would be played at the school. And after that, another quarter century would pass before Notre Dame football would create campus-wide electricity.

Notre Dame, the educational institution, thus existed long before Notre Dame, the football team, and Notre Dame was *not* the cradle of the American college game: The Ivy League filled that role. Yet Notre Dame has been just about everything else to the game. And vice versa. For the better part of the university's modern life, football has been entwined with its educational identity. As all will acknowledge, it has been a wonderfully successful mix.

To the credit of the fathers running the school, they have striven to maintain a perspective. Over the years, they haven't surrendered the University's ethics to the football program. Likewise, they haven't destroyed the football program with pettiness. Perhaps that, more than anything, is the supreme achievement of Notre Dame football. Where so many other American universities seem to have lost sight of their educational mission while pursuing a winning football team, Notre Dame's administration has endeavored to achieve a detachment from the school's athletic success.

"I'm not concerned about football," Rev Theodore M Hesburgh, Notre Dame's president for 35 years, said shortly before his retirement in 1987. "If we win, hooray! If we don't, fine." Hesburgh and his primary assistant, Rev Edmund P Joyce, who oversaw the school's athletic programs during the rise of modern sports, never for a moment forgot the importance of not allowing football to overshadow religion and education.

That doesn't mean that religion and this most powerful of football mythologies haven't had their confusions. One example of this is the 132-foot-high stone mosaic of Christ on the south side of Hesburgh Library. The figure, with hands upraised, faces Notre Dame Stadium. The placement has led to the figure's popular nickname, "Touchdown Jesus," suggesting that Christ is signaling yet another score for the Irish. Just west of the library is a bronze statue of Moses with his right hand and finger upraised as he chastises the Israelites for succumbing to idolatry. With their own idolatrous sense of humor, Notre Dame fans have dubbed the statue the "We're Number One Moses." With the same humor fans have tagged another statue on campus, that of former university president Rev William J Corby, as "Fair-Catch Corby." Indeed, Corby, posed with his arm upraised, seems to be signaling for an eternal fair catch.

Such fun aside, Notre Dame entered the second century of its football program in 1987 firmly astride its principals. "Football is bad only when it is perverted and misused," Hesburgh said. "But football can be done honestly,

Opposite left: *The Reverend Edmund P Joyce who, along with Reverend Theodore M Hesburgh, the president of Notre Dame, administered the school's sports program from 1950 to 1987.*

Opposite right: *Notre Dame cheerleader Joe Gargan helped provide cheers for old Notre Dame in the early part of the twentieth century.*

Right: *Jack Snow and John Huarte of the 1964 Fighting Irish offense pose in front of the bronze statue of "We're Number One" Moses.*

and this place has proved it. And we don't want to be third-rate in anything."

Over the decades of the twentieth century the university has offered a rich mix of tradition – religious, educational, athletic. Seldom, if ever, in American higher education has such balance met with such success. And it has bred a school spirit that would be hard to duplicate anywhere else. The Irish don't love their school because of its football. It's the other way around. But football is certainly a potent symbol of that deeper affection.

"Cheer, cheer for old Notre Dame, wake up the echoes cheering her name." That simple college ditty stirs vast emotion on home-game Saturdays in Notre Dame Stadium, driving a chorus of 59,075 voices intent on waking up echoes

8

52
KIEL
5
37

Opposite top: *Coach Frank Leahy watches from the bench on 15 November 1948. In Leahy's 11 seasons as head coach at Notre Dame (1941-43 and 1946-53), he compiled a career record of 87-11-9 which included six undefeated seasons and five national championships.*

Opposite bottom: *Coach Gerry Faust paces the sidelines. As head coach from 1981-85, Faust put together a 30-26-1 record.*

Right: *The Reverend Theodore M Hesburgh, president of Notre Dame from 1952-87, carried on the school's tradition of placing equal emphasis on education, religion and athletics.*

that since 1887 have never really been allowed to sleep.

Oh, there's been a bit of snoozing now and then, a recent example being the Gerry Faust teams of 1981-85. Yet even Faust finished his Notre Dame coaching tenure with a winning record (30-26-1 in five fretful seasons). It's just that winning isn't nearly enough in the domain of Touchdown Jesus. The aspiration must be Greatness: The Notre Dame tradition demands it. Anything less than legendary status is unacceptable.

Since it began play in 1887, Notre Dame has compiled a regular-season record of 659 wins, 201 losses and 40 ties, for a winning percentage of .754, making it the winningest team in college football history. Big chunks of that success came under Knute Rockne (a lifetime record of 105-12-5 for an .881 winning percentage, the highest ever for a college or pro coach); under Frank Leahy (a Notre Dame career record of 87-11-9); and under Ara Parseghian (95-17-4 in 11 years at Notre Dame). "I can't live up to all the expectations," Coach Lou Holtz warned after he was named to replace Faust in 1986. "I look at those records put up by Rockne, Leahy and Parseghian, and I swear to gosh it's a misprint. Nobody can win that many games." All three are, of course, Hall of Famers.

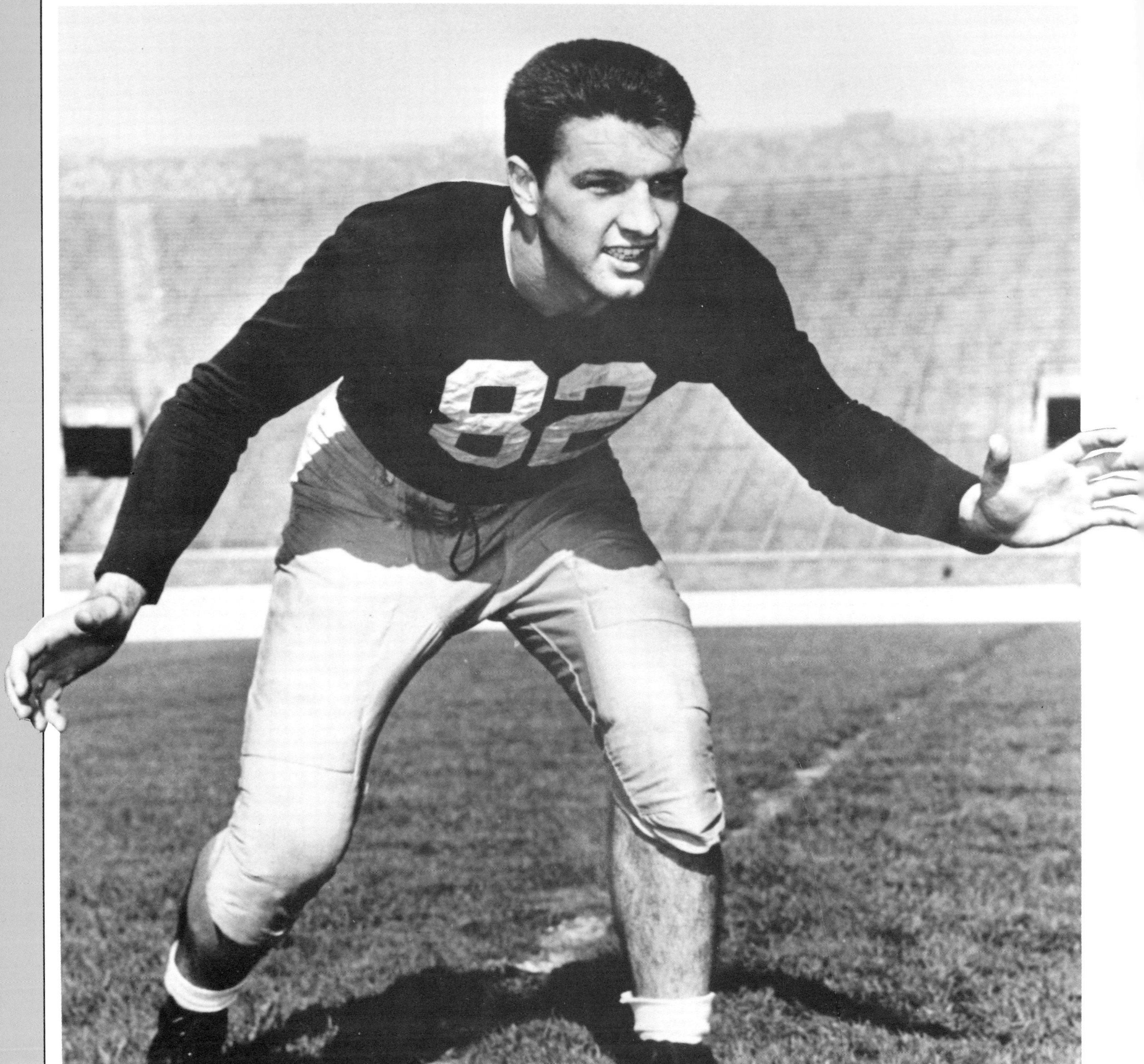

The academic record of Irish athletes compares favorably with its football success. In the 1980s Notre Dame has won five College Football Association Awards for the graduation rates of scholarship players. Of the nearly 500 scholarship athletes since 1965 who remained four years at the school, fewer than 10 have failed to graduate. All the same, it would be difficult not to categorize Notre Dame as a football factory, although not in a negative sense of the image. All factories are judged by their products, and Notre Dame has

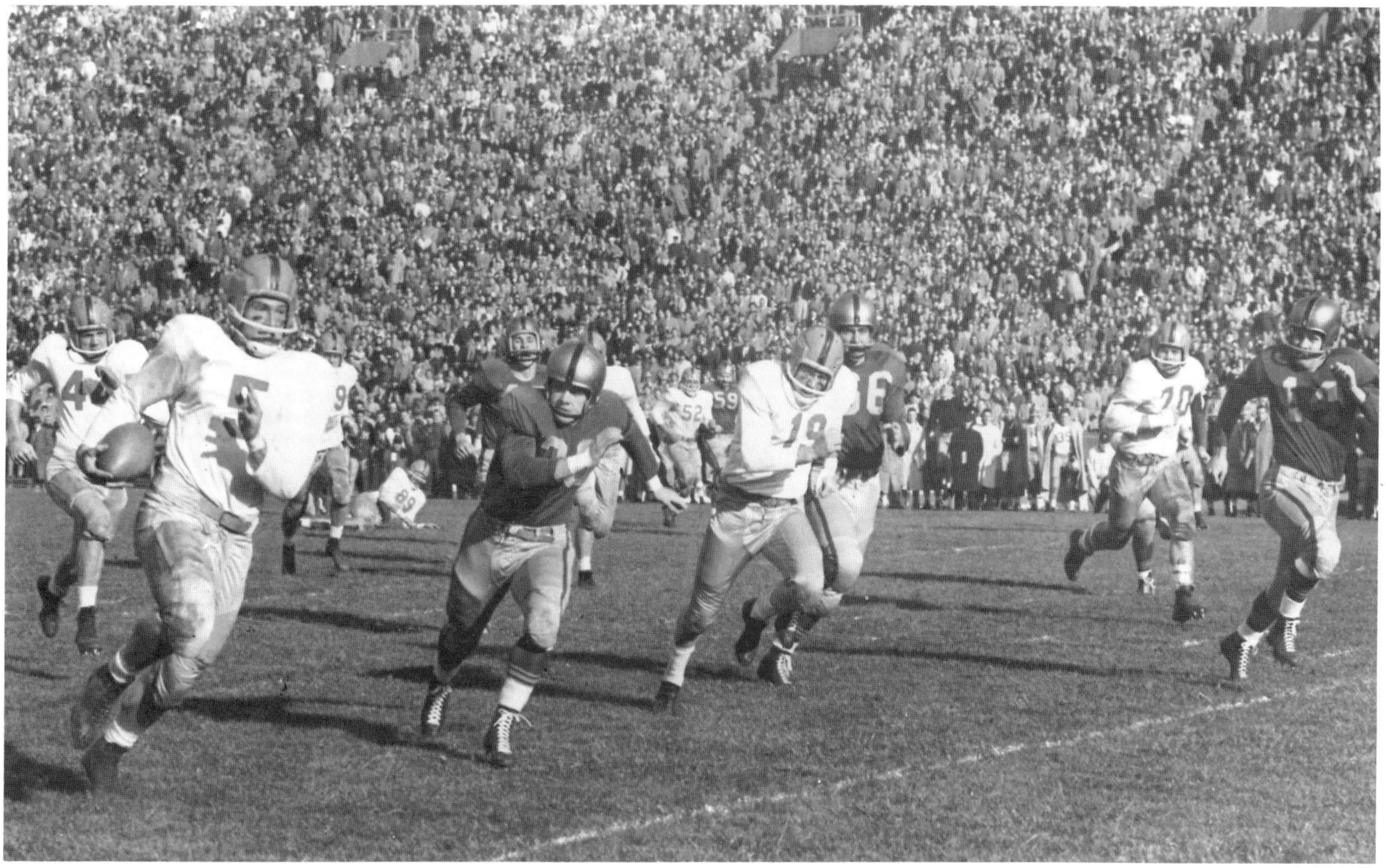

Opposite: *End Leon Hart was the Heisman Trophy winner in 1949.*

Above: *All-American Paul Hornung (5) is touchdown-bound against Pitt in this 1956 game. He won the Heisman Trophy that year.*

Left: *The legendary Knute Rockne (here shown teaching the fine art of tackling) was head coach at Notre Dame from 1918 to 1931. Considered one of the greatest coaches of all time, his career record of 105 victories, 12 defeats and five ties included five undefeated seasons.*

turned out some of the best. Consider. Seven Heisman Trophy winners – Angelo Bertelli, John Lujack, Leon Hart, John Lattner, Paul Hornung, John Huarte and Tim Brown. Two Lombardi Award (outstanding linemen) winners – Walt Patulski and Ross Browner. Three Outland Trophy (outstanding interior linemen) winners – George Connor, Bill Fischer and Ross Browner. Twenty-nine inductees into the National Football Foundation Hall of Fame, and nearly 70 consensus All-Americans. An impressive output, to say the least.

Consider, too, the long roster of Notre Dame players who have gone on to make their mark as professionals: Joe Montana, Paul Hornung, Mark Bavaro, Joe Theismann, Daryle Lamonica, Dave Casper, George Connor, Leon Hart, Wayne Millner, Rocky Bleier, John Lujack, Frank Tripucka, Alan Page, Nick Buoniconti, Dave Duerson, Eddie Anderson and numerous others.

As a team, Notre Dame has won seven Associated Press national championships, more than any other college. In fact, it is difficult to think of the years when Notre Dame has not been somebody's choice as the nation's top team. Truly, judging from the product, Notre Dame is the ultimate football factory, with the ultimate quality control.

Above: *Lou Holtz took over coaching duties in 1986.*

Top right: *Joe Montana called the signals from 1975 to 1977.*

Right: *Lineman Walt Patulski won the Lombardi Award in 1971.*

Opposite top: *Cotton Bowl action in 1978 versus the Texas Longhorns.*

Opposite left: *Ara Parseghian.*

Opposite right: *Joe Theismann was the QB from 1968 to 1970.*

J.BROWNER
89

89

7

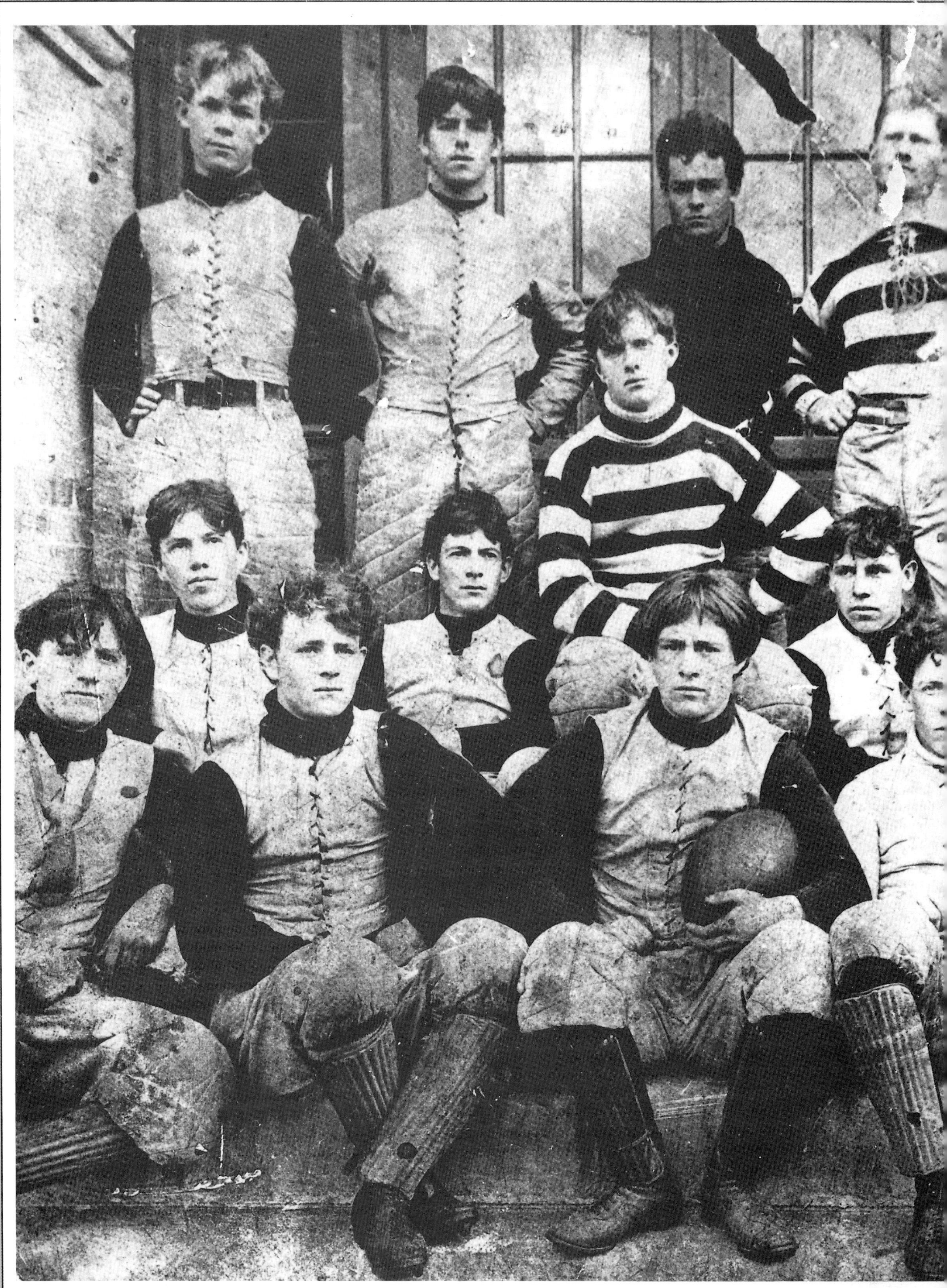

RIVALRY

1887-99

Previous pages: *The 1896 Notre Dame football team. Under player/coach Frank E Hering Notre Dame played an expanded schedule of seven games, winning four and losing three.*

Above: *This 1870 engraving shows a game of rugby at the Rugby school for boys in England. American football evolved as a combination of this sport and association football, or soccer.*

It's only fitting that Notre Dame's football history begins with the University of Michigan. Since the two schools met for Notre Dame's first game in November 1887, their football programs have struggled for the position atop the all-time standings of American college football. Certainly their athletes and coaches carry great traditions on their backs each time they take the field. You might say they play for more than the moment: They play for the ages. With 683 victories, Michigan has won more games than any other college football team. Notre Dame is second in total victories with 659, yet the Irish hold the top spot in the all-time standings by virtue of their winning percentage, .754 to the Wolverines' .742.

Against just about all of its major competitors over the decades, Notre Dame maintains a solid winning edge. (The Irish are slightly behind Penn State with a 5-6-1 record against the Nittany Lions over the years.) Only Michigan has enjoyed long-term success in meetings with Notre Dame. The Wolverines are 13-6 against college football's best team.

Michigan had been playing football for a decade or so when, in November 1887, its team leaders suggested the Wolverines travel to South Bend to give the Notre Dame boys a lesson in the game. Although the Ivy League, particularly Yale and Walter Camp, ruled over college football in the 1880s, Michigan had begun to establish its football tradition in 1887. The Wolverines fancied themselves "the champions of the West" and showed a readiness to demonstrate their prowess across the region. According to some, the Notre Dame boys were eager to try the new game and agreed to the meeting if their visitors would take time to teach them the rules and demonstrate plays before the competition began.

College football in the late 1880s was just a decade or so old and embroiled in its evolution from English rugby and soccer. Although the college game officially sets its beginning at 1869, with a contest between Princeton and Rutgers, that game for the most part was a soccer match. Football as Americans know it made its appearance in an 1875 game between Harvard and Yale, where rugby rules allowing players to run with the ball were in effect.

College football in the 1870s was played on a long, wide field (140 by 70 yards), which was unmarked save for the goal and mid-field stripes. The number of players on a side numbered 15. By the early 1880s the size of the field was decreased to 110 by 53 yards,

Left: *This 1887 woodcut by Frederic Remington, called "a tackle and a ball down," depicts a scene from an early college football game. Note the size of the football.*

Below left: *This late nineteenth-century Remington woodcut illustrates the straight arm, a dangerous maneuver characteristic of early football games.*

and the number of players was trimmed to 11 per side. To catch something of the atmosphere of those early games a modern observer need do no more than visit a Sunday afternoon rugby match on any of America's college campuses. The game's early participants liked to be known for their rakish toughness. They disdained padding as something for sissies and wore instead sweaters or canvas jerseys (and were often called canvasbacks). There was no headgear, so the players grew their hair long to pad their skulls when they smacked heads. The art of tackling was in its rudimentary stages. As a result, the games were often rough affairs of pushing and punching. Noses were broken, teeth knocked out, heads and limbs bruised – all badges of courage to be worn proudly after the game.

A Yale graduate, Walter Camp spent the 1880s overseeing the development of rules of American amateur football. By the time Notre Dame played its first game, the concept of a line of scrimmage had evolved. No longer did action begin with a rugby scrum. It had been established that each team would have three downs to gain five yards for a first down. And to help matters, the field was marked off with lines every five yards, bringing the concept of gridiron to young college football minds. By that November 1887 the scoring system allowed four points for a touchdown, five for a field goal, two for a point after and two for a safety.

The Wolverines came to South Bend on the Wednesday morning of 23 November. In a nice gesture that has somehow been lost over the decades, a committee of Notre Dame students met the Michigan players and took them on a tour of the campus. With those preliminaries concluded, these young players unceremoniously initiated college football's greatest tradition. First, for demonstration purposes, the teams were divided into two groups, mixing Notre Dame and Michigan players. After some minutes of running practice plays and demonstrating the rules, the schools broke off to their original sides and played what was termed an "inning" of ball.

Not wanting to seem ungracious guests, the Wolverines ran up a respectable 8-0 score, then retired to the dinner table, where Notre Dame's President Walsh thanked them for the demonstration. The Michigan players still had time to catch the train for Chicago, where they were scheduled to play an Ivy League alumni group the next day. That first Notre Dame team, outfitted with jackets with ND on the chest, included H B Luhn, Joe Hepburn, Hal Jewett, George Houck, Frank Fehr, Ed Hawkins, Joe Cusack, Pat Nelson, Gene Melady, Frank Springer and Ed Prudhomme.

The event was such a success that the two schools resumed it the following April in a two-game series. Again, the Wolverines traveled to South Bend, where the Notre Dame team had arranged to play the game in Green Stocking Ball Park. Reports have estimated the crowd at more than 400. What they witnessed was a display of Michigan's experience. The Wolverines won, 26-6, sowing more than a bit of irritation in the Irish soul.

The next noon, the Michigan boys came to the campus for a meal and a ride on the lake. Whatever strands of civility that held the afternoon in place were broken later that day on the football field. One of the Michigan players had been injured in the first game, and it was decided that he would trade

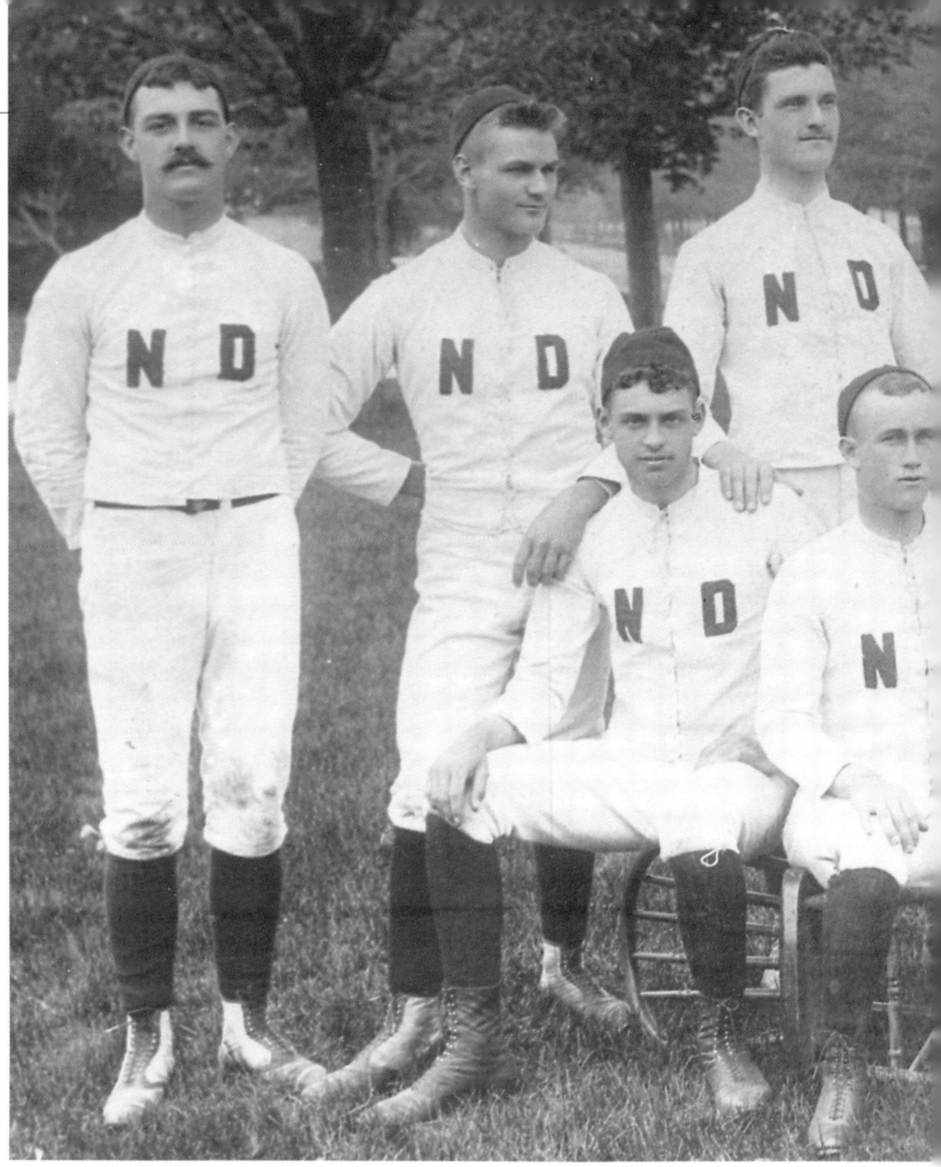

Above: *The first Notre Dame football team took on the University of Michigan Wolverines on 23 November 1887 in South Bend. The Wolverines won 8-0, and the two teams then dined together before the Wolverines departed for another game in Chicago.*

Left: *Father Thomas Walsh, the president of Notre Dame from 1881 to 1893.*

places with the referee, Edward Sprague, who would then suit up for Michigan. Fired by their humiliation the day before, the Irish lads toughened in the second game. While they hadn't yet figured the intricacies of offense (there were few in the early version of football), the Notre Dame boys put up a fine defense that April afternoon. But

Below: *Well-dressed fans at a typical college football game of the 1880s.*

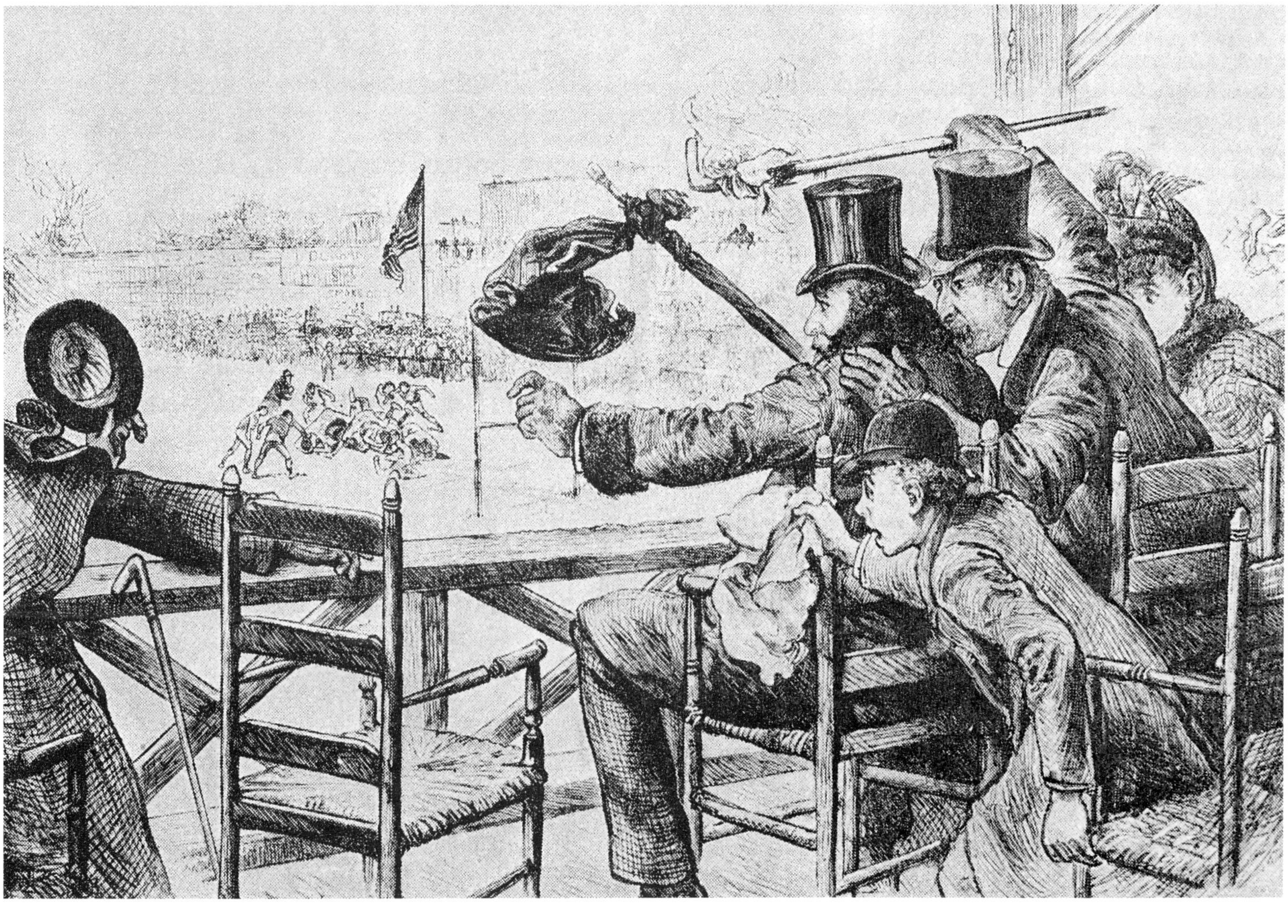

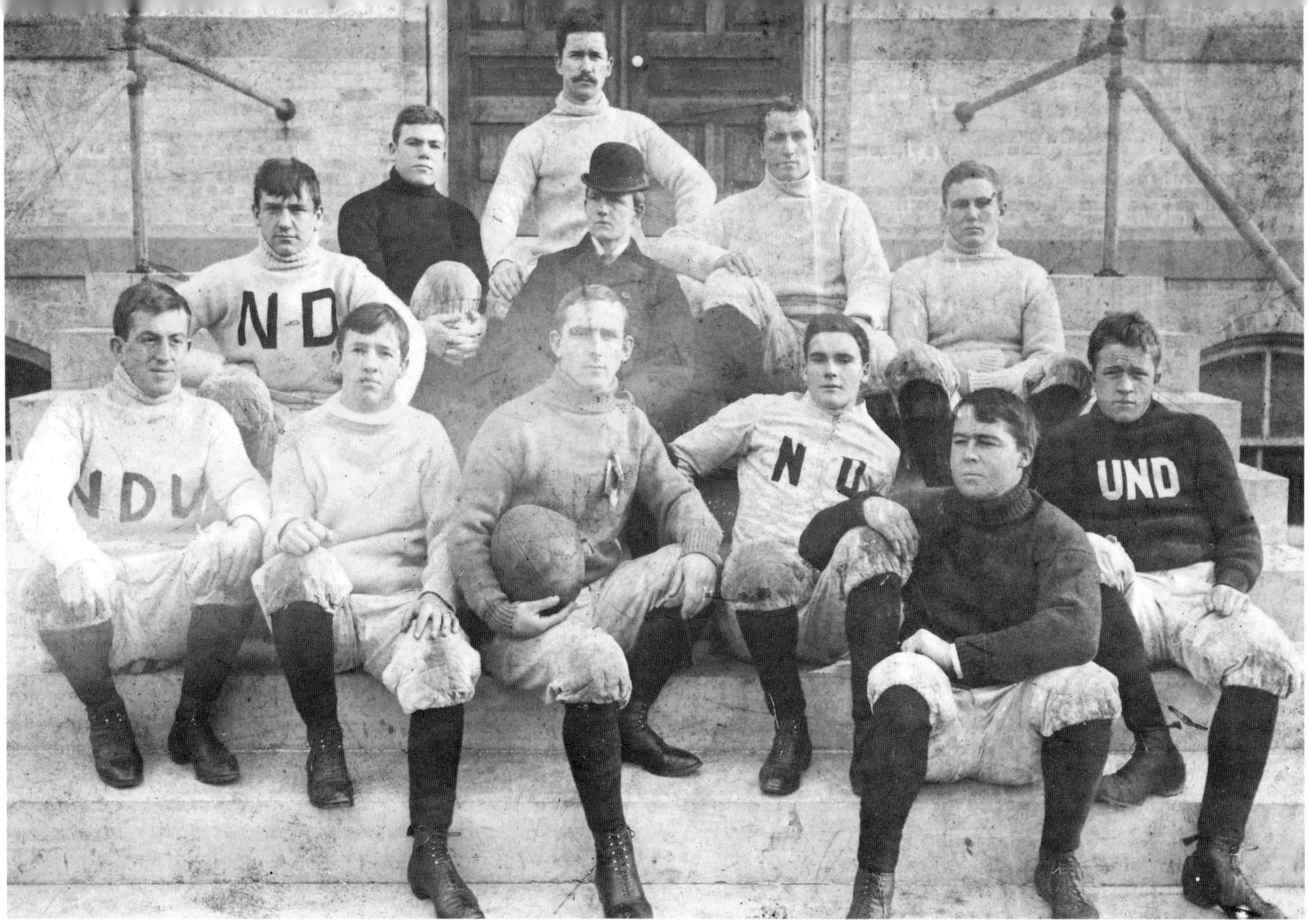

Above: *The 1893 Notre Dame football team played five games, winning four and losing only one, to the University of Chicago on New Year's Day, 1894.*

another in a string of disputes broke out with about two minutes to play. While the teams argued, Sprague snatched the ball from the referee's hands and raced for a touchdown. The Notre Dame players argued vociferously and claimed Sprague had stepped out of bounds. The referee, however, allowed the play to stand, and the Wolverines went on to a 10-4 victory.

Notre Dame next played that December, when Harvard School in Chicago came to South Bend for a game. The Irish, captained by Edward Prudhomme, won 20-0, for their first victory. That next spring, Prudhomme and his teammates sported new gold and blue uniforms with a trace of padding on the shoulders.

They had hopes of a rematch with Michigan. But the Michigan program had fallen into some disorganization, and a game couldn't be arranged, leading to Notre Dame howls that the Wolverines had backed down. Notre Dame finally arranged a match at Northwestern University in November 1889. Again Prudhomme was captain (there was no coach), and again the Irish won, 9-0.

Football was still little more than a club sport in those early years, and as such, the teams struggled as organizations. Notre Dame played no intercollegiate football in 1890-91. Then, in 1892, Captain Pat Coady helped reorganize the team with a two-game schedule, both at home. Eager for a rampage, Notre Dame indulged in a common college practice of that era and whipped up on South Bend High School, 56-0, on 19 October.

The test that season was to come several weeks later when, just before Thanksgiving, the Irish entertained Hillsdale. That game ended in a 10-10 tie. Despite the big victory over South Bend, the frustration was high for James Kivlan, a Notre Dame faculty member who took an interest in the football team. He went so far as to write Walter Camp for help in improving the team.

Still, time was the largest factor in the team's early development. The 1893 schedule was ambitious, four games from 25 October to 30 November, then a fifth game on New Year's Day 1894. Played at home, the first four brought Notre Dame a winning streak. In succession, the Irish defeated Kalamazoo 34-0 and Albion 8-6; then, despite a snow-covered field, they trounced DeLaSalle 28-0 and Hillsdale 22-10. The New Year's game at the University of Chicago brought Notre Dame's only loss, 8-0.

The taste of victory only increased Notre Dame's thirst for more, and the next season team leaders brought in a former player from Michigan, James L Morison, as the team's first coach. He quickly put together a five-game schedule. His team opened the season on 13 October with a 14-0 home win over Hillsdale. The resulting excitement

died a bit when Albion tied the Irish a week later in another home game, 6-6. Nearly a month later Notre Dame defeated Wabash 30-0, and then Rush Medical 18-6. A few days after Thanksgiving, Albion returned for a rematch and whipped Notre Dame 19-12.

After finishing 3-1-1, Morison moved on to coach Hillsdale. He was replaced by H G Hadden in 1895, and Notre Dame finished 3-1 against an interesting collection of club teams – Northwestern Law, Illinois Cycling Club, Indianapolis Artillery and Chicago Physicians and Surgeons. The artillery boys pounded the Irish 18-0.

It is fitting that the idea man for Mother's Day, Frank E Hering, was also a Notre Dame alum. Beyond that, he served as an important building stone in the foundation of the Irish football program. He had performed his undergraduate work at the University of Chicago, where he played football under the famous Amos Alonzo Stagg. Hering entered Notre Dame to study law and served as player/coach of the football team (intercollegiate rules on undergraduate eligibility had yet to be adopted). Under Hering, the schedule was expanded to seven games for 1896, all of them at home. Hering, a strong student and leader, gained almost immediate popularity, despite opening with two losses, to Chicago Physicians and Surgeons and the University of Chicago. His first win came against South Bend Commercial Athletic Club, 46-0. After a win over Albion and a loss to Purdue, Hering's edition of the Irish murdered Highland Views 82-0 and edged a semiprofessional team from Beloit, Wisconsin, 8-0 in a cold rain.

Hering brought stability to the club team by remaining three seasons as coach. Beyond that, his major accomplishment was an upgrading of the schedule. For 1897 Notre Dame finished 4-1-1 against a slate that included Michigan State, Chicago and DePauw. The season marked the scoring of Notre Dame's first field goal, a 35-yarder booted by Mike Daly against Chicago. Hering's biggest coup came in 1898, his last season, with the resumption of the Michigan rivalry, which had been on hold nine seasons since the dispute of 1888. Unfortunately, the Wolverines continued their dominance, 23-0, in Notre Dame's first game at Michigan. The 1898 schedule also included Illinois, Michigan State, Indiana and DePauw. Hering closed out his career at Notre Dame with a 60-0 win over Albion.

The schedule expanded to 10 games in 1899, as James McWeeney took over as coach. The Irish finished 6-3-1 but lost another away game to Michigan, 12-0, leaving another bitter cud to chew over the winter. Notre Dame had yet to gain a win over the Wolverines. But that and much more would come.

Above: *In 1894, Notre Dame finished 3-1-1 under new coach James L Morison.*

TURN OF THE CENTURY

1900-09

College football was a long way from being a respected sport at the outset of the twentieth century. It was a time of transient, semi-professional athletes and coaches, moving from one college team to another. Athletic clubs, which often paid players in hopes of building strong teams, had sprung up around the country, creating the first network of professionalism. Athletes often played under aliases for two or more teams at a time, suiting up for a college squad during the week and an athletic club on Sunday.

"Football today is a social obsession," remarked Shailer Matthews, dean of the Chicago Divinity School. "Football is a boy-killing, education-prostituting, gladitorial sport. It teaches virility and courage, but so does war. I do not know what should take its

Previous pages: *The 1900 Notre Dame football team.*

Bottom left: *Walter Camp, "Father of American Football."*

Left: *Fullback and team captain Louis "Red" Salmon led the Irish to their first undefeated season in 1903. He went on to coach for his alma mater.*

place, but the new game should not require the services of a physician, the maintenance of a hospital and the celebration of funerals.'' Many people agreed with him.

Pat O'Dea, an Australian who had gained fame as the ''Kangaroo Kicker'' for the University of Wisconsin, coached Notre Dame in 1900-01. His first team finished 6-3-1 but lost to Michigan again. Even worse, O'Dea's alma mater humiliated Notre Dame 54-0 in Madison. Michigan was dropped from the schedule the next season, and Notre Dame opened with a scoreless tie with the South Bend Athletic Club. But from there on the team played well, losing only to Northwestern 2-0 in a heavy rainfall. The team's big victory came over Indiana, 18-5, in the rain.

The one-eyed James F Faragher replaced O'Dea as Notre Dame coach for 1902. An Ohio native, Faragher had played football at West Virginia, Nebraska and Duquesne before coming to Notre Dame in 1900 to participate. Faragher, who had lost his eye in a football game, had played two seasons for the Irish, then became coach. He was a spirited, enthusiastic teacher of the game. His 1902 team finished 6-2-1, with a loss to Michigan and a tie with Purdue. On 15 November the Irish defeated American Medical 92-0!

Success would grow in the 1903 season, Notre Dame's first undefeated. Led by 175-pound fullback Louis ''Red'' Salmon, the Irish rang up 292 points over nine games while holding their opponents scoreless. Unfortunately, Michigan and most other state universities weren't on the schedule, which included a collection of graduate schools and club teams. The only blemish was a scoreless tie with Northwestern on 14 November.

Regardless of the schedule, the season brought the first national recognition to South Bend, as team captain Salmon was named to Walter Camp's All-America third team. In four varsity seasons (1900-03), Salmon had scored 250 points – 36 touchdowns, 60 extra points and two field goals. The scoring system was different in that early era, but Salmon's scoring mark would stand 80 years until Allen Pinkett scored 320 points in a four-year career, 1982-85.

Faragher went on to become a campus cop the next season, a post that he would hold for years, and Salmon assumed the coaching duties. His 1904 team finished 5-3, with lopsided losses to Wisconsin, Kansas and Purdue, the only major teams on the schedule. The season highlights included a 107-yard return of a fumbled punt by Frank Shaughnessy against Kansas (the field was 110 yards). ''Shag'' Shaughnessy went on to a career as a professional baseball player and executive.

In 1905 Notre Dame again whipped a series of club teams and graduate schools. The Irish rolled up 121 points against American Medical during a 25-minute first half on 28 October. After they ran the score to 142-0 eight minutes into the second half, the game was ended, which allowed the medical students to eat before catching their train to Chicago. ''The Doctors,'' needed their meal. Notre Dame, however, lost four games that year, most of them with other university teams. An offshoot of the blowout victories was a record-setting 16 touchdowns rushing by Notre Dame back Bill Downs. Six of Downs' touchdowns came against DePauw.

Above: *Frank ''Shag'' Shaughnessy played on the 1904 Notre Dame squad and went on to gain fame in professional baseball.*

While the Irish had become mired in mediocrity, college football was caught in its bad-boy image. A change for the good came in 1905 when President Theodore Roosevelt saw a photograph of a bloodied Swarthmore player being carried from the field. Outraged, he demanded that college football clean up its act or face abolition. The resulting reforms made for a better game. The evolution of football had become mired. In 1897, for example, Pop Warner had outfitted his Carlisle Indians with headgear, but the adoption of safety equipment was a gradual process over the next three decades.

The immediate result of the Roosevelt uproar was a White House conference between the President and representatives of the Ivy League's Big Three – Harvard, Princeton and Yale. From there, the football powers of the East agreed to form a new rules committee with a goal of opening up the game, taking it out of the rowdy rut it had fallen into.

Walter Camp, who had lobbied long to remove football's nastiness, said, "We have lost the Homeric thrill of human action, the zest of out-of-doors, the contest of speed, of strength, of human intelligence, of courage. Unless steps are taken to reform the sport, we shall discover that our precious football is being relegated to the ash heap of history. Brutality has no place in this sport. This is a game that must train its followers, its players and its spectators in the qualities of successful character."

The committee met in 1906 and offered several new rules, the most memorable being legalization of the forward pass. The pass had been used irregularly in games for years, and the rules members agreed it was time to make it official. They also strapped it with enough restrictions to chill its impact. First, the ball could be thrown forward only when the thrower had moved laterally five yards from the center of the line of scrimmage: Thus the field was marked off with hash lines to show the throwing zone. Once it had been touched by a receiver, an incomplete pass, like a kick, resulted in a loose ball that could be recovered by either side. If the pass went out of bounds, it was given to the defense where it went out, which gave the pass the same use as a coffin-corner punt in the modern game. The earliest passes were hurled end over end (the passer would cup a hand over the blunt nose of the ball). Downfield, the blockers would gather around the receiver to protect him from defenders while he attempted to catch the punt-like toss.

Although the pass proved its usefulness and eventually caught on at colleges across the country, it was viewed for years as a sissified thing.

The real contribution the 1906 rules committee made toward lessening the violence in football was the establishment of a 'neutral zone' on the line of scrimmage. Theretofore linemen had battered each other before the ball was snapped, which led to much fighting and slugging. But the neutral zone forbade offsides contact until the ball was put into play.

The rules committee, however, might as well have tried to stamp out the male ego as to eliminate brutal toughness from football completely. In 1908, before Harvard's legendary Percy Haughton coached his first game against Yale, he was said to have brought a bulldog into the locker room at Yale Field, where, as his players watched aghast, he strangled the animal. "There," he said after ridding his hands of the lifeless creature. "That's what I want you to do to

Opposite: *In January 1906, President Theodore Roosevelt convened a meeting of college football representatives to discuss the increasing violence in college football. The forward pass was introduced, and a neutral zone was established on the line of scrimmage, to lessen the brutality of the game. These rules would help football to evolve into the modern game we know today.*

Above: *Pop Warner, head coach of the Carlisle Indians, was the first to give his team members helmets as a safety precaution.*

those Yale bastards out there this afternoon."

In 1910 the rules were further amended to add a fourth offensive down, a factor that increased the use of the pass. (Third down quickly gained recognition as the passing down.) The new rules also disallowed linemen lining up in the backfield unless they were positioned five yards behind the line of scrimmage. This eliminated the hurtling, smashing interference that caused so many injuries.

Grudgingly, the oldtimers recognized that an offshoot of the improved forward pass was the opening up of the game, which in turn added a new defensive wrinkle. The center in the defensive line was forced to begin hanging back to defend against passing plays. The evolution of the game is no better exemplified than by the center rising from all fours to a crouch that allowed him to read offenses. It wasn't long before coaches and players identified the position as a 'roving' element in the defense: The modern linebacker had been born.

In those seasons of reform Father John Cavanaugh, Notre Dame president, kept a loving, watchful eye on the football program. Tom Barry, a Brown University alumnus and law-school graduate, served as coach for the 1906 and 1907 seasons and produced two fine teams with large lines (averaging better than 210 pounds) and swift, efficient backfields. The roster included Allan Dwan, who went on to become a movie director in Hollywood. The '06 team lost only to Indiana, and the only setback for the '07 unit was a scoreless tie with the Hoosiers, giving Indiana a temporary edge over Michigan as Notre Dame's most intense rivalry. The highlights of the '07 season included Dom Callicrate's 95-yard kickoff return against Olivet.

Victor Place, a Dartmouth product, replaced Barry as coach for 1908, and the Notre Dame success continued. The Irish solved the Indiana riddle 11-0 but lost once again to Michigan in mid-October. The Wolverines had kicked three field goals, but halfback Paul McDonald made a long run for a Notre Dame score. Then the referee ruled that he had stepped out of bounds. The Irish argued unsuccessfully, and Michigan had won yet another, 12-6.

Above: *Harvard coach Percy Haughton is said to have strangled a dog in the locker room before a Yale game to inspire blood lust in his players.*

Right: *The Reverend John W Cavanaugh, Notre Dame president from 1905 to 1919, avidly supported the school's football program.*

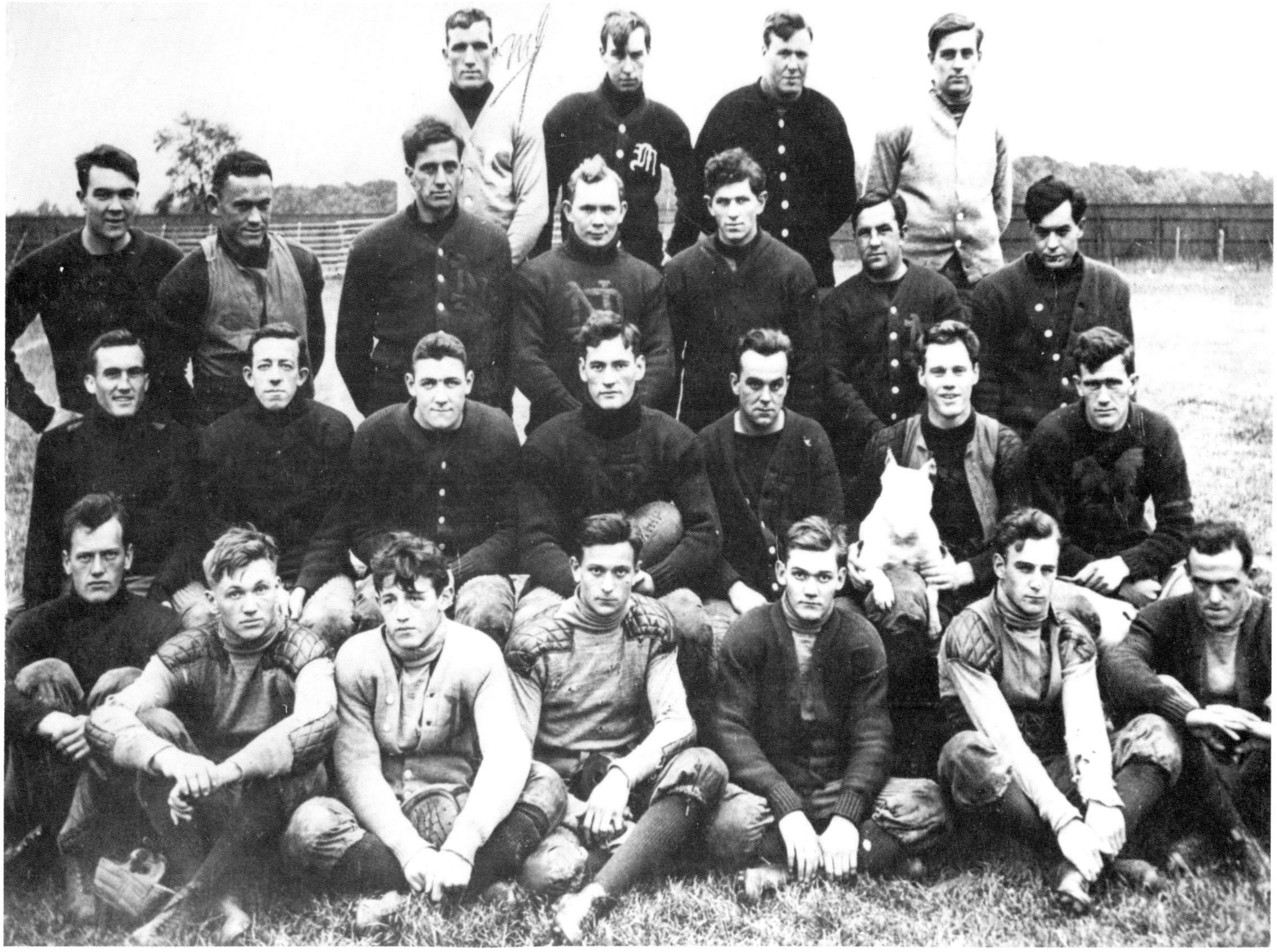

Above: *The 1909 Notre Dame team was undefeated, winning seven and tying one. The season's most exciting victory was over the Wolverines, 11-3, in Ann Arbor.*

Frank "Shorty" Longman, a University of Michigan man, moved in as Notre Dame coach for 1909 and finally ended the drought against the Wolverines. The Irish beat Michigan 11-3 in Michigan, and when they returned home elated students met them at the train and paraded them through the town. All in all, it was a banner year, as Notre Dame won the first seven games, outscoring opponents 236-14. Hopes of a perfect season died with the last game, a 25 November meeting with Marquette that ended scoreless. Still, regional newspapers bestowed the unofficial "champions of the West" distinction on the Irish. Even Walter Camp joined in the chorus, at least to the extent that he could for a little-known team out of the Midwest. He named Notre Dame halfback Harry Miller to the third team of his All-America squad. Against Olivet that season, Miller had returned a punt 95 yards, yet failed to score. He was tackled on the five-yard line.

The next season, a scrawny and unheralded freshman end, Knute Rockne, would join the team, and the football world would never be the same.

THE YOUNG KNUTE

1910-17

The legend of Knute Rockne has always loomed over American college football, even through the decades of change since his death in 1931. The son of a Norwegian carriagemaker and engineer, Rockne spent his boyhood in the Logan Square Park area of Chicago. His father had traveled to the United States for the 1893 World's Fair and had decided to stay. Rockne, his mother and three sisters immigrated a short time later. It wasn't long before the young Norwegian was plunged into the world of vacant-lot football, a world where a kid had to tape his ears to keep opponents from pulling at them. He came home so beat up after one game that his parents refused to let him play football again. Baseball would have to be his game, they said. Several days later a fight broke out at a baseball game, and another boy smashed Rockne across the nose with a bat, sending him home with a bloodied schnoz that would be misshapen the rest of his life.

Later, at Chicago's Northwest High School, he distinguished himself in track as a pole vaulter and half-miler. After high school, he had hopes of attending the University of Illinois, but family money was scarce. So Rockne took a job as a postal clerk, with the notion of saving for college. With the badgering of his sister, he put aside money, only to fall about $1000 short of his tuition. Several teammates from the Illinois Athletic Club had decided to attend Notre Dame, where costs were lower, and they influenced Rockne to do the same. He still needed prep courses to gain admittance, but after passing those the 22-year-old Rockne traveled to South Bend and began life as a freshman in Brownson Hall. His roommate was an energetic 18-year-old Wisconsin native, Gus Dorais. One of college football's great passing combinations had made its first connection.

Dorais would develop into a fine quarterback, and the 150-pound Rockne into a crafty

Previous pages: *End Knute Rockne clears the way for fullback Ray Eichenlaub versus Marquette at White Sox Park, Chicago, on Thanksgiving Day, 1912. The Irish walloped the Warriors 69-0, to break a three-year string of tie games.*

Top left: *Knute Rockne as a young man. A track star at Chicago's Northwest High School, he enrolled at Notre Dame in 1910.*

Above: *Team captain Gus Dorais takes a kick during a practice in 1912. He quarterbacked his team to a perfect season that year.*

end. But before that happened, Notre Dame's legend had to endure his time as a scrub. His under-financed education left him with one suit and two shirts. In the winter, he borrowed an old oversized coat. To earn spending money, he entered prize-fights in South Bend and found he was a winner. At one point that first year Rockne was almost expelled from school after being accused of stealing wine from a chemistry lab. Making the necessary adjustments to smooth away his rough edges, he somehow stayed in school.

He failed in his first tryout with the football team, so Rockne turned his attention back to track, where his speed convinced coach Frank Longman that the little Norwegian might make a football end after all. Meanwhile, Dorais, who had a reputation as a fine baseball pitcher, was also impressing the coach and eventually made the starting lineup.

Against a mild schedule, the 1910 Irish finished 4-1-1, with a loss to Michigan State and a tie with Marquette. Longman left after the season and was replaced by John Marks, a former halfback at Dartmouth. In two years he never lost a game as Notre Dame coach. The Irish scored 222 points in 1911 and gave up only 9, finishing 6-0-2. The record included an 80-0 win over Loyola of Chicago (Art Smith scored seven touchdowns on the day, a Notre Dame record) and scoreless ties with Pittsburgh and Marquette. Against

Top: *Knute Rockne (left) with teammates Plant and Pritchard on the Notre Dame track team in 1911.*

Above: *Notre Dame vs St Bonaventure, 1911. The 1911 team went 6-0-2, scoring 222 points against its opponents' 9.*

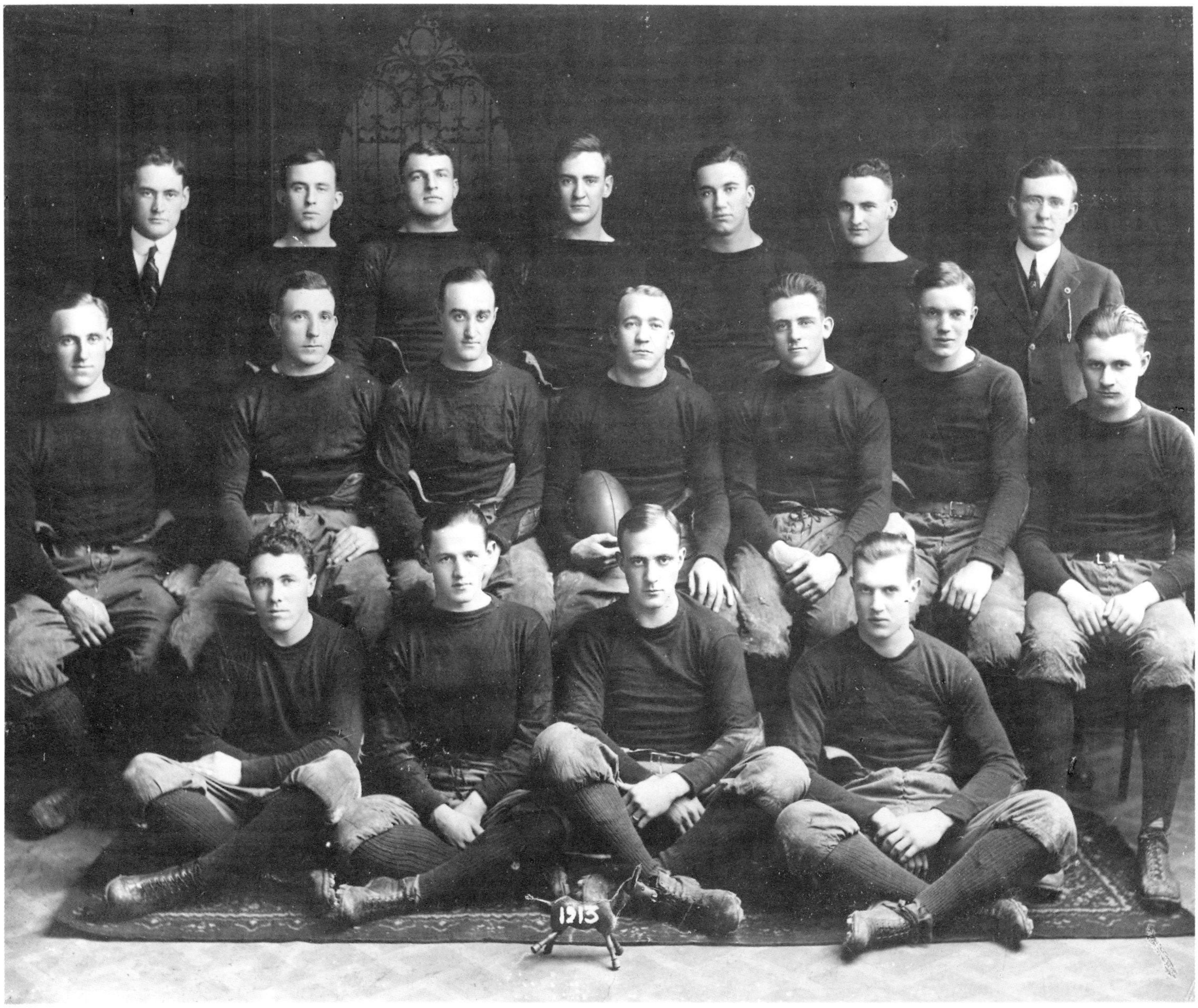

Above: *The 1913 Notre Dame football team, captained by Knute Rockne (holding football) went 7-0-0 for a second consecutive untied, unbeaten season. Rockne and teammate Gus Dorais (at Rockne's left in team photo) developed a passing combination that defeated a powerful Army team and launched Notre Dame to national fame.*

Loyola, Alfred Bergman set a school record by returning a kickoff 105 yards.

With Dorais as captain, Notre Dame opened the 1912 season with a 116-7 win over St Viator. From there a collection of clubs and small colleges fell until a midseason game at Pittsburgh in the snow, which the Irish only narrowly won, 3-0. At season's end Notre Dame finally ended a three-year streak of tie games with Marquette, slashing past the Warriors 69-0, and finished the school's first unbeaten, untied season at 7-0. Along the way, Marks had even allowed Rockne and Dorais to work on their passing act. But the real point man for the Irish was Alvin Berger, who scored 78 points in seven games, an 11.1 per game average.

Jesse Harper was named Notre Dame football coach and athletic director for the 1913 season. Harper had played under Amos Alonzo Stagg at the University of Chicago, then established himself as a coach at Alma and Wabash colleges. The big excitement of his first year came when Army needed a team to replace Yale on the schedule. To the eastern football establishment Notre Dame was a little-known team out of the Midwest. The Spalding Football Guide of 1912 reported that Notre Dame had been undefeated, so Army athletic officials reasoned that the match-up would be good competition. They first tried to lure Harper to West Point with a $600 guarantee, but the Notre Dame coach held out for $1000. Army reluctantly agreed, and the game that would launch Notre Dame's reputation was on.

Eager to prepare, Harper reportedly met many of the Irish players at the train station as they returned to school that fall. Over the summer Dorais and Rockne had taken jobs at a resort in Cedar Point, Ohio. In their off hours they turned their attention to passing. Dorais had been working to perfect a spiral with his throwing. (It has often been reported that Dorais was the innovator of the spiral, yet the technique was in use else-

Right: *Gus Dorais, one of the first college quarterbacks to effectively use the spiral, led the 35-13 upset of Army in 1913 with 14 of 17 passes completed for a total of 243 yards. End Rockne was there to receive his share of passes, as Dorais mixed passing plays with running plays to show the football world its future.*

Below: *Jesse Harper became head football coach and athletic director at Notre Dame in 1913. In five years he compiled a 34-5-1 record, setting a precedent for winning for future coaches.*

Above: *Halfback Alvin Berger was a key player on the 1912 Notre Dame team, the first undefeated, untied team in the school's history.*

where in college football: Dorais' contribution was that his use of the spiral was publicized and dramatized, thus convincing other young quarterbacks of its effectiveness.) As the story goes, that summer at Cedar Point Rockne and Dorais worked and reworked their passing combination to precision. Their effort is also credited with producing the buttonhook play, where the receiver curls back to take the pass while using his body to shield the ball from the defender.

The fall brought ample evidence of Rockne's development at Notre Dame. He had become an honors chemistry student and was selected captain of the football team. In addition, he was a flutist in the student orchestra, wrote for the student newspaper and yearbook and acted in several Notre Dame theater productions. He also held a part-time job as a research assistant to Professor Julius Nieuwland, who pioneered the development of synthetic rubber. His prowess was even exhibited in the campus

Below: *Head coach Jesse Harper (left), assistant coach Knute Rockne (center) and freshman team coach Deak Jones (right) in 1915.*

Bottom: *Captain Knute Rockne carries the ball onto the field followed by his team at the 1913 season opener against Ohio Northern on 4 October. Notre Dame won in no uncertain terms, 87-0.*

marble tournament, where he reached the finals, only to lose.

On the field, Harper's team tested its power against Midwest opponents while continuing to develop its secret weapon for the 1 November game against Army. The Irish opened with an 87-0 butchering of Ohio Northern, then followed by downing South Dakota 20-7. When Army coaches scouted the third game, against Alma on 25 October, they saw Notre Dame's power ground attack – built around 6-foot-3, 225-pound fullback Ray Eichenlaub – romp, 62-0. The Cadets were expecting more of the same the next week at West Point. The Army team enjoyed a position as one of the darlings of the New York press. And while Notre Dame was known to be a potent little team from the Midwest, neither Army officials nor the eastern football writers figured the visitors would provide much of a challenge. As a result, the game drew only 3000 spectators. The hayseed image of the Irish was reinforced when they arrived with 18 players and only 14 pairs of cleats. They had ridden the train all night and arrived tensed up, not having slept much. Despite their nervousness, the Notre Dame team showed the football world its future that day – the effectiveness of an offense balanced between running and passing.

The lesson, however, didn't begin immediately. The Irish fumbled on the opening series, and Army took over inside the Notre Dame 30. The Irish defense allowed only a yard and regained the ball. There, the Cadets immediately packed their defense in tight to stop Notre Dame's powerful linebacks. So Dorais crossed them up with an 11-yard pass to Rockne. Mixing passes with runs from Ray Eichenlaub, the Irish moved the ball across midfield. On the next play Rockne faked an injury, showing Army's

Above: *Crowds gathered by radios to hear the play-by-play of the 1913 contest between Notre Dame and Army. South Benders were jubilant at the 35-13 upset by the Irish.*

defensive back a limp, then suddenly broke open in the secondary to take in a pass from Dorais for a 40-yard touchdown.

Army then scored twice but missed an extra point and led 13-7. Notre Dame answered with a drive and a score by halfback Joe Pliska to lead 14-13, an edge they held at the half. During the break the Irish rested on their bench with blankets over their shoulders, while Army coach Charles Daly adjusted his defense to a five-man front line. The Cadets, with one of their stars, Dwight Eisenhower, injured and watching from the bench, had reason to worry. They, too, were one of the best passing teams in the East, but their air game was the stilted version used by most teams of that era, reserved mostly for desperation situations.

Unfortunately for the Cadets, their situation did become desperate in the second half, and even their passes didn't do them any good. They opened with a strong drive to the Notre Dame goal, but Dorais intercepted a pass to prevent a score. Then he turned on an air show such as football had never seen. He completed 13 second-half passes. (For the day he completed 14 of 17, for 243 yards, amazing totals for 1913, or 1989, for that matter.) The effect of Dorais's success was that he opened up the power of the ground game, and the Irish double-punched the Cadets the rest of the way, winning, 35-13.

"Notre Dame Open Play Amazes Army," The *New York Times* declared the next day. Suddenly the little team from the Midwest was no longer an unknown. In fact, Dorais, Rockne and company had sown the seed of Notre Dame's nationwide following. James A Farley, who would later become postmaster general of the United States, covered the game as a young newspaper reporter that day. He and many others like him became Notre Dame fans for life. When the team

Below: *Back Ray Eichenlaub ran the ball for the undefeated 1913 Notre Dame team.*

Bottom right: *Back Joe Pliska scored Notre Dame's second TD in the 1913 upset over Army.*

returned on Monday to South Bend they were met by a crowd with bands playing. Then came speeches, cheers, a parade and more speeches.

The Irish marched with that ebullient step over their final three opponents, Penn State, Christian Brothers of St Louis and Texas, to finish 7-0-0, the second consecutive untied, unbeaten season. Gus Dorais was named to the first team of Frank Menke's All-America squad and received the same honor from the International News Service (later to be a part of United Press International). Walter Camp selected Eichenlaub for his second team and Rockne for the third. There was little doubt that Notre Dame football had arrived at the big time.

That spring Rockne graduated magna cum laude, with honors in biology, bacteriology and chemistry, and entertained thoughts of going to medical school. He was accepted at St Louis University and planned to finance his education by coaching high school football. But when university officials learned of his plans, they turned him down. That fall of 1914 he was back at Notre Dame as a chemistry instructor, with duties as assistant football coach and head track coach. With a $2500 salary, he felt secure enough to propose marriage to Bonnie Skiles, a sweetheart he had met while working at Cedar Point.

Depleted by the graduation of Rockne and Dorais, Jess Harper's Notre Dame machine sputtered a bit in 1914 and finished 6-2. The disasters came in a return to the East, where Yale unloaded on the Irish 28-0 and Army gained revenge 20-7. Notre Dame did close the season with wins over Carlisle and Syracuse, and earlier in the year they had whipped Rose Poly 103-0.

Above: *Diehard Notre Dame fans wait for their team to return after a 28-0 loss to Yale in New Haven in 1914.*

The 1915 season held nothing but promise, although it dimmed a bit in the third game, when Notre Dame traveled to Nebraska and lost a close one 20-19. Still, Harper's third club gained another victory over Army 7-0, then bombed Creighton, Texas and Rice to finish 7-1.

They came close to perfection again in 1916 but they lost their fourth straight game at Army 30-10, to finish 8-1. Still, that finish was enough to bring Notre Dame another round of national recognition. Halfback Stan Cofall was selected to the Menke and INS All-America first teams. And Walter Camp singled out guard Charlie Bachman for his second-team All-America unit. In three varsity seasons Cofall had scored 246 points – 30 touchdowns, 60 extra points and two field goals – nearly breaking the career scoring record set by Red Salmon. Cofall did set a record for points per game during his career, 246 in 24 games, for a 10.3 average. It has stood for seven decades.

Notre Dame's 1916 freshman team included an eccentric older player, George Gipp. He had come to school with a reputation as a fine baseball player and might have remained a baseballer if assistant coach Knute Rockne hadn't caught sight of him drop kicking a football one September afternoon. He quickly made a hit in the freshman lineup and marked the season by winning a game for the freshmen with a 62-yard drop kick.

Gipp moved to the varsity for the 1917 season, Harper's last, but he wasn't *the* star. That status belonged to center Frank Rydzewski, who would make the Newspaper Enterprise Association and INS All-America first teams. (Ever the pessimist about "Western" football, Camp picked Rydzewski for his second team.) The Irish ran to a 6-1-1 record after an early tie with Wisconsin and a 7-0 loss to Nebraska. The high point of the season was a 7-2 upset of Army and its great Elmer Oliphant.

At age 33, Harper decided he'd had enough football after the 1917 season and went home to Sitka, Kansas, to manage his 20,000-acre ranch. In five years at Notre Dame he had compiled a 34-5-1 record, setting the school's dynasty in motion. He was elected to the National Football Foundation Hall of Fame in 1971.

As for Knute Rockne, he had just begun to earn his honors.

THE ROCK AND THE GIPPER

1918-20

Previous pages: *Notre Dame coach Knute Rockne (left) and George Gipp (right), the triple-threat halfback whose wildfire style captured the imaginations of football fans everywhere.*

Below: *Gipp played baseball in Michigan before accepting a baseball scholarship to Notre Dame in 1916. Here he is shown (fourth from right, standing) with the Michigan team.*

Opposite top left: *Rockne (at right) spotted Gipp practicing drop-kicks in the fall of 1916 and recruited him to the freshman football team.*

Opposite top right: *The 1918 Notre Dame team featured freshman fullback Curly Lambeau, who later founded the Green Bay Packers.*

Opposite bottom: *The 1919 Notre Dame football team was Coach Rockne's first undefeated, untied squad, with a record of 9-0.*

The George Gipp story was a sizable enough sports legend in its own right, but Hollywood made it bigger. Ronald Reagan, the young actor, played the part of George Gipp in the 1940 film *Knute Rockne, All American.* It was one of Reagan's more successful roles, and he played it right down the path to the presidency in 1980, for the Gipper in Reagan's political persona came to represent his American idealism, his projection of old-fashioned values.

Like many American heroes, the real George Gipp had his rough edges. He was a 21-year-old taxi driver in his hometown of Laurium, Michigan, in 1916, when a friend talked him into accepting a baseball scholarship to Notre Dame. He never did fulfill his baseball dream after Knute Rockne discovered him drop-kicking that football the fall of his freshman year. From a strong showing on the 1916 freshman team, Gipp graduated to a prominent role as a sophomore on the 1917 varsity. But America's involvement in World War I had brought some turmoil to Notre Dame football: Several Irish players were headed for the service. And Knute Rockne had grown weary of his role as assistant coach and planned to take the head coaching job at the University of Michigan.

Then, abruptly, a family death brought the resignation of Jesse Harper. Before leaving, Harper argued to Father John Cavanaugh, Notre Dame president, that Rockne should be the next coach. Finally, Cavanaugh agreed. The decision would pay its dividends in trophies. National championship selection fell to a variety of parties in that era, as news agencies, publications, statistics professors and foundations picked a winner at the close of each season. Six times during his coaching tenure – 1919, 1920, 1924, 1927, 1929, 1930 – Rockne's teams were somebody's choice as national champions.

Yet even Rockne wasn't an overnight sensation. The ongoing war meant that the 1918 season would be abbreviated to six games. In retrospect, it probably allowed the young coach to gain his footing. In addition to Gipp, Rockne's first team featured a strong freshman fullback, Curly Lambeau, who would leave school after one season and return home to Wisconsin to become the founder of the Green Bay Packers. In the first game, against Case Tech, Gipp showed his triple threat versatility. He rushed for 88 yards and two touchdowns, passed for 101 yards, kicked two extra points and punted eight times for 304 yards, as the Irish won 26-6. In the third game, the Irish tied the Great Lakes Naval Station Training Team 7-7. That Great Lakes team featured future

Victorious.
19 Foot-Ball Squad 19
NOTRE DAME

pro football Hall of Famers George Halas, Paddy Driscoll and Jimmy Conzelman and would go on to win the Rose Bowl at the end of the season. The next week, Rockne's team was upset by Michigan State in the rain, and after adding another victory, it closed the season with a scoreless tie against Nebraska. The 3-1-2 record was the last Rockne would see of mediocrity for a decade.

The 1919 team was flush with talent, including a number of veterans returning from the war. George Trafton, who would go on to greatness in the pros, played center. Hunk Anderson was a guard. Roger Kiley, Bernie Kirk and Eddie Anderson rotated at ends. Quarterback Pete Bahan was captain.

Gipp opened the 1919 season by rushing for 271 yards in two games. Then, in the third game, he passed for 124 yards, as Notre Dame beat a strong Nebraska team 14-9 at

Right: *Paddy Driscoll was one of the future pro football Hall of Famers who played on the Great Lakes Naval Station Training Team which met the Irish in 1918. The game ended in a tie, 7-7.*

Below and opposite: *The first All-America football player at Notre Dame, George Gipp was a strong runner, passer and kicker who led the Irish to two perfect seasons (1919 and 1920). During his best season, 1920, Gipp averaged an amazing 8.1 yards per carry, and over the course of his 27-game career he averaged an incredible 86.7 yards rushing.*

Nebraska. His best effort came toward the end of the game, when he used his skill to run out the clock and protect the lead for the tired Irish. After that came wins over Western Michigan and Indiana and a meeting with Army. Gipp rushed for 70 yards and a touchdown and threw for 115 yards against the Cadets, as Notre Dame earned its sixth victory 12-9. He intercepted two passes and threw a touchdown pass in a 13-0 win over Michigan State, and followed that by completing 11 of 15 passes for 217 yards and two touchdowns in a 33-13 pasting of Purdue. When the Irish closed out their schedule with a 14-6 win over Morningside, Knute Rockne had his first unbeaten, untied season, 9-0. Strangely, there were no national honors for Irish players afterward.

Rockne was fired with anticipation for 1920. That cooled considerably the next fall when team captain Gipp ran into academic troubles and faced suspension from school. Rockne, however, interceded with Father James Burns, the school president, who allowed Gipp to retake an oral exam in a law class. Given a second chance, Gipp passed the test. He and the Irish were now ready to soar into the realm of legend.

In Notre Dame's first two wins of 1920 Gipp rushed for 306 yards and three touchdowns. In the third win, 16-7 over Nebraska, he passed for 117 yards and gained another 70 running. Then, against Valparaiso, he passed for 102 and rushed for 120 and two touchdowns. He bettered that against Army, rushing for 150 on 20 carries and throwing for 123 and a touchdown in a 27-17 win. He also returned eight kickoffs for 157 yards and two punts for 50 yards and kicked three extra points. The New York newspapers trumpeted his play the next day, a factor that would lead to a spate of honors after the season. "It was a show of immortality," commented the *New York Journal-American*. The performance set off a wild celebration back in South Bend.

The next week against Purdue he rushed 10 times for 129 yards, including one 80-yard run to break the Boilermakers' spirits, and completed four of seven passes for another 128. Only an injury could stop him, and it did in the next game. Gipp hurt his shoulder early and watched from the bench, his shoulder taped to his body, as the Hoosiers held a 10-7 lead into the fourth quarter. With Notre Dame's unbeaten streak threatened and the crowd chanting his name, Gipp returned to the game as the Irish marched to the Indiana goal. He ran the five yards for the winning touchdown.

Unable to play the next week against Northwestern, he still dressed and put on a drop-kicking exhibition for the Northwestern crowd before the game. Late in the game, with their team losing badly, the home crowd began chanting for a token appearance by Gipp. Finally, he and Rockne complied, and he promptly threw a 50-yard touchdown pass. Before the game was over he would finish with 157 yards passing, as the Irish won 33-7 to finish their second perfect season under Rockne. On that last day Eddie Anderson had caught three touchdown passes, a Notre Dame record equalled but never bettered. After the game, Gipp remained in Evanston to give a local high school team some pointers on punting.

Apparently, he contracted strep throat over the Northwestern weekend, and the ill-

ness persisted. Gipp begged off early from the team banquet two weeks later, and the next day he was hospitalized. He was too ill to enjoy his selection to Walter Camp's All-America first team, the first Notre Dame player so honored. Camp also distinguished

Opposite: *The Gipper was immortalized by Ronald Reagan (left) in the 1940 film* Knute Rockne, All American. *Hollywood has made legendary the words supposedly spoken by the dying football star to Knute Rockne: ". . . win just one for the Gipper."*

him as the nation's outstanding player. For the season, Gipp had averaged 8.1 yards per carry, a record that still stands at Notre Dame. His record for rushing yards per game over the course of his 27-game career, 86.7, stood until Allen Pinkett bettered it (96.1) in the 1980s.

With the infection and complications of pneumonia, his condition worsened. On 14 December, at age 25, George Gipp died. Rockne had a private visit with the athlete on his deathbed. Although there were no witnesses to their conversation, its content has become legendary. "I've got to go, Rock," Gipp was supposed to have told his coach. "It's all right. I'm not afraid. Some time, Rock, when the team is up against it, when things are wrong and the breaks are beating the boys, tell them to go in there with all they've got and win just one for the Gipper. I don't know where I'll be then, Rock. But I'll know about it, and I'll be happy."

The school and the entire football world sank into mourning. From a memorial service at Sacred Heart Church in South Bend, the football team and student body carried his coffin through a snowstorm to the train station for burial in his hometown. The honors continued to mount as INS and NEA both named him first-team All-America, making him Notre Dame's first consensus selection. In 1951 Gipp was voted into the National Football Hall of Fame.

Below: *The Gipp Memorial at Notre Dame commemorates the tragic death, at age 25, of Notre Dame's most famous football star.*

THE FOUR HORSEMEN

1921-24

The Fighting Irish entered the Golden Age of Sports in 1921 with an 18-game winning streak. It would be a grand decade for the Golden Dome, with each season bringing a new harvest of victories. Even better, the era would mark the appearance of the next constellation in Notre Dame's firmament of legends: The Four Horsemen.

Despite the loss of Gipp, Rockne had plenty of veterans returning for 1921, including Roger Kiley and Eddie Anderson at ends, Buck Shaw and Hunk Anderson on the offensive line and Chet Wynne at fullback. Chet Grant had moved to the starting slot at quarterback, with Danny Coughlin and Johnny Mohardt taking over as the halfbacks.

They extended the winning streak to 20 games by blasting Kalamazoo and DePauw, then traveled to Iowa where the spell died at the hands of the Hawkeyes, 10-7: The Irish had moved into scoring position inside the 10 on four occasions but got nothing. To their credit, they regrouped quickly, beating Purdue soundly and powering past Nebraska 7-0 at Homecoming in South Bend. They followed with an impressive string of wins, blasting Indiana, then humil-

Previous pages: *The Four Horsemen of Notre Dame: (l-r) Don Miller, right halfback; Elmer Layden, fullback; Jim Crowley, left halfback; and Harry Stuhldreher, quarterback. The potent backfield combination wreaked havoc for the Irish in 1924 and became yet another Notre Dame legend.*

Above: *The 1921 Notre Dame squad included such veterans from the 1920 championship team as Roger Kiley, Eddie Anderson, Buck Shaw, Hunk Anderson, Chet Wynne, Chet Grant, Danny Coughlin and Johnny Mohardt.*

Left: *Halfback Danny Coughlin was one of the veterans who led the 1921 edition of the Fighting Irish to a 10-1 season.*

iating Army 28-0 at West Point, before finishing off Rutgers, Haskell, Marquette and Michigan State to ring up a 10-1 record.

There was no championship for his team, but Rockne was aglow and remarked privately that the 1921 bunch had developed into one of his best. Apparently the football world agreed and handed out a round of individual honors to Notre Dame players. Kiley, the repeat All-American, was the most honored, with INS and NEA selecting him first team and Camp and the *Football World* magazine according him second-team recognition. Hunk Anderson was a first-team pick by INS and the football magazine. Camp added Mohardt to his second team: The halfback had turned in one of the finest seasons in the early history of college football, completing 53 of 98 passes for 995 yards and nine touchdowns and rushing for another 781 yards. His Notre Dame passing records would stand for two decades, until Angelo Bertelli came to prominence in 1941. Mohardt also rushed for 12 touchdowns.

Eddie Anderson made INS's first team and *Football World* magazine's second. Buck Shaw was picked for the magazine's second team, and halfback Paul Castner was honored by INS. Never had Notre Dame had such a broad array of players cited. Just about all of the group would go on to make names in coaching.

Rockne's 1922 team would move on an infusion of sophomore talent, particularly the Four Horsemen, although it would be toward the end of the season before they would play together as a unit and two more seasons before they would earn their nickname. The four sophomores, of course, were Elmer Layden, who started at left half; Jim Crowley, who backed him up; Don Miller, who started at right half; and Harry Stuhldreher, a backup quarterback. None of the four weighed more than 165 pounds or was taller than 5-foot-11. And only Layden, who was reportedly timed at 10-flat in the 100-yard dash, had any speed. Yet, Rockne would mold them into a finely timed unit, capable of brilliant displays of ball handling.

In one way or another, all four had been drawn to Notre Dame by the allure of its football mystique. Miller, from Ohio, had several relatives who had played for Notre Dame, including his brother Red, a stalwart of the 1909 Irish. Stuhldreher was from that cradle of pro football, Massillon, Ohio,

Top: *Game action from the 1921 game versus the University of Iowa Hawkeyes which broke Notre Dame's 20-game winning streak. They lost 10-7.*

Above: *This 1921 game versus Rutgers ended in victory for the Irish.*

Far left: *Fullback Elmer Layden, speediest member of the famous Four Horsemen combo, was their star defenseman. His knack for intercepting passes led to two touchdowns in the 27-10 Notre Dame victory over Stanford in the 1925 Rose Bowl.*

Left: *Quarterback Harry Stuhldreher was the first of the future Four Horsemen to catch Coach Rockne's eye, in 1921. A natural leader, he had the mental acuity to read the other team's strategy, as well as being a good blocker, tackler and runner.*

where as a youngster he had seen Knute Rockne play as a part-time pro on weekends. Crowley had played his high school ball in Green Bay, Wisconsin, and had been recruited for Notre Dame by Curly Lambeau, the player/coach of the Green Bay Packers. Rockne had used an old recruiting trick to attract Layden from Davenport, Iowa: He hired Layden's high school coach, Walt Halas, brother of Chicago Staleys player/coach George Halas.

The Irish bulled past their first six opponents, struggling only with Georgia Tech, 13-3, then faced off Army in a scoreless tie. The next week, against Butler, Rockne lost Paul Castner, his triple-threat fullback, to a broken hip. The coach then shifted Layden to fullback, and the next week, against Carnegie Tech, the new backfield had its first playing time together. Notre Dame won 19-0, and Rockne had a glimpse of his squad's future. But the picture dimmed a bit the next week, with a season-ending 14-6 loss to Nebraska. Still, the Notre Dame coach was reasonably pleased. He had finished 8-1-1.

As for Castner, his hip injury had brought an early close to a brilliant career. In three years at Notre Dame he had punted 84 times, averaging just shy of 40 yards. In the 1922 season he had returned 11 kickoffs for 490 yards and two touchdowns, an incred-

Opposite top left: *End Eddie Anderson, captain of the 1921 team.*

Opposite top right: *Halfback Don Miller was the star ball carrier for the 1924 Four Horsemen backfield.*

Opposite bottom: *Guard Ed DeGree set a school record with a 74-yard punt in a game against Nebraska in 1922. That year he also made All-America.*

ible average of 44.5 yards per return and a Notre Dame record that still stands.

In fact it was a season of big returns for Notre Dame. Castner ran a kickoff back 95 yards against Kalamazoo; Don Miller did the same against St Louis, and Bill Cerney equalled their feat against DePauw. Not to be outdone, guard Ed DeGree had punted the ball 74 yards against Nebraska, a record that stood until Bill Shakespeare broke it in 1935. After the season DeGree was named to INS All-America first team, and Castner was named to Camp's third team.

Although college football coaches were becoming infatuated with the single wing formation, Rockne focused on developing the traditional T formation through a series of innovations. To make his young backs faster, he sought lighter equipment and less padding. (Not satisfied with his speed,

Stuhldreher did away with his padding altogether.) Rockne knew the secret to their success was timing, and heading into the 1923 season he drilled them repeatedly. From their T they would move into their Notre Dame shift, Stuhldreher moving just back of guard and tackle, Miller relocating at wingback, Crowley stepping in at tailback and Layden lining up behind the other tackle. From this formation the backfield dazzled opponents with slick ballhandling and lightning execution. In another innovation, Miller became the team's primary receiver, making him one of the first, if not *the* first, running back in all of football to take on the role of pass receiver.

In what was becoming characteristic Notre Dame fashion, the Irish ran past their first six opponents, scoring 195 points and allowing only 16. Then, for the second year in a row, they were upset by a larger Nebraska team. From there they finished off Butler, Carnegie Tech and St Louis to end the year 9-1. Notre Dame had lost two games in two years, both to Nebraska. They were determined not to lose to the Cornhuskers again.

Nineteen twenty four was a glorious season for college football. Red Grange at Illinois thrilled crowds in the Big Ten. Ernie Nevers worked a similar magic for Pop Warner's Stanford Indians. And by the third game of the season, the Four Horsemen, with the help of sportswriter Grantland Rice, would grab the nation's attention. Just about everywhere, throngs were packing stadiums to witness the deeds of "greats." Where the Irish had previously played before crowds of 10,000 to 20,000, that began to change with the coming of sport's newfound popularity. Americans had found a new toy, the million-dollar stadium. When Notre Dame met Army at the Polo Grounds in New York in October there were 55,000 in the stands, the largest crowd ever to witness a Notre Dame game up to that time. Over the next few years, the crowds at college games would swell from 80,000 to 120,000 for key rivalries.

The Irish worked their ballhandling magic on Army on 18 October, winning 13-7. Grantland Rice dubbed the backfield the "Four Horsemen," and the Notre Dame publicity office posed them on horseback. From then on the season moved at a gallop. Soon the offensive line – Chuck Collins, Ed Hunsinger, Rip Miller, Joe Bach, John Weibel, Noble Kizer and Adam Walsh – was tagged the "Seven Mules."

Above: *The scene at the Polo Grounds before the 1924 Notre Dame-Army game. The Irish won 13-7.*

Left: *Grantland Rice, the famed sportswriter who invented the name "the Four Horsemen."*

Below: *Game action from the 1923 meeting of Notre Dame and Army.*

Right: *Team captain Adam Walsh led the offensive line, the "Seven Mules," for the 1924 squad.*

Left: *Noble Kizer was another member of the so-called Seven Mules of 1924.*

Below: *Halfback Jim Crowley leaves his opponents in the dust and heads downfield. One of the Four Horsemen of 1924, Crowley was an agile runner and a nimble wit. In his three varsity years, he carried the ball for a total of 1932 yards.*

The next week they beat a good Princeton team 12-0 before another Eastern crowd of 40,000, then subdued Georgia Tech and Wisconsin before another meeting with Nebraska. This time, the Cornhuskers came to South Bend, and the Irish took their revenge 34-6. A highlight of the rout was when Stuhldreher connected with Crowley on a 75-yard scoring pass. The next week brought a brief letdown against Northwestern before 45,000 at Soldier Field in Chicago, but Notre Dame still survived, 13-6. With a late win over Carnegie Tech, they stood 9-0 and earned an invitation to meet Nevers and Stanford in the Rose Bowl on New Year's Day 1925, the only bowl in college football at the time. Warner, purveyor of the single-wing, unbalanced line, was eager to test his Indians against Rockne and Notre Dame.

Miller, who had been an INS first-team All-American for 1923, didn't repeat in 1924, despite rushing for a team-leading 763 yards and making another 297 yards in receptions. But the other members of the backfield took up where he left off. Stuhldreher was a first-team consensus pick of *Liberty* magazine, INS, NEA, Walter Camp, the All-America Board and *Football World*. Crowley made four first teams and Camp's second. Layden made three first teams, including INS. Adam Walsh, the center of the Seven Mules and team captain, was named to the NEA and INS second teams and Camp's third.

With his flair for theatrics and surprise, Rockne started his second team in the Rose Bowl in Pasadena. Warner and Stanford responded to that by driving for a field goal and a 3-0 lead on their first possession. The Indians would dominate the statistics the rest of the way, but the luck of the Irish brought them all of the big plays. In the second quarter Notre Dame worked a 46-yard drive, and Layden scored on a 3-yard dive. When Crowley's kick failed, the Irish led 6-3. Minutes later, Layden intercepted a Nevers pass and returned it 78 yards for a 13-3 Notre Dame advantage.

Rockne's defense turned up another score in the third quarter, when Ed Hunsinger picked up a fumbled punt and ran 20 yards for the touchdown. Finally, Stanford drove and scored with a minute left in the third quarter, closing the gap to 20-10. Stanford pushed right back down to the Notre Dame goal line early in the fourth, but the Irish held Nevers on downs. "It was one of the greatest plays in football history," Rockne later said of the fourth down when Nevers was stopped inches short.

Top: *A view of the crowd at the 1925 Rose Bowl in Pasadena.*

Above: *Harry Stuhldreher leaps to intercept a Stanford pass during the 1925 Rose Bowl. The Irish pulled out all the stops to beat the Indians 27-10.*

The Indians were driving again late in the fourth period, when Layden intercepted another Nevers pass and returned it 70 yards to extend the lead to 27-10, the final margin. "It was true we got the breaks," Rockne told reporters afterward, "but we would have won anyway. It is one thing to get the breaks and another to take advantage of them."

The Indians had amassed 17 first downs to Notre Dame's 7. They had run up 316 yards in total offense to 186 for Notre Dame. But the Irish had intercepted five passes and returned them for 139 yards. Rockne later declared that the Four Horsemen and Seven Mules were his all-time favorite team. Across the football world, thousands of fans were making the same declaration.

APOTHEOSIS

1925-30

Previous pages: *Notre Dame kicks off before a full house in Baltimore at the 1929 Navy game. The Irish won 14-7.*

Above: *Notre Dame vs Army, 1925. The Cadets surprised the Irish with a 27-0 victory before a crowd of 65,000 at Yankee Stadium.*

Right: *Rockne had much rebuilding to do with the departure of the Four Horsemen and the Seven Mules. Yet the 1925 team turned in a decent 7-2-1 record.*

The magic figures of Knute Rockne's 1924 squad were graduated, taking with them Notre Dame's depth and experience. Gone were the Four Horsemen. Gone were the Seven Mules. Gone were the top dozen substitutes. In came a set of new faces – Christie Flanagan at left half; Red Edwards at quarterback, backed up by little Art Parisien; Tom Hearden at right half; Rex Enright at fullback.

Just like the typical Irish team, the 1925 edition opened with a storm, blowing past the early patsies on the schedule – Baylor, Lombard and Beloit. The difference came against Army in the fourth game, before a crowd of 65,000 at Yankee Stadium: The Cadets took the wind out of Notre Dame 27-0. The Irish regrouped from there, beating Minnesota and Georgia Tech before settling for a scoreless tie with Penn State. After victories over Carnegie Tech and Northwestern, they ended the season with another loss to Nebraska 17-0. Their record, 7-2-1, wasn't bad for a rebuilt team.

Still, the players thought Rockne had acted strangely, and the sports world was stunned to learn in December that he had signed a contract package to coach at Columbia University and to work as a chemist for Union Carbide. The furor died down when Notre Dame officials reminded their coach

Above: *Notre Dame halfback Ray "Bucky" Dahman collars Northwestern's Moon Baker during the first half of the 1926 game played in Evanston, Illinois.*

Above: *Center Art Boeringer was All-America in 1926.*

that he still had eight years remaining on his contract at South Bend, a contract that forbade him leaving without a written release.

Embarrassed, Rockne swore his allegiance to the alma mater and attributed his decision to leave to tiredness. Despite the embarrassment, he mustered the energy to prepare the Irish for another season. It was a grand one. In 1926 they ripped Beloit (as Vince McNaily returned two kickoffs for touchdowns), Minnesota and Penn State in quick succession, then ran aground briefly against Northwestern. But little Art Parisien came off the bench to throw a touchdown pass for a 6-0 win to keep the streak going. They belted Georgia Tech and Indiana before their rematch with Army in Yankee Stadium. There, a crowd of 65,000 watched Notre Dame avenge the 1925 humiliation 7-0. After a Homecoming victory over Drake in the snow, Rockne was feeling confident. His team was 8-0 and scheduled to play little-regarded Carnegie Tech in Pennsylvania the next weekend. Rather than make the trip with his team, he decided to scout the Army-Navy game in Chicago.

The Irish were shut out that afternoon 19-0, bringing a shock to Rockne and the sports world. He later apologized to his team for his lack of judgment. At 8-1, Notre Dame traveled the next week to Los Angeles to play Southern California. A late score by USC gave the Trojans a 12-7 lead, bringing Rockne to call once again on little Art Parisien, the 5-foot-7 reserve quarterback. He responded by passing the Irish downfield to the game-winning touchdown, 13-12.

The 9-1 finish was followed by All-American honors for center Art Boeringer, who was named to the first teams of the Associated Press, NEA, INS, *Colliers* magazine and the All-America Board. Halfback Christie Flanagan was picked for the All-America Board's second team.

Rockne used the summer of 1927 to catch up on his rest. That fall a veteran team returned, led by Christie Flanagan in the backfield and John Smith on the line. The Irish tuned up on Coe and Detroit in early October, then hit the stretch of their schedule and ran through Navy, Indiana and Georgia Tech. In an early November snowstorm at South Bend, Minnesota shocked them with a 7-7 tie. Army, with a veteran team led by Red Cagle and Moe Daly, followed that with an 18-0 whipping in Yankee Stadium before 65,000 witnesses. After blowing out Drake (little-used sophomore substitute Jack Elder returned an interception 90 yards for a score in that game) the Irish met Southern Cal at Soldier Field and attracted an astounding crowd of 120,000 (the paid attendance was only 95,000). Notre Dame held a 7-6 lead late in the game when Charlie Riley fumbled a punt out of his own end zone. When the referees decided the play was a touchback instead of a score for the Trojans, a fight broke out. The decision, however, stood. Notre Dame won its seventh game to finish 7-1-1.

Somehow *The Football Thesaurus,* a popu-

Left: *Quarterback Charlie Riley lent his superior running and accurate punting and passing to the 1927 team.*

Left: *The referee prepares to flip the coin before the Notre Dame-USC game on 26 November 1927. John "Clipper" Smith, Notre Dame captain, is at left, and USC captain Morley Drury is at right. The Irish went on to win a 13-12 squeaker.*

Below: *Members of the 1928 Irish offense: (l-r) Tim Moynihan, Jack Chevigny, Frank Carideo, Butch Niemiec and Fred Collins.*

lar publication of the period, decided the Irish should be national champions. Christie Flanagan was named to the United Press and NEA All-America first teams. Smith was named to six All-America first teams, and tackle John Poliskey was named a second team selection by a newspaper group.

The 1927 season was followed by Rockne's worst record. When his 1928 squad sank to the lowest his program had been in a decade, he played his desperation card, the George Gipp request. The Irish had opened the season with a win over Loyola of New Orleans, then had promptly suffered an upset by Wisconsin, 22-6. They whipped Navy the next week at Soldier Field but were shut out by Georgia Tech on the road on 20 October. After wins over Drake and Penn State, the Irish were 4-2 and facing Army. Army was undefeated at 6-0, the powerhouse of the East that year, and again led by Red Cagle, who had destroyed Notre Dame the year before. Accounts vary as to when and how Rockne made his "Win One For The Gipper" speech. Some say he made it before the game, some say at halftime with the game scoreless. What seems certain is that Rockne related his deathbed talk with Gipp and told his players of the request: "Someday, Rock, when things on the field are going against us, tell the boys . . . ." Various witnesses said that players and coaches openly wept.

Another certain part of the record is that

Left: *Game action from the 1928 Notre Dame-Penn State game played in Philadelphia. The Irish eleven took home a 9-0 victory.*

Opposite bottom: *The Notre Dame defense gives a Navy rusher a hard time in the first period of the 1927 Notre Dame-Navy game in Baltimore. The Irish sank the Midshipmen 19-0.*

Notre Dame played an inspired second half that November afternoon, despite giving up a third period touchdown by Army's Cagle to fall behind 6-0. The Irish battled back with two scores to win 12-6. Running back Jack Chevigny scored first from one yard out and reportedly told his teammates, "That's one for the Gipper." The clinching score came when reserve Johnny O'Brien, inserted for one play, caught a 32-yard touchdown pass from halfback Butch Niemiec, bringing a round of celebration on the Irish sidelines (O'Brien would be known forever as "One-play O'Brien"). Cagle, however, returned the ensuing kickoff 55 yards, and Army immediately threatened. Moments later, when Cagle was removed from the game due to exhaustion (he had played the entire afternoon), Army could drive no deeper than the Notre Dame one, where time expired. "Gipp's Ghost Beats Army," The *New York Daily News* declared on its front page the next day. Perhaps never in the history of sport has an event soared so rapidly into the realm of legend.

But from that grand moment Irish fortunes again plummeted, as Carnegie Tech humiliated them at South Bend the next week 27-7, Notre Dame's first home loss since 1905. Southern Cal added to their woes a week later, dousing them 27-14, as Notre Dame finished with a 5-4 record, Rockne's worst. The lone consolation of the season was the naming of tackle Fred Miller to the INS All-America first team. Lost in the disappointing close was the fact that Christie Flanagan was graduated after averaging 6.4 yards per carry over his career.

If Rockne seemed down for the 1928 season, things seemed even worse for the 1929 campaign, for college football's coaching celebrity was struck with painful, life-threatening phlebitis. But as Rockne had done in the past, he rallied, using the worst circumstances as the very material to motivate his men. The magic of 1929 was that he was able to sustain that motivation over the course of the season. Confined to a wheel chair and limited in his travel, Rockne spent much of the season bedridden. Much of the credit belongs with Tom Lieb, an assistant coach who had played as a lineman for Rockne in the early 20s. The Irish also were

Right: *Butch Niemiec drops back to make a pass in the 1928 Notre Dame-Army game. Rockne gave his famous "win one for the Gipper" speech before the game.*

Top right: *Jack Chevigny carries the ball during the 1928 Notre Dame-Army game. Chevigny's first touchdown was for the Gipper; ND won 12-6.*

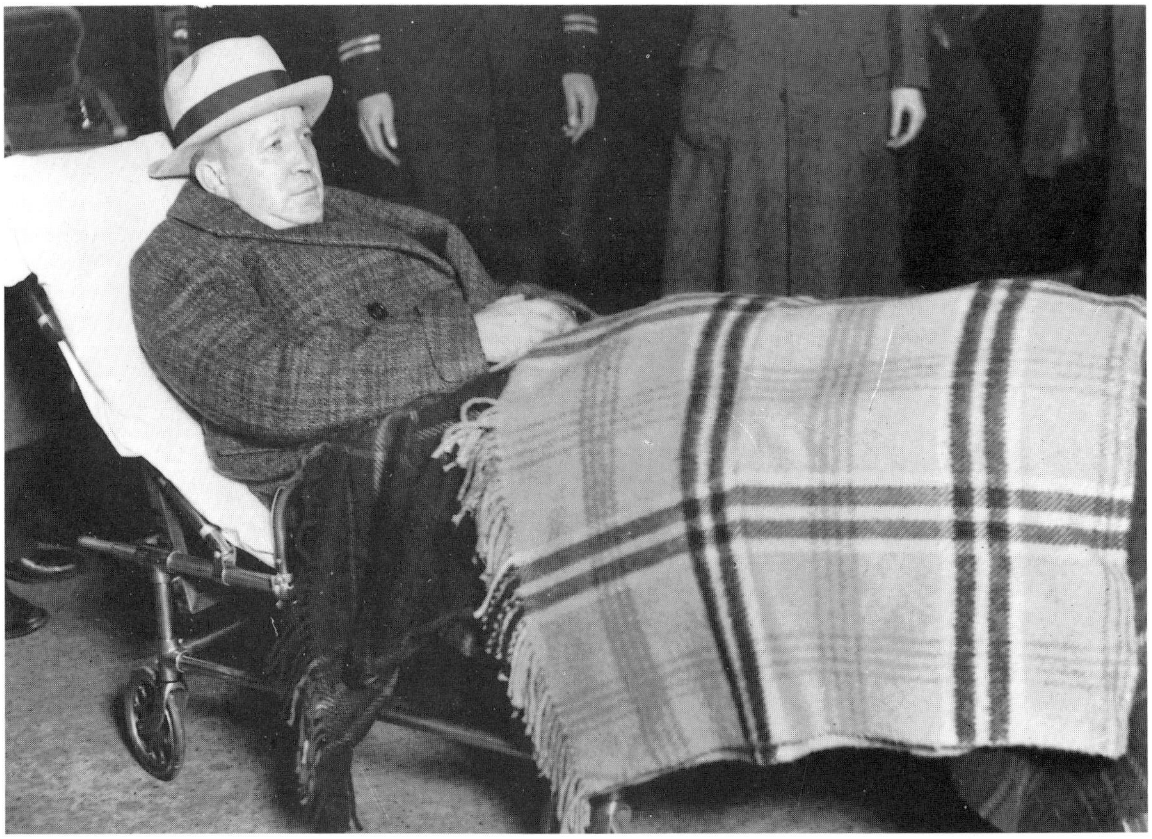

Left: *An ailing Knute Rockne watches the 1929 Notre Dame-USC game from a wheelchair. The Irish were tied with the Trojans at halftime 6-6, but a visit to Soldier Field by the Rock gave the team new spirit and they returned to win the game 13-12.*

Below: *Tackle Fred Miller was named first team All-American in 1928.*

helped by an immensely talented group of rising juniors, including Frank Carideo at quarterback, Moon Mullins at fullback, Marty Brill at right half, Tom Conley at right end. Another junior, tackle Frank Leahy, played as a substitute but would later emerge as one of Notre Dame's finest sons.

Unlike most seasons, this one began with no easy tune-up games. And because Notre Dame Stadium was under construction, the Irish played no home games. Jack Elder, a senior, had developed into a classy sprinter and needed all of his speed to dispatch Indiana 14-0 in the opener. He scored both touchdowns, setting a big-play tone for a big-play season. The poignant scene of the year came in an away game the next week against Navy in Baltimore. There, the players filed past a phone booth before the game, each to have a word with Rockne back home. With that inspiration, they toughed out a 14-7 win. After that Wisconsin fell 19-0 before a crowd of 90,000 at Soldier Field, and the Irish squeezed past Carnegie Tech 7-0 in a road game. They followed that with a convincing 26-6 win over Georgia Tech, also on the road.

After dismissing Drake 19-7, they faced Southern Cal before 112,000 at Soldier Field. As usual, the two teams burned a barn or two. USC scored first on a long pass play, then Elder answered with a long pass for Notre Dame to tie it at 6. A halftime visit by Rockne in his wheelchair has been cited as

Above: *Notre Dame has possession of the ball in this scene from the 1929 game versus Drake University. ND won 19-7.*

the turning point for Notre Dame. They drove for a score, and Carideo kicked the extra point for a 13-6 lead. Then the Irish had their enthusiasm cooled with a 92-yard touchdown run by USC halfback Russ Saunders. When the Trojans missed the extra point, Notre Dame held on for a 13-12 win. They also beat Northwestern on the road to head into the season-ending Army game at Yankee Stadium with an 8-0 record.

Nearly 80,000 fought off the 8-degree weather to watch the two teams slip and slide on the frozen field. The signal event of the game was another big play by Jack Elder. As Army was driving to score in the second period, he intercepted a Red Cagle pass and returned it 90 yards for a touchdown. The 7-0 lead was all Notre Dame needed as the weather lined up with their defense.

A round of publications and foundations and systems awarded the Irish the national championship after the season. Carideo and guard Jack Cannon were consensus choices as first-team All-Americans. Tackle Ted Twomey was cited as second-team material by two other groups. On the season, Carideo had intercepted five passes and returned them 151 yards. He was also well on his way as Notre Dame's career punt-return leader. Against Georgia Tech alone, he had returned five punts for 110 yards.

The national championship was met by other good news heading into the 1930 season. Rockne had regained his health, and the stadium he had wanted so badly had been completed. Although Elder, the big-play man, had been graduated, Notre Dame's talented underclassmen returned as veterans. Then, just before the season began, starting tackle Frank Leahy was lost with a knee injury.

In the first game in new Notre Dame Stadium Carideo started things off right against Southern Methodist, returning one punt 45 yards for a touchdown and passing for another, as the Irish won 20-14. The next week they dedicated the stadium with a crowd of 40,000, special ceremonies and a 26-2 demolition of Navy in which Joe Savoldi scored three touchdowns. While the home fire was still hot, they burned Carnegie Tech 21-6, then took their act on the road to beat Pitt 35-19. Returning home the next week, they blanked Indiana 27-0 and followed that by drilling Penn 60-20 at Franklin Field in Philadelphia. Marty Brill, a transfer from Penn, marked the day with three long touchdown runs.

The controversy of the year arose before the next game when news broke that fullback Joe Savoldi had separated from his young wife, leading to his being expelled from school. Savoldi went on to play professional football, join the pro wrestling circuit and become a hero in World War II.

Even without him the Irish smashed their way to another national championship, first with easy wins over Drake and Northwest-

Left: *The Irish in action against Penn State on 8 November 1930. This second-quarter play resulted in a 60-yard run and a touchdown for Notre Dame. Penn was overwhelmed 60-20.*

Below: *Senior Jack Elder's powerful sprinting helped Notre Dame to an undefeated season in 1929.*

Above: *Quarterback Frank Carideo was a consensus All-American in 1929 and 1930. He led Notre Dame to undefeated seasons both years.*

ern, then with another squeaker over Army in the rain and sleet of Soldier Field before a crowd of 110,000. Notre Dame scored when Marchy Schwartz, the left half, ran 54 yards for a touchdown and a 7-0 lead. Minutes later, the Cadets blocked a Carideo punt and recovered the ball in the end zone. The Irish responded by blocking Army's extra point kick. The Cadets couldn't recoup in time, and the Irish had a 7-6 win.

They closed out the season on the road at undefeated Southern Cal. Expecting a tough game, the Irish turned it into a 27-0 rout to claim their second national championship.

Again Carideo was everybody's consensus as a first-team All-American. Schwartz was also named to five first teams. A host of Notre Dame players – Marty Brill, guard Bert Metzger, end Tom Conley, tackle Al Culver, even Savoldi – received All-America second-team mention. Metzger was named to the AP and UPI first teams.

It had been a happy season for Rockne, perhaps the happiest of his life. On 31 March he boarded Transcontinental-Western Flight 599 from Kansas City to Los Angeles, heading for the West Coast to make an instructional film on football. Not long after becoming airborne the plane encountered a storm and crashed in a wheat field just outside Bazaar, Kansas. All on board were killed.

"We owe him more than he could know," humorist Will Rogers eulogized from Los Angeles. "His last football game was played in Los Angeles last December, and it kept us from contracting the worst case of swelled head the world has ever known. He cured us in a business-like fashion when Notre Dame licked Southern California. If Rock's boys hadn't won that game we would have thought every man east of the Mississippi was anemic."

"He was the best after-dinner speaker we had," Rogers added. "I would have hated to have to follow him. He told me many stories in my dressing room. I got 'em for nothing and then retold 'em and collected. If there was anybody I owed royalties to it was Rock."

For Notre Dame, April was a cruel month. Its first day brought Rockne's body on the train into Chicago, where 10,000 or more came to Dearborn Station in mourning. Four days later, with 1400 squeezed into Sacred Heart Church and a throng listening at the loudspeakers outside, the Notre Dame community held services for Rockne. Six of his players – Carideo, Brill, Conley, Schwartz, Mullins and Tommy Yarr – carried his casket to Highland Cemetery. The proceedings were broadcast over national radio.

In his statement Father Hugh O'Donnell, university president, said: "Nothing has ever happened at Notre Dame that has so shocked the faculty and student body. Everybody was proud of him. Everybody admired him. More than that, we loved him . . . He was a great personality, with attributes of genius. His loss in many ways is irreparable."

Top: *The wreckage of the tragic plane crash in Kansas in which Knute Rockne lost his life on 31 March 1931.*

Above: *The crowd outside Sacred Heart Church in Chicago during Knute Rockne's funeral on 5 April 1931.*

Left: *The great Rockne as he is remembered. A popular personality and an electrifying coach whose style led his teams to dominate the college football world in the 1920s, Rockne was revered by students, alumni and "subway alumni" alike.*

THE THIRTIES

1931-40

Previous pages: *Coach Hunk Anderson (center) watches his team hold the Kansas Jayhawkers to a scoreless tie in the first game of the 1933 season, played in South Bend.*

Above: *The unenviable task of taking over coaching duties for the late Knute Rockne fell to Hunk Anderson, who had played for Rockne from 1918 to 1921. Winning seasons in 1931 and 1932 yielded to a shocking 3-5-1 record in 1933 which cost him his job.*

The task of following Knute Rockne fell to his assistant, Heartly "Hunk" Anderson, the All-American guard who played for Rock from 1918-21. He had worked into college coaching part-time while playing professional ball for the Chicago Bears. He then became head coach at St Louis University for two seasons, 1927-28, before returning to the Alma Mater as Rockne's assistant for the 1929 season. If the challenge of replacing Rockne seemed difficult to Anderson, Father Charles O'Donnell, the university president, made it even more so in announcing Anderson's promotion to the team at the opening of spring practice. "There will never be a head coach but Rockne at Notre Dame," Father O'Donnell told the players. "Anderson will be in charge, but he will be the senior coach, and Jack Chevigny the junior coach. Rockne cannot be displaced as head coach. The eyes of the football world are on Notre Dame. It wants to know what Notre Dame will do without Rockne. You will answer. So carry on."

Carry on they did – at least as well as possible under the circumstances. To give Anderson administrative support, Notre Dame officials brought back former coach Jesse Harper from his ranch in Kansas to serve as athletic director. But within three seasons the demanding Notre Dame alumni would call for Anderson's removal. Considering the weight of the job, he would fill in admirably, but again, Notre Dame football, particularly the 1930s version, dealt not in what was admirable, only in what was great.

The 1931 team jelled around senior center and captain Tommy Yarr, a future All-American. The other veterans on the line included Ed Kosky, Al Culver and Joe Kurth. Marchy Schwartz, who had averaged an incredible 7.5 yards per carry while rushing for 927 yards in 1930, returned at left half.

They whipped Indiana on the road 25-0 for their first win, then saw their streak die in the rain with a scoreless tie with Northwestern before 65,000 at Soldier Field. From there, good things resumed with successive wins over Drake, Pitt, Carnegie Tech, Penn and Navy. Going into their 21 November home game with Southern Cal, they were 6-0-1 and favored. The Trojans attracted the first capacity crowd (50,731) in the short history of Notre Dame Stadium. They watched the Irish control for three quarters, mounting a 14-0 lead well into the third quarter. USC scored but muffed the conversion, to pull to 14-6 about halfway through the final period. They held Notre Dame on downs, regained the ball and drove for the score to pull within one at 14-13. Again Notre Dame couldn't get a first down, and the capacity crowd sat silent and stunned as the Trojans completed a long pass to set up the winning field goal as time expired. That loss was followed by a season-ending defeat at the hands of Army in Yankee Stadium. Coming out of the Rockne tragedy, Anderson's first team had finished 6-2-1, fine for most American colleges but the kind of record that brought nothing but grumbles from the alumni.

Schwartz, who had averaged 4.7 yards per carry over the season, was again a consensus All-American. Joe Kurth made four first teams, including United Press. Karr made three first teams, including the Associated Press. Guard Nordy Hoffmann also made the AP first team.

In 1932 Kurth led a returning group of veterans that included fullback George Melinkovich, quarterback Chuck Jask which and end Ed Kosky. They outscored their first three opponents – Haskell, Drake and Carnegie Tech – 177-0 before being upset by coach Jock Sutherland's Pitt Panthers in a

Left: *(L-r) Jesse Harper, coach Hunk Anderson, assistant coach Jack Chevigny and team captain Tommy Yarr in 1931.*

Above: *Action from the 1931 meeting of Notre Dame and Navy on 14 November. The Fighting Irish were victorious.*

Below: *The scene at Soldier Field during a rainsoaked game between Notre Dame and Northwestern in 1931.*

Left: *Steve Banas of the Fighting Irish carries the ball for a nine-yard gain in the first quarter of the 1932 game versus Carnegie Tech played in South Bend. Notre Dame won 42-0.*

Opposite top: *Team captains Hugh Devore (right) of Notre Dame and Jablowski (left) of Army shake hands before the 1933 game.*

Opposite bottom: *The opening kickoff at the 1933 Notre Dame-Army game at Yankee Stadium. A crowd of 80,000 saw the Irish come from behind in the fourth quarter for a 13-12 victory.*

Below: *Tackle Ed "Moose" Krause was on the 1932 squad that finished 7-2, losing only to Pitt and USC.*

road game 12-0. The Irish rebounded with wins over Kansas, Northwestern, Navy and Army before losing yet another season-ending game to Southern Cal 13-0, to finish 7-2. (With the victory, the Trojans extended their winning streak to 19 games.) Kurth, a 6-foot-2, 204-pound tackle, was an easy consensus All-American, with Melinkovich, tackle Moose Krause and Kosky receiving mention on several second teams.

While Anderson hadn't won championships in his two seasons, he had at least established a sense of status quo. Yet all of that fell apart with remarkable rapidity in 1933. The Irish opened the season with a scoreless tie with Kansas, then righted their floundering ship by whipping Indiana, only to stumble into the worst losing streak in school history. First was a 7-0 upset by Carnegie Tech on the road. Then Pitt humiliated them 14-0 in Notre Dame Stadium, followed by a loss to Navy and, the last straw, in-state rival Purdue winning at Notre Dame Stadium 19-0, leaving the Irish scoreless at home in three games. They beat Northwestern on the road 7-0, but then got shut out at home again by Southern Cal 19-0, leaving them 2-5-1 going into their final game with Army at Yankee Stadium. Although it wasn't announced, the season had already cost Anderson his job. Elmer Layden, the fullback of the Four Horsemen and successful coach at Duquesne, came to New York to discuss the coaching vacancy with Notre Dame officials the weekend of the Army game.

The Irish appeared headed for a final insult when the Cadets took a 12-0 lead in the third quarter. Nothing was mentioned about the Gipper, but he probably smiled again somewhere as, toward the end of the period, the Notre Dame offense found its footing to begin a drive culminating in a scoring dive by senior fullback Nick Lukats early in the fourth period. With the score 12-7 the Irish defense toughened, and several minutes later Notre Dame end Wayne Millner blocked a punt and recovered it in the end zone, and although the conver-

sion failed, it was enough for a 13-12 victory. "It was a grand game," Anderson told reporters afterward, "and I don't mind saying how delighted I am. It was a beautiful ball game and I'm just tickled to death that we won."

Army coach Gar Davidson entered the Notre Dame locker room and congratulated Anderson. "That was as fine a Notre Dame team as I have ever seen play," he said. "I don't see why you people always save it up for us. But we are proud to lose to a team as good as yours. I played against the Four Horsemen and against two Notre Dame teams that followed them. I also have scouted Notre Dame on numerous occasions in the last decade, but the Notre Dame team that licked us today had the greatest spirit of any Notre Dame team that I have ever seen."

Later that night at the Hotel McAlpin, the New York Notre Dame Club held a dinner

Above: *Delirious Notre Dame fans tear down the goalposts at Yankee Stadium after the 13-12 come-from-behind victory over Army on 2 December 1933. The final big win was still not enough to redeem the disastrous 3-5-1 season.*

for the team. "As far as speech-making is concerned . . ." Anderson began his after-dinner talk, then broke down before being able to continue. "The Notre Dame team made it for me this afternoon at the Yankee Stadium. I thank you from the bottom of my heart." Back in South Bend, students and alumni, eager for any reason to celebrate, snake-danced through the streets, chanting, "We Were Down, But We Weren't Out." After that the jubilation got out of hand, with the crowd tearing down the city's Christmas decorations and hauling off the displays of a local theater.

A week later, Father John O'Hara, Notre Dame's interim president, announced what had been rumored: "The University of Notre Dame has accepted the resignation of Jesse Harper and Heartley Anderson as athletic director and head football coach and has signed Elmer Layden for a contract that governs both positions. The university also has approved the selection of Joseph Boland as assistant football coach."

Upon hearing the news reporters rushed Layden in Pittsburgh. "It's true, and I think I'll accept," he told them. "I have the greatest admiration for my predecessor, whose resignation placed me in the position of refusing a call from my alma mater or accepting one of the hardest jobs in the country. All I can promise is that I will do my best, and the Notre Dame authorities tell me that is all they want."

Notre Dame had hitched its future to one of its surviving legends. But while Layden returned the Golden Dome to the habit of winning, he still failed to deliver that unbeaten, championship perfection that the alumni had grown accustomed to under Rockne. More than anything, Layden failed to produce the type of superlative offensive performer, or offensive-minded team, needed to lift the Irish to greatness. Nothing, perhaps, is more indicative of this than the fact that his most heralded player was Bill Shakespeare, who finished third in the 1935 voting for the Heisman Trophy.

Shakespeare, a 5-foot-1, 180-pound left half, affectionately dubbed "the Bard" (he was reported to have struggled with English classes), was known primarily for his punting. In fact, he holds the record for the two longest punts in Notre Dame history: 86 yards against Pitt in 1935 and 75 yards against Navy the same season.

All in all, the offense was anemic during Layden's seven-season tenure as Notre Dame coach. The only major offensive records set during that time were for punting, fewest first downs, fewest penalties and fewest offensive plays in a game. Not once in Layden's time as coach did a Notre Dame ball carrier gain more than 450 yards in a season, and only once did a passer throw for more than 400 yards.

On the other hand, his defenses were exceptional. His 1937 secondary allowed only 27 pass completions in nine games, and for the season Layden's defense allowed only 61 first downs, a modern record. Against his 1938 defensive backfield opponents completed only 30 percent of their passes. His seven-season record of 47-13-3, a winning percentage of .770, is excellent. It's just that it can't compare with those of Notre Dame's coaching legends – Rockne, Leahy and Parseghian.

Above: *Elmer Layden, former member of the famous Four Horsemen backfield, signs a two-year contract to return to his alma mater as athletic director and head football coach in 1933. At his left is the Reverend John F O'Hara, acting president of Notre Dame.*

Left: *Coach Elmer Layden lasted for seven seasons (1934-40) and compiled a 47-13-3 record for a .770 winning percentage. Only at Notre Dame would such a strong record be deemed mediocre.*

Layden lost his first game 7-6 to Texas, coached by Hunk Anderson's former assistant, Jack Chevigny. By mid-season the Irish were 3-3. They trailed Northwestern 7-0 in the second half and appeared headed toward more disappointment, when they suddenly broke loose for a 20-7 win. With solid wins over Army and Southern Cal, they finished 6-3.

That spring brought more sad news with the death from pneumonia of captain-elect Joe Sullivan. With the players dedicating their efforts to him, the winning streak carried right on through into 1935, as they rolled past Kansas, Carnegie Tech, Wisconsin, Pitt and Navy. Sporting a 5-0 record they faced unbeaten Ohio State in a road game on 2 November. The Buckeyes were favored and pushed to a 13-0 lead by the end of the third quarter, as the Irish offense struggled. At the half, Layden had announced he would start the second half with the second team. Substitute left half Andy Pilney replaced the ineffective Shakespeare, and the fourth period opened with Pilney having sparked a Notre Dame drive to the Ohio State 12. Two plays later, Steve Miller scored on a dive. The conversion kick

Top: *Coach Elmer Layden (right) looks over his 1934 first string team as training begins: (L-r, line) Captain Dominic Vairo, John Michuta, Paul Schrenker, Harry Pozman, Rocco Schiralli, Ken Stilley and Wayne Millner; (L-r, backfield) Al Costello, Bud Bonar, Don Elser and Andy Pilney.*

Above: *Halfback Bill Shakespeare goes over for a touchdown in the second quarter of the 1935 game against Pittsburgh. Marty Peters kicked a last-minute field goal to give the Irish the game 9-6.*

failed, but the Irish trailed only 13-6 with plenty of time left. Moments later, Notre Dame again drove to the Ohio State goal, only to watch Miller fumble into the end zone. They got the ball back at their own 20 with three minutes left, and Pilney, who had remained on the bench behind Shakespeare much of his career, promptly moved them across midfield, where he threw a 33-yard touchdown pass to Mike Layden, the coach's brother. Again Notre Dame muffed the conversion and trailed, 13-12.

Ohio State quickly covered the onsides kick and needed only to run 90 seconds off the clock to win. But Pilney hit Buckeye fullback Dick Beltz hard as he drove off tackle and caused a fumble, recovered by Henry Pojman, a Notre Dame second-stringer. With Layden puffing cigarettes nervously on the sidelines, Pilney dropped back to throw, found his receivers covered and broke loose for a scramble down to the Buckeye 19, where he was forced out of bounds. The tackle on the play caused a career-ending knee injury for Pilney, and he was unable to continue.

Shakespeare entered the game with less than 30 seconds remaining and promptly threw the ball right to Ohio State's Beltz, but the defender was so surprised he dropped the ball. Given a reprieve, Shakespeare found end Wayne Millner in the end zone for the winning touchdown on the next play. "I've thought a lot about the pass," Shakespeare said later. "But I wake up nights dreaming about the one before it – the one the Ohio State guy had in his hands and dropped."

The Irish were unexpectedly 6-0 and seemed headed toward a banner season. Then came an unexpected home loss to Northwestern, followed by a 6-6 tie with Army in Yankee Stadium. They finished 7-1-1 after a season-ending win over Southern Cal in Notre Dame Stadium. Shakespeare, Millner and Pilney all received some mention on post-season teams, and Shakespeare finished third in the voting for the first Heisman.

The 1936 and 1937 seasons were bittersweet for Layden as both teams finished 6-2-1, both with losses to Jock Sutherland's Pitt powerhouses. The highlight of 1936 was a 26-6 upset of top-ranked Northwestern in Notre Dame Stadium.

The 1938 team was obviously Layden's best, using a sound defense to rip off eight straight wins. By the seventh week of the season the Irish had moved to the top spot in the polls. For Notre Dame's 300th all-time victory, they hammered 12th-ranked Minnesota 19-0. Next they slipped past 16th-ranked Northwestern 9-7 and needed to beat eighth-ranked USC in the final game to claim the national championship. The Trojans, however, completely dominated, 13-0,

Above: *Action from the 1935 game against the undefeated Ohio State Buckeyes in Columbus. Before a full house, Bill Shakespeare threw a touchdown pass in the final 30 seconds to upset the Buckeyes 19-13.*

Left: *Coach Elmer Layden in 1934.*

Right: *Mr Jackson, the Army mule, and Clashmore Mike, Irish terrier mascot of the Notre Dame team, are introduced by their respective cheerleaders before the 1939 Notre Dame-Army game, won by the Irish 14-0 in Yankee Stadium on 4 November.*

to dash the Irish hopes completely.

Layden finished his tenure with another pair of book-end seasons in 1939 and 1940. Both teams finished 7-2. In 1939 the Irish had risen as high as number two in the rankings until they faced Iowa and Nile Kinnick, who won the Heisman at the end of the season. Kinnick scored and kicked the conversion to give the Hawkeyes a 7-6 upset. Despite seven wins, Notre Dame scored only 100 points on the season. The point output improved for 1940, but the record didn't.

Layden had worked under long-term contracts at Notre Dame, but when school officials offered him only a one-year deal at the end of the season he decided to accept the post of commissioner of the National Football League. Once again, school officials began combing the ranks of its former players who had gone on to coaching success. As always, Notre Dame was looking for its next legend.

Left: *Former coach Elmer Layden (right) bids farewell to the 1941 Notre Dame team as he leaves for a new position as commissioner of the National Football League.*

Opposite: *Halfback Andy Pilney spent much of his college football career in the shadow of star Bill Shakespeare. His brilliant performance at the Ohio State game in 1935 redeemed much for him.*

THE LEAHY LADS

1941-45

48
75
70
42

Previous pages: *The 1942 Notre Dame football squad: (L-r, back row) Earley, Cowhig, Zilley, Bertelli, Miller; (L-r, back to front) Murphy, Neff, Rymbus, Wright, Dove and Ziemba.*

Left: *Another chapter of Notre Dame football history was begun on 15 February 1941 when Frank Leahy signed a contract as coach and athletic director. At his left is president the Reverend J Hugh O'Donnell.*

Opposite top: *Halfback Angelo Bertelli (48) shakes off an Arizona tackler as he rushes for a gain in the 1941 game behind the interference of Maddock (left) and Murphy. Bertelli completed 11 of 14 passes for the day to lead Notre Dame to a decisive 38-7 win.*

Below: *Two great coaches confer: Notre Dame's Frank Leahy (left) and Army's Red Blaik.*

Notre Dame officials were of course expecting another Knute Rockne when they hired Frank Leahy to run their football program in 1941. From the perspective of history, it seems they got that and more. Rockne's winning percentage was slightly better. But in 11 seasons Leahy gave the Golden Dome six undefeated seasons, five national championships, four Heisman Trophy winners and another grand chapter in the Irish book of legends.

Despite the dislocations of world war, Leahy accomplished all that with a personal drive that burned so hot it almost consumed him. "I used to think I was the most intense coach in the business," Army's Red Blaik once said of Leahy. "But I'm about ready to concede that Frank eats his heart out even more than I do."

His background offered an interesting mix for a football coach. Raised in Winner, South Dakota, he picked up the roping and ranching skills of a cowpoke, yet spoke with a heavy Irish brogue. (Throughout his coaching career Leahy referred to his players as "lads.") At Winner High, where he was coached by Rockne disciple Earl Walsh, Leahy was a talented three-sport athlete, a natural for Notre Dame. But his playing career for the Irish was first interrupted, then ended, by a series of injuries. After ruining his knee just before the start of his

senior year (1930), he spent the season assisting Rockne in coaching duties, taking notes and using the opportunity to absorb much of the master's approach.

Upon graduation he went to Georgetown University as line coach in 1931 and Michigan State in 1932, then was lured to the same position under Jim Crowley at Fordham. Leahy coached Fordham's legendary "Seven Blocks of Granite," including a stubborn young Vince Lombardi. In 1938 he was hired as the head coach of Boston College and promptly coached the Eagles into the Cotton Bowl. In his second season Boston College won the Sugar Bowl. In two years, he had compiled a 20-2 record, enough to make him the top choice when his alma mater began looking. Although he had just signed a new long-term contract with Boston College, Leahy gained his release and accepted when Notre Dame came courting.

His first priority was to rebuild the Irish offensive, which he accomplished without changing Notre Dame's single-wing, shifting formation. The secret was a sophomore tailback, a 6-foot-1, 173-pound Italian kid from Springfield, Massachusetts, Angelo Bertelli. Throwing from the tailback slot, Bertelli became Notre Dame's first 1000-yard passer, completing 70 of 123 attempts (.569 percentage) for 1027 yards and eight touchdowns, enough to lead the Fighting Irish to

Right: *Ace QB Angelo Bertelli shows his passing form during a workout before the 1941 Army game.*

an unexpected 8-0-1 season.

It was an error-free year for the most part. The Irish fumbled just six times, a school record low. They opened the year unranked, but quickly earned national respect with wins over Arizona, Indiana and Georgia Tech. By early November they were ranked sixth in the Associated Press poll and faced 14th-ranked Army in Yankee Stadium. Notre Dame punted a record 16 times that day, as the teams battled to a scoreless tie, the only blemish on the 1941 record. The Irish finished the year ranked third in the AP poll, and end Bob Dove was named a consensus All-American. Although Bertelli received no serious mention on the All-America teams, he finished second in the Heisman voting behind Minnesota's Bruce Smith.

Leahy's great move came in his planning for the next season. The game of college football was changing, and he saw the need to discard Notre Dame's traditional offense. Bertelli was a fine passer but a mediocre runner, and Leahy felt the new T-formation with split wings would serve his talents better. Bertelli could function as a drop-back passer after taking the ball under center. Soon sportswriters were marveling at this new concept, a "pocket" formed by blockers from which Bertelli could pass. There was some grumbling among Notre Dame supporters, and it grew louder when the Irish tied Wisconsin in the first game and were upset by Georgia Tech in the second. The third game, however, made converts as Bertelli threw a school-record four touchdown passes and kicked three extra points in a 27-0 defeat of the Stanford Indians, coached by Marchy Schwartz. At one point Bertelli com-

Above: *The 1943 coaching squad: (l-r) Hugh Devore, Jake Kline, head coach Frank Leahy and Ed McKeever.*

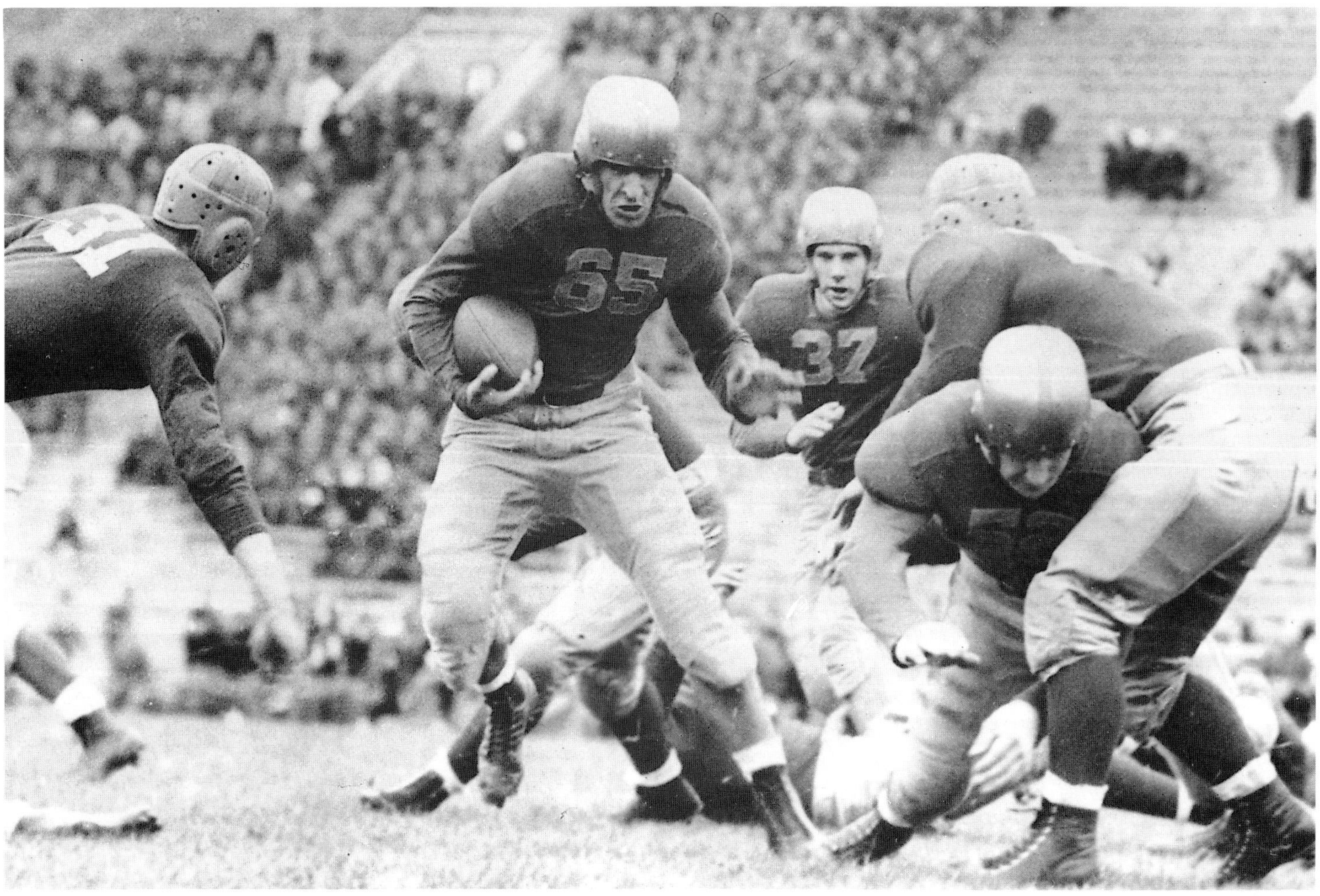

Below: *ND back Jim Mello (65) comes through for a nine-yard gain during the 50-0 rout of the Wisconsin Badgers on 18 October 1943.*

Left: *Johnny Lujack (32) kicks for the extra point after Notre Dame's first touchdown in the Army game at Yankee Stadium in 1943. The kick was wide, but the Irish forged ahead to blast the Cadets 26-0.*

pleted 10 consecutive passes, a feat not equalled until Joe Montana did it against Georgia Tech in 1978.

After whipping the Iowa Pre-Flight School, fifth-ranked Illinois, Navy and 19th-ranked Army, the Irish rose to fourth in the Associated Press rankings, with a 5-1-1 record, only to be beaten 32-20 by sixth-ranked Michigan in Notre Dame Stadium. That setback was followed by victories over Northwestern and 14th-ranked Southern Cal and a season-ending tie with the Great Lakes naval training team, a squad stocked with talent. Notre Dame's Corwin Clatt had run 81 yards from scrimmage for a touchdown to help the Irish gain the tie, and Notre Dame had rushed 25 times for 250 yards, the 10-yard-per-carry average being the best in modern school history.

The Irish finished 7-2-2, and Bertelli had thrown for another 1044 yards and 11 touchdowns. He finished sixth in the Heisman voting and received mention on several All-America teams. Bertelli also intercepted eight passes over the season, a school record. End Bob Dove was again a consensus choice, making the first unit of six different teams.

The next year might have been all Bertelli had there not been a war going on. Across the country, players were leaving the ranks of their college teams for military service. Bertelli lasted the first six games of 1943 before being drafted into the Marine Corps, enough time to burn Notre Dame's first six opponents for 511 yards passing and 10 touchdowns. The top-ranked Irish outscored their first six opponents – Pitt, Georgia Tech, Michigan (Creighton Miller rushed for 159 yards and two touchdowns), Wisconsin (Notre Dame intercepted seven passes against the Badgers), Illinois and Navy – by a combined total of 261-31.

Bertelli was then replaced by sophomore John Lujack, a Pennsylvania schoolboy wonder. In his first game against third-ranked Army, Lujack ran for one touchdown, passed for two more and intercepted

Below: *Corwin Clatt ran 81 yards for a touchdown to help the Irish to tie the talented Great Lakes Naval Training Team in 1942.*

a pass, as Notre Dame won 26-0. With that confidence, Lujack directed the Irish to wins over eighth-ranked Northwestern and the second-ranked Iowa Pre-Flight School, 14-13. But a late score by the Great Lakes team ended Notre Dame's hopes of a perfect season with a 19-14 loss. Regardless, the Irish at 9-1 were the unanimous choice as national champions.

Despite missing the last four games, Bertelli was the runaway winner of the Heisman, polling 648 votes. Teammate Creighton Miller, who had rushed for 911 yards and 13 touchdowns and had intercepted six passes, finished fourth, with 134 votes. In fact, it was the threat of Miller's ground game that made Notre Dame's passing so effective. Without a doubt Leahy considered Miller's performance in 1943 one of his all-time favorites.

When the Downtown Athletic Club requested Bertelli's presence at their award ceremonies, the Marine Corps wired back: "Regret to advise you impracticable to grant request for presence of Pvt Angelo Bertelli at Downtown Athletic Club. Bertelli now undergoing training at Parris Island, where he is competing against many other men for assignment to candidates class for commission. Any absence for even limited time materially affects his chances for selection in first group to go to candidates class, in view of which it is necessary to disapprove request."

Although Bertelli was named to the second-team Associated Press All-America squad, he finished first on most other lists. Miller, end John Yonakor (who caught 15 passes for 323 yards and four touchdowns), tackle Jim White and guard Pat Filley were all named to one or another All-America first teams.

As it did everywhere, World War II brought its turmoil to Notre Dame football in 1944 and 1945. Both Leahy and Lujack went into the service, along with a host of other Notre Dame players. Frank Dancewicz became quarterback for 1944 and threw for 989 yards. Ed McKeever, Leahy's assistant, served as coach for a season of highs and lows. By blistering their first five opponents, the 1944 Irish shoved their way to the top

Top left: *Angelo Bertelli won the Heisman Trophy in 1943.*

Above: *Coach Leahy left his job to enter the Navy in 1944 and 1945 but returned to bring more glory to the Irish in 1946.*

Opposite top: *The 1945 Notre Dame eleven: (l-r, front row) Dick Cronin, Pete Berezney, Fred Rovai, Bill Walsh, John Mastrangelo, Ed Meiszkowski and Robert Skoglund; (l-r, back row) Elmer Angsman, Frank Dancewicz, Frank Ruggiero and Phil Colella.*

Opposite bottom: *Departing coach Frank Leahy (left) shakes hands with assistant coach Ed McKeever, who would take over in 1944.*

ranking in the polls, only to fall in a 32-13 upset to sixth-ranked Navy. The next week, the new number-one team, Army, and the great Doc Blanchard humiliated Notre Dame 59-0. The Irish regrouped for three final wins to finish 8-2, but the memory of the Army defeat would stew until the next season, when the Cadets repeated the trick.

Hugh Devore, a co-captain of Notre Dame's 1933 team and onetime Irish freshman coach, served as head coach for 1945 and watched his squad work its way up in the polls to number two with a series of five impressive wins. The surge stopped when the Irish tied third-ranked Navy 6-6 in Cleveland. Then once again Blanchard and Army humiliated Notre Dame in Yankee Stadium 48-0. The Irish won two more from there before closing the season with a 39-7 loss to Great Lakes. Devore's team finished 7-2-1.

The war had thrown Leahy's great program into turmoil, but upon his return the Notre Dame coach would astound the football world with how quickly he could reassemble his powerhouse.

NOTRE DA
65TH. SEAS

THE PRICE OF PERFECTION

1946-53

Previous pages: *Carrying a shillelagh, Irishman Jack Sand follows team captain Don Penza and mascot Mike as they lead the squad to the first practice session of 1953.*

Opposite top: *Halfback Emil Sitko runs back an intercepted Navy pass for 20 yards during the first quarter of play in the 1946 game. The Irish downed the Middies 28-0.*

Opposite bottom left: *Lujack, All-America quarterback for 1946 and 1947 and Heisman Trophy winner in 1947, led the offense that helped give Notre Dame two consecutive national championships.*

Opposite bottom right: *Tackle George Connor was one of the outstanding Irish linemen who received All-America honors for 1946.*

Below: *Coach Leahy and star QB Johnny Lujack.*

Frank Leahy and Johnny Lujack were among the luckiest of veterans returning from World War II service, for they were able to come back to their former lives and pick up the good fortune they had left behind. Lujack would realize his boyhood dream of becoming a Notre Dame star, perhaps its brightest ever. Leahy, for whom football perfection had always seemed just beyond his reach, would be able briefly to attain his goal. But upon achieving it, Leahy would find that perfection carried a heavy price, much heavier than even he had ever imagined.

For Lujack the Notre Dame experience held the wonder of a Pennsylvania boyhood dream. Irish football was all he had thought about as a youngster growing up in Connellsville, Pennsylvania. His accomplishments as a high school athlete and class president meant that dozens of colleges wanted to offer him an athletic scholarship in 1942. The most tempting was an appointment to the US Military Academy, but Lujack held fast to his dream and turned down the West Point offer. The more he dreamed his dream, the better it seemed to get. The Notre Dame coaches recognized his talent and spent hours grooming and instructing him to be their T-formation, hoping to make him the quarterback of the future. When his chance finally arose during his sophomore year in 1943, he responded with a brilliant performance, to defeat Army and lead the Irish to a national championship. The 1946 season brought nothing but more opportunity for stardom.

Lieutenant Frank Leahy returned from the Navy in November 1945 to find a program well stocked with talent. For the 1946 season Leahy resumed his duties, and Hugh Devore, the war-time coach, moved on to become head coach at St Bonaventure. In Leahy's 1946 line-up Lujack headed a backfield of young talent with freshman halfback Emil Sitko and sophomore Terry Brennan. Behind them was nothing but pure depth, including speedster Coy McGee, Bob Livingstone and Corwin Clatt. Fullback John Mello had spent his war years playing with the Great Lakes Naval Station team coached by Paul Brown and would turn his experience and power into a key element in the Notre Dame offense. The line was a thing of veteran precision, with tackle George Connor, guard John Mastrangelo, center George Strohmeyer, guard Bill Fischer, tackle Ziggy Czarobski and end Leon Hart all on their way to earning All-America honors.

The tendency is to cite the offensive prowess of the 1946 Irish, but defensively they were vicious, allowing only 40 first downs rushing the entire season. In nine games, they allowed the opposition only 24 points and one touchdown pass, both modern Notre Dame records. Beginning the season unranked, they blistered Illinois, Pitt, Purdue, 17th-ranked Iowa and Navy to move to the number-two spot in the AP poll heading into their November 9 game with top-ranked Army at Yankee Stadium. The Notre Dame offense was hitting on all cylinders.

As for the Cadets, they were riding a 25-game winning streak and had a pair of high-powered Heisman winners in their backfield in Glenn Davis and Doc Blanchard. They had generated 107 points against the Irish over the past two seasons. The sports minds of the day expected an offensive clash between Army and Notre Dame, and even Leahy suggested the two teams would score liberally. Instead, the teams produced one of the finest defensive struggles in college football history.

The drama surrounding the event was substantial for the period. The game had been a sell-out for months, and more than a half million dollars in refunds were given to fans who couldn't get tickets. There was little standing room among the 74,000 in Yankee Stadium. To make sure his team was fired up, Leahy had posted the game scores from the two previous seasons in the locker

Opposite top: *Arnold Tucker, Army quarterback, is rushed by ND tackle George Connor (81) in the first quarter of the 1946 game against top-ranked Army on 9 November. A crowd of 74,000 at Yankee Stadium watched the game turn into a defensive battle that ended in a scoreless tie.*

Opposite bottom: *This third-quarter play in the 1946 Notre Dame-Army game shows the famed Notre Dame T-formation in execution. Quarterback Johnny Lujack hands off to halfback Emil Sitko as their outstanding linemen go into action.*

room. During practice, his players chanted, "Fifty-nine and forty-eight, this is the year we retaliate."

But the energy of both squads stifled the power of their offenses that afternoon. Neither team mounted a successful scoring drive. At one point the great Blanchard broke into the open, apparently headed for a score, but Lujack raced across the field and wrapped him up with a precise tackle at the Irish 37. With that threat snuffed, the game ended in a scoreless draw.

"They said Blanchard couldn't be stopped one-on-one in the open field, yet I did it," Lujack told reporters afterward. "I really can't understand all the fuss. I simply pinned him against the sideline and dropped him with a routine tackle." Commented Major General Maxwell D Taylor, superintendent of the United States Military Academy, "It was a very fine game. I'm proud of both teams."

Such opinions aside, the game did nothing to determine the best team in college football, and both coaches made no attempt to hide their disappointment. "There is no jubilation in this dressing room," Army Coach Red Blaik told reporters. Leahy said he definitely wasn't enthusiastic. "I suppose I should be elated over the tie. After all, we didn't lose. But I'm not," he told reporters. "You know, of course, that I had expected to lose this game, but five minutes after the start, after we had stopped Army in the first period, I had a feeling that we might win."

Yet, the game would prove to be a hinge in Notre Dame's swing toward the national championship. The Irish resumed their pace afterward, nailing Northwestern, Tulane and 16th-ranked Southern Cal by big scores. Leahy missed the USC game because of illness, and Moose Krause took charge of the team, turning loose substitute Coy McGee, who ran for two touchdowns, including a 77-yard sprint early in the game.

On the other hand, Army barely struggled past Navy 21-18 in a late game, and that played a major factor in the minds of the pollsters. They unanimously voted Notre Dame the champions at the end of the season. The Cadets' Glenn Davis won the Heisman, with Lujack finishing third in the voting. On the season, Lujack had passed for 778 yards and six touchdowns.

It was announced before the 1947 season that the upcoming game between Army and Navy would be the last for awhile. Irish fans suggested that Red Blaik had grown weary of battling Frank Leahy's teams. In fact, so had some others. Coaches in the Midwest, particularly the Big Ten, had grown weary of the battering their teams were taking from his high-powered squads. Even on the campus in South Bend the faculty and administration began to show resentment of his success and the attention it brought. Part of the reward of perfection was a ripple of com-

Below: *Halfback Terry Brennan is stopped by Army's Arnold Tucker after a nine-yard gain in the first quarter of the 1946 Notre Dame-Army game.*

plaints and jealousies. Leahy worked as a man possessed, unsmiling, self-consumed, driven. He worked incredible hours to assure the success of his teams. It has often been said that he was respected but not loved.

If anything, that situation worsened with the 1947 season, perhaps Notre Dame's finest ever, as Leahy extended his unbeaten streak to 18 games. The nine opponents on the schedule fell by thundering scores – Pitt 40-6, Purdue 22-7, Nebraska 31-0, Iowa 21-0 and Navy 27-0 – leaving the Irish 5-0 and top-ranked heading into the Army game. There Brennan returned the opening kickoff 97 yards for a touchdown, and the Irish finally quenched their thirst for revenge against the Cadets, 27-7. The big win was followed by a letdown and the season's only really close game, a 26-19 squeaker on the road against Northwestern. The Irish dropped to number two in the polls but regained their top spot two weeks later by whipping third-ranked Southern Cal 38-7 in a game highlighted by Bob Livingstone's 92-yard touchdown run.

The Irish claimed several national championships, including the prestigious Associated Press award, but undefeated Michigan also received the top nod from three ratings systems. Lujack also outpolled Michigan's Bob Chappius for the Heisman Trophy in a year where Doak Walker of SMU, Charley Conerly of Mississippi, Bobby Layne of Texas and Chuck Bednarik of Penn all finished in the top eight. In addition to being voted the AP's male athlete of the year, Lujack was selected a consensus All-American. Other Irish getting All-America mention were Bill Fischer, a consensus AP and United Press first teamer, and Leon Hart, George Connor and Ziggy Czarobski. For the year, Brennan led the team in scoring, with 11 touchdowns, and Sitko led the rushing statistics, with a little under 500 yards.

Although Lujack graduated to stardom with the Chicago Bears after the '47 season, the 1948 Irish followed up his act with an outburst of offense, gaining a school-record 3194 yards rushing. At the center of the show was Emil Sitko, who again led the team on the ground. Against Michigan State he carried 24 times for 186 yards and a touchdown, a 7.8 per carry average on the day. He bettered that against Navy with 172 yards and a touchdown down in only 17 carries, a 10.1 per carry average. Frank Tripucka had moved into Lujack's quarterback slot, and while he could pass with the best of them, he

Above: *Halfback Emil Sitko (14) bulls his way over the goal line from the six-inch line in the first quarter of the 1948 season opener versus Purdue. The Irish beat the Boilermakers 28-27.*

Opposite top: *End Leon Hart (82) waits to receive Frank Tripucka's pass from the nine-yard line for Notre Dame's first score in the 1948 meeting with Pitt. The Irish went undefeated for the season.*

Opposite bottom: *Frank Tripucka, backup quarterback in 1947, with Coach Frank Leahy on the sidelines of the Notre Dame-Army game. Tripucka took over full-time quarterbacking duties in 1948.*

offered little as a runner. Still, he threw for 660 yards and 11 touchdowns, despite missing some playing time due to injury.

Purdue gave the Irish a real fight in the first game before succumbing 28-27 when the Irish blocked a kick and fullback John Panelli ran for the winning touchdown. From there, the scores turned gaudy again as Pitt, Michigan State, Nebraska, Iowa, Navy and Indiana all fell by big margins. Only eighth-ranked Northwestern presented a problem. The Irish prevailed 12-7 when Bill Gay scored a late touchdown. After that, Washington was obliterated 46-0, and the Irish needed only to defeat unranked Southern Cal on the road to finish another perfect season. Instead, Notre Dame had to score in the final minute, then convert the extra point to earn a 14-14 tie and a 9-0-1 finish for the season, giving the Irish 28 straight games without defeat.

Fischer, Sitko, Hart and guard Marty Wendell all received All-America mention after the season. Michigan, however, claimed the national championship, with Notre Dame finishing second in the AP poll. Between 1946-48, the Irish had won 21 consecutive games, a school record, and were well on their way toward an eventual unbeaten streak of 39 straight.

Opposite top: *Team captain Jerry Groom (50) leads the Notre Dame squad to the opening practice session in September 1950. The Irish entered the season unbeaten for 38 straight games.*

Opposite bottom: *End Leon Hart (82) is trapped by Skeet Hesmer and Tom Stevens of North Carolina after snaring a pass from quarterback Bob Williams in the second quarter of the game at Yankee Stadium in 1949. The Irish outscored the Tarheels 42-6.*

The Notre Dame fortunes fell into the hands of junior quarterback Bob Williams in 1949. And he used the opportunity to carry Notre Dame to yet another undefeated season while rewriting the school passing records. For the season, he would complete 83 of 147 passing attempts with only seven interceptions, for 1374 yards and 16 touchdowns and a rating of 161.4, a school record that still stands. As a team, the 1949 Irish averaged a 6.02-yard gain on every offensive play, another modern record. Against Navy, they averaged a whopping 10.2 yards per play. They scored a modern-record 53 touchdowns over the season.

Emil Sitko rushed for 712 yards, leading the Irish in that category for the fourth straight year. He also scored nine touchdowns. But the real sensation of the season would be end Leon Hart, who caught 19 passes for 257 yards and five touchdowns, in addition to holding down defensive chores. At season's end the 6-foot-4, 245-pounder from Turtle Creek, Pennsylvania would receive a unique award for a lineman, the Heisman Trophy. He gained this status in the dying days of one-platoon football (he and tackle Jim Martin were among the last of the two-way performers for Notre Dame), when an end could be appreciated for the "whole" game, blocking on offense and rushing on defense. He would earn four letters at Notre Dame without ever experiencing defeat. There would be other grand honors for him in 1949, including the Associated Press male athlete of the year award and the Maxwell Award as the top player in college football. Williams and Sitko would finish fifth and eighth respectively in the Heisman voting. And Hart would go on to an all-pro career with the Detroit Lions.

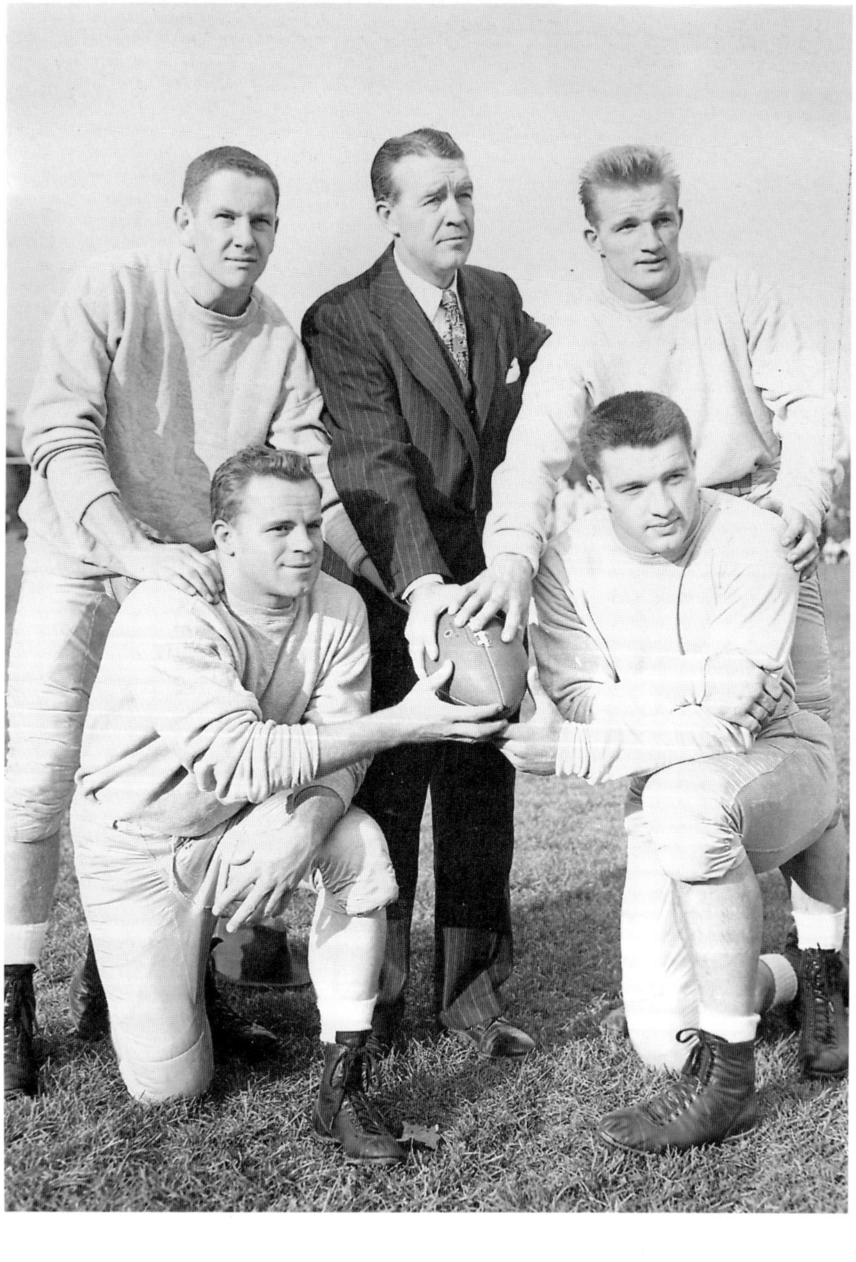

On the field, it was another high-octane season for Notre Dame. They outscored their opponents 360-86 and won all 10 games, extending their streak of unbeaten to 38. The first nine on the schedule, including fourth-ranked Tulane, tenth-ranked Michigan State and 17th-ranked Southern Cal, were all felled with apparent ease. Only the final game, a 27-20 struggle with SMU in Dallas, pushed the Irish to the edge. The Mustangs' Kyle Rote had an explosive day, scoring two touchdowns to help SMU overcome a 14-0 deficit to tie the game at 20. Only a late drive and score by Bill Barrett salvaged the perfect season.

The perfect season, however, had anything but a perfect aftermath. In fact, Leahy later remarked to confidants that he wished

Left: *Coach Frank Leahy poses with some of the players on his 1949 team: (l-r, standing) Quarterback Bob Williams and tackle Jim Martin; (l-r, kneeling) halfback Emil Sitko and end Leon Hart.*

the 1949 season had been his last. The orgy of winning proved to be the last straw among the anti-football forces on Notre Dame's faculty. To them, it seemed the school had gotten far more recognition for its sports programs than for its excellent scholarship. They used their influence to force the administration to drop the number of football scholarships to 18, from a high of 32. Perhaps the only thing that kept Leahy from resigning was a promise to 1950 team captain Jerry Groom that he would stay through the player's senior season.

To ease the burden on Leahy, Notre Dame promoted Moose Krause to the position of athletic director, thus freeing the coach from the business distractions of managing the athletic department. Still, 1950 was a season to be missed. Notre Dame opened as the nation's number one team but barely squeaked past 20th-ranked North Carolina 14-7 for the 39th consecutive unbeaten game (the longest, by far, in school history). That streak abruptly ended in the rain at Notre Dame Stadium against Purdue the next week when the Boilermakers gained an overdue revenge, 28-14. The Irish also lost to Indiana and Michigan State, to stand 2-3 at midseason. They whipped Navy and Pitt, then tied Iowa and, despite allowing just one first down, lost to Southern Cal 9-7, to finish the year 4-4-1.

Bob Williams had passed for another 1035 yards and 10 touchdowns, enough to become a consensus first-team All-American, and Groom made the United Press first team. Yet there was little else to say for the season, the first time in 17 years Notre Dame had failed to field a winner.

Leahy was left wrestling with a destructive self doubt. He had worked incredibly long hours, endured huge levels of stress to build the program. Those around him worried about his health. As for the ever-demanding fans, they offered nothing but grumbles. Father John Cavanaugh, university president, released this statement shortly after the season: "Leahy is blamed for wrecking the Notre Dame schedule by developing teams that win most of their games. He was brought here to win and to achieve excellence. If he didn't win, they would be asking to fire him. His was, indeed, an unsolvable problem. At Notre Dame we have no apologies about wanting winners. We want our students to win debates, in the classroom, on the baseball diamond, and in the more important battles of life. The football team is a great example of how perfection may be attained."

Leahy turned his frustration into effort and returned a team re-stocked with talent to the playing field in 1951. John Petitbon and Billy Barrett ran at halfback, with a sophomore substitute named John Lattner waiting in the wings. Neil Worden was the fullback, and John Mazur started at quarterback, with an eager young Ralph Guglielmi pushing him.

For the season, Worden would lead the team in scoring, with eight touchdowns, but he got four of them in the second quarter of the first game, against Indiana, as the Irish unleashed their pent-up anger and pelted the Hoosiers 48-6. They treated Detroit in the same fashion, but then were upset by SMU 27-20, as the Mustangs' Fred Benners threw four touchdown passes in Notre Dame Stadium. After big wins over Pitt, Purdue and Navy, the Irish suffered the worst loss of Leahy's long and distinguished career, 35-0, to fifth-ranked Michigan State. They achieved the 400th victory in the school's history with a 12-7 win over North Carolina the next week, then scored late to tie Iowa in Notre Dame Stadium. Having struggled back to respectability, the Irish closed a 7-2-1 season with a 19-12 win over Southern Cal and Frank Gifford.

While 1952 would bring no immediate relief from the task of rebuilding, it was a benchmark year in another way. Reverend

Above: *Irish end Jim Mutscheller (85) is given a short ride by North Carolina center Irv Holdash after taking a pass from quarterback Bob Williams in the second quarter of the 1950 game in South Bend. The play picked up 11 yards. Notre Dame eked out a 14-7 victory.*

Right: *Back Neil Worden slants off tackle in the first quarter of the 1951 game against Pitt. The Irish won 33-0.*

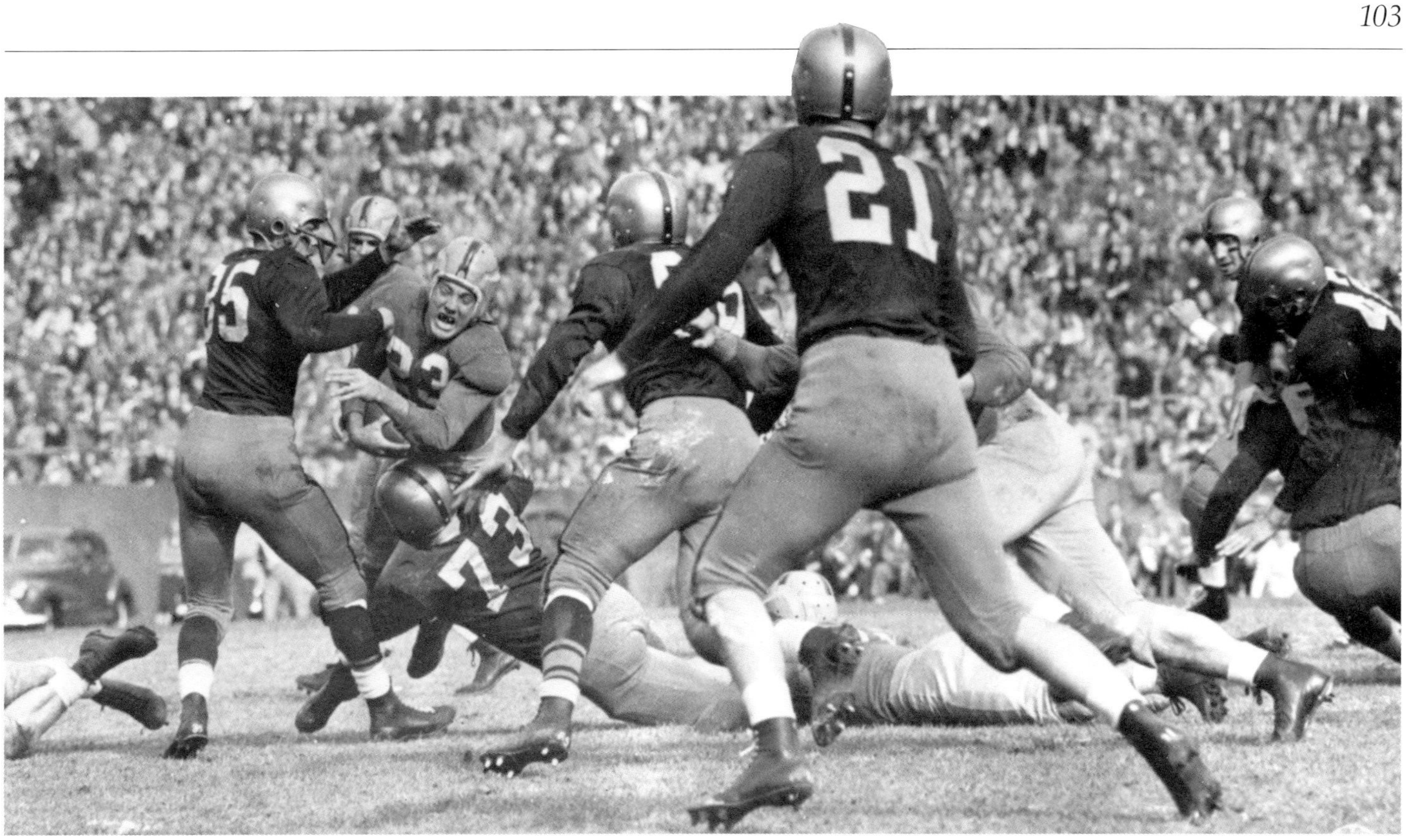

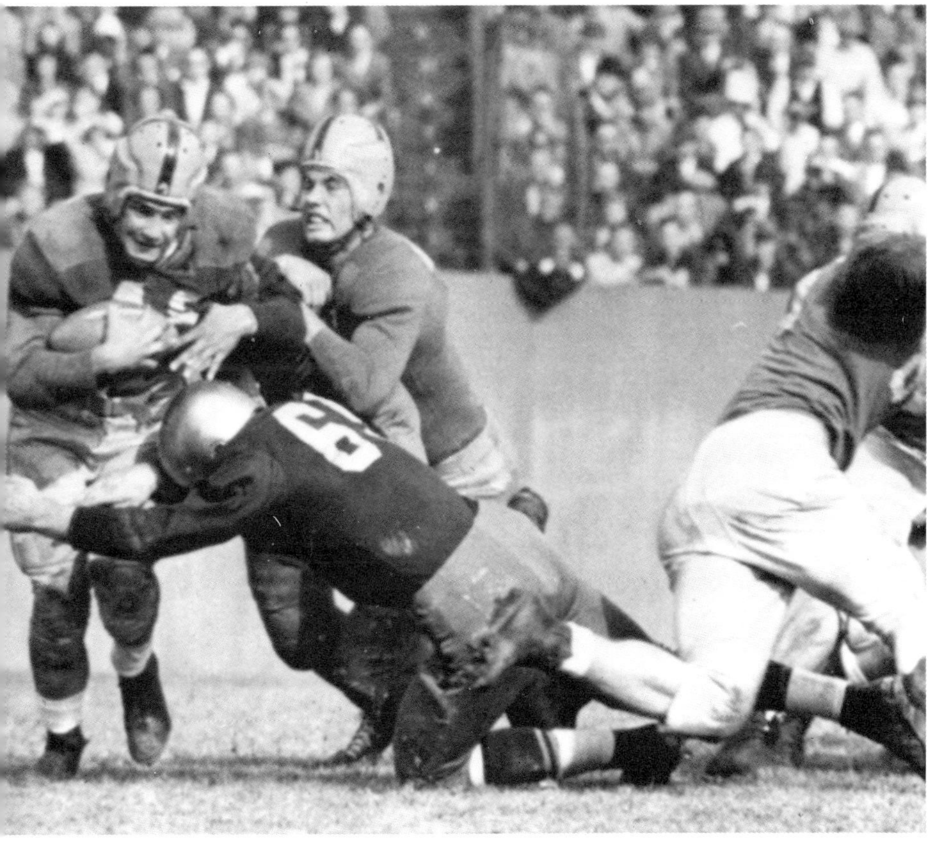

Top: *Halfback John Petitbon (23) is stopped by Pitt's Joe Zombeck (85) and Bob Brennan (73) after a seven-yard gain in the first quarter of the 1951 Notre Dame-Pitt game in Pittsburgh.*

Theodore Hesburgh came to the presidency of Notre Dame, bringing with him Reverend Edmund Joyce as administrative vice president and chairman of the athletic board. Under Hesburgh, the university would prosper, and Notre Dame athletics would eventually find its modern athletic identity. It would be accurate to say that the two men helped guide the institution toward a balance that made the school a model for other universities. That, however, wasn't accomplished without occasional faltering in the athletic programs. Apparently their promotions in 1952 brought an easing of the tension between academics and athletics in South Bend. On the field, however, the proceedings were infected with a severe case of fumblitis.

Record fumblitis, to be exact, by both the Irish and their opponents. Over the season, Notre Dame fumbled a record 57 times, losing a record 29 of them. The Irish fumbled 10 times each against Oklahoma and Purdue and lost a record seven fumbles against Michigan State. Not to be outdone, Purdue fumbled the ball right back 11 times, another record, and Notre Dame recovered eight of them, yet another record. On the season, their opponents fumbled 51 times, losing 28.

Such statistics lead one to wonder how a team with that many turnovers could finish 7-2-1, yet they did. A large part of the answer was the emergence of a 6-foot-1, 190-pounder out of Fenwich High on Chicago's West Side, John Lattner. He mastered several trades for the Irish, running, catching and punting, enough to earn the Maxwell Award as college football's top player for 1952, his junior season. He also excelled as a defensive back, intercepting 13 passes during his three-year varsity career.

With Lattner in the offensive backfield were quarterback Ralph Guglielmi, left half Joe Heap and fullback Neil Worden. Art Hunter returned to lead the offensive line, moving from center to end. On defense, the main man was linebacker Dan Shannon.

Above: *Fullback Neil Worden flies high for a plunge over the backs of Irish guards Jack Alessandrini (left) and Tom Seaman (right) during a September workout in 1952. Notre Dame entered the season ranked tenth in the nation and ended it with a 7-2-1 record.*

Leahy braced for what he figured to be his worst season. First, the scholarship reduction had begun to take its toll just as the schedule became much tougher. When all was said and done, and Notre Dame had survived, Leahy ranked 1952 as his best coaching job. Considering he spent much of the year plagued by nervous exhaustion, it easily was.

The Irish opened the season ranked as the number 10 team in the polls and promptly tied Pennsylvania, the 12th-ranked team, 7-7. The next week they upset fifth-ranked Texas 14-3, and were upset in turn the following week by Pitt 22-19. From there, they whipped ninth-ranked Purdue, North Carolina and Navy, to stand 4-1-1 going into their 8 November game with fourth-ranked Oklahoma, led by Billy Vessels, the eventual Heisman winner.

Vessels had a Heisman-type day against the Irish in Notre Dame Stadium, carrying the ball 17 times for 195 yards. He scored three touchdowns, but it wasn't enough. Neil Worden scored two for Notre Dame, and Tom Carney scored the game winner in the fourth period, as the Irish ended Oklahoma's 13-game winning streak 27-21. It was a great win, but top-ranked Michigan State doused their enthusiasm the next week, 21-3. Rebounding, they whipped Iowa and upset second-ranked USC, to close out a good year. Lattner's all-around performance was enough to place him on everybody's All-America first team.

Leahy's health might have been bad, but he only had good feelings about his 1953 team. The entire backfield and just about all the line returned. (Among the line substitutes was Wayne Edmonds, Notre Dame's first black varsity player). The sports media acknowledged the Irish potential by ranking them number one heading into the season. Still, it was a strange year. College football underwent a swift reversal in 1953 when the major rules that liberalized substitution were repealed. Just as football had entered the age of two platoons, it was thrust back into the medieval times of one platoon again. The Irish opened the schedule with an immediate test, a road game with sixth-ranked Oklahoma. It was a seesaw afternoon, with Notre Dame scoring first and the Sooners playing catch-up. The score was last tied at 14. On the day, Guglielmi threw three touchdown passes to Heap, as Notre Dame won, 28-21. After that Pitt and Purdue were the victims. Then the Irish faced fourth-ranked Georgia Tech in Notre Dame Stadium. The Wreck was sporting a 31-game unbeaten streak, but Lattner returned the opening kickoff 80 yards to get the Irish going. On the sidelines during the first quarter Leahy was stricken with severe chest pains and retreated to the locker room. There his condition worsened to the point that Father Joyce administered last rites. Word of his condition broke among the players, charging them to a 27-14 win.

Leahy was hospitalized but was back out the following week. Friends and administrators tried to convince him that it wouldn't be so bad if Notre Dame lost a game or two. For him, there was little worse, and the team seemed to agree. From there, they ripped Navy, Penn and North Carolina, then stalled amid controversy and flat play against 20th-ranked Iowa in Notre Dame Stadium. The controversy came when Leahy, out of timeouts, had tackle Frank Varrichione fake an injury to get an official timeout so that Leahy and quarterback Ralph Guglielmi could discuss a play. The

Above: *Fullback Neil Worden (48) takes advantage of Notre Dame's forward wall and races eight yards for a touchdown against North Carolina in 1952. The Irish won 34-14.*

Right: *Coach Frank Leahy and team captain Jack Alessandrini pose with the 1952 Notre Dame squad for a pre-season photo.*

press got hold of the story after the game, and the headlines howled about it across the nation the next morning. As it was, the Irish needed a last-second score to finish with a 14-14 tie, but it kept them in the running for the national championship.

The next week Heap ran 97 yards for a touchdown as Notre Dame demolished Southern Cal 48-14. Then Worden closed out his career scoring three touchdowns in a 40-14 destruction of SMU. With that, the Irish finished 9-0-1 and claimed several national championships. Maryland, however, with a 10-1 record was voted tops by both AP and UPI.

Regardless, Notre Dame football was back on top. Lattner was again a consensus All-American and claimed the Heisman in close voting over Minnesota's Paul Giel. Tackle Art Hunter and end Don Penza also were mentioned among the All-America teams.

The coaching clock, however, had run out for Leahy. Early in 1954, he issued this statement: "The doctors advised me after my experience between the halves of the Georgia Tech game to give up coaching. Before making up my mind I wanted to get some

Above: *Halfback John Lattner won the Maxwell Award, given to college football's top player, in 1952, and the coveted Heisman Trophy in 1953. An impressive runner, receiver and punter, he made All-America in both 1952 and 1953.*

Right: *Dan Shannon receives a pass from quarterback Ralph Guglielmi to register a touchdown that brought the Irish within one point of Iowa in the closing seconds of the 1953 game. The conversion made it 14-14, the tie game breaking Notre Dame's seven-game winning streak.*

Opposite top: *Coach Frank Leahy addresses a crowd of 2000 Notre Dame students in an emotional farewell at his retirement in February 1954.*

Opposite bottom: *Halfback Joe Heap (42) takes a pass in the Oklahoma end zone during the first quarter of the 1953 game in Oklahoma City. Notre Dame took home a 28-21 victory.*

rest and think over the move very seriously. Notre Dame means more to me than I can ever express, not only because of the opportunities it gave to me as a student and later on as athletic director and coach, but because of all that the university stands for."

And Notre Dame followed with this release: "The University of Notre Dame regretfully announces the resignation of Mr Frank Leahy for reasons of health. Mr Leahy has rendered valiant service to the University since 1941 as head football coach, and for a while, also as director of athletics. Coach Leahy's record during his eleven-year tenure rivals even that of the immortal Knute Rockne. More important, he has distinguished himself as a fine Christian gentleman who represented Notre Dame's ideals to millions of Americans, young and old."

When they hired Frank Leahy, Notre Dame officials were seeking another Knute Rockne. This is how Leahy's record compares with Rockne's:

Rockne . . . Won 105, Lost 12, Tied 3, Winning Percentage .875.

Leahy . . . Won 87, Lost 11, Tied 5, Winning Percentage .813.

DOWNTURN

1954-63

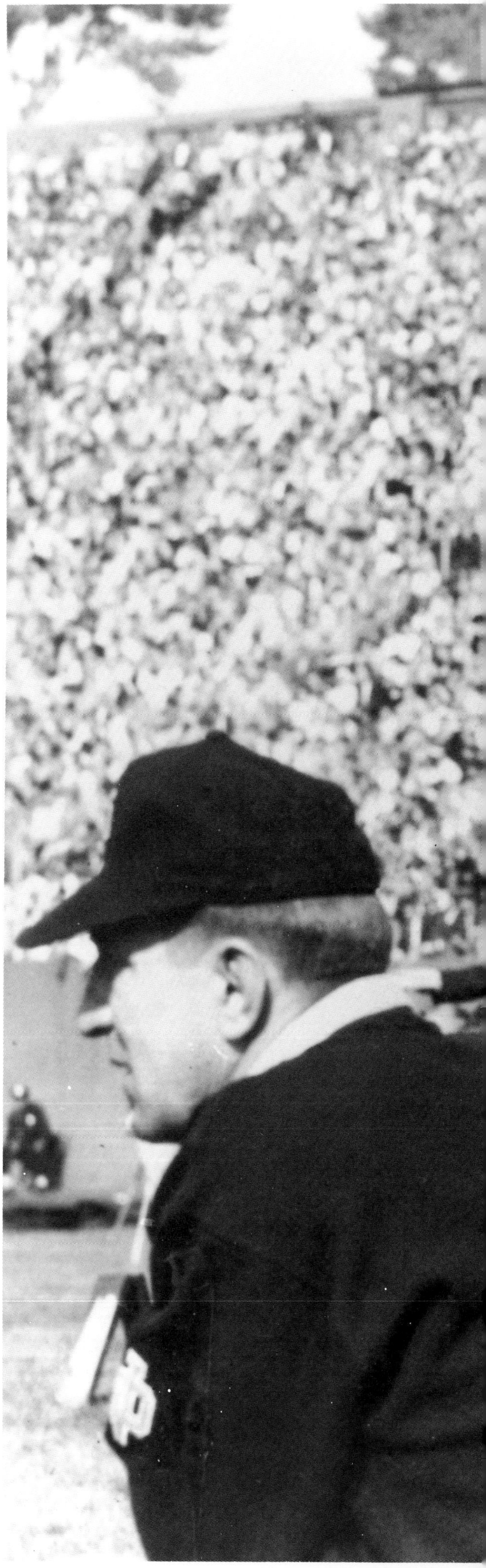

Previous pages: *Coach Terry Brennan stands up to cheer his team on during the 1954 game against Pitt. The Irish won 33-0.*

Opposite top: *Ralph Guglielmi (3) intercepts a pass intended for Texas' Howard Moon during the 1954 season opener at South Bend. The Irish blanked Texas 21-0.*

Opposite bottom: *Coach Terry Brennan talks to his starting eleven before the start of the 1955 season: (l-r, linemen) Bob Scannell, Wayne Edmonds, Ray Lemek, Jim Mense, Pat Bisceglia, Gene Martell and Jim Munro; (l-r, backs) Paul Reynolds, Paul Hornung, Don Schaefer and Jimmy Morse.*

Notre Dame stunned the sports world in early 1954 by announcing the hiring of 25-year-old Terry Brennan, the Irish freshman coach, to replace Leahy. "Terry is a very talented young man who borders almost on the genius as a coach," Leahy said after the announcement. "I have no doubt that he will do an outstanding job."

Despite the surprise of the public, Brennan had displayed just the type of character that Notre Dame wanted in its next coach. A three-year starter in Leahy's backfields of 1946-47-48, Brennan had been graduated in 1949 with a degree in philosophy. Perhaps Brennan had won the job during his playing days when he was taught religion by Father Theodore Hesburgh. Brennan answered the call nicely when Notre Dame officials were challenged to produce a football player who could discuss Aristotle intelligently for a radio program. After graduation he received a law degree in Chicago while coaching football at Mount Carmel High School, where his teams won three straight city championships. He returned to Notre Dame in 1953 as the freshman coach, only to find himself with the top job a year later. Upon his hiring, he made sure he kept as much as he could of Leahy's winning formula, including top assistants Johnny Druze, George Dickson, Francis Johnston, Bill Earley and Bill Fischer.

From Johnny Lattner and Neil Worden in the backfield to Art Hunter on the line, Notre Dame has lost six All-Americans from its 1953 team. Yet Leahy's rebuilding efforts left the team with a substantial mix of young talent and veterans. Ralph Guglielmi returned at quarterback, and with him in the backfield were Joe Heap, Don Schaefer and several others. Most important, the offensive and defensive lines were stocked with veterans, including ends Dan Shannon and Paul Matz, guard Pat Bisceglia and tackle Frank Varrichione. The gem among the newcomers was a sophomore from Louisville, Paul Hornung, whom Leahy had projected as a future great for Notre Dame. His performance against the Old Timers in a spring game as a freshman had led to his nickname, "The Golden Boy." For the season, the offense was again potent, as Schaefer would rush 141 times for 766 yards, a 5.4 average gain. And Guglielmi would throw for 1162 yards, completing 68 of 127 passes for six touchdowns.

On reputation alone the Irish began the

Below: *Coach Terry Brennan with four of the previous season's strongest players, in 1954: (l-r) Quarterback Ralph Guglielmi, fullback Don Schaefer, halfback John Gaffney and halfback Joe Heap.*

year as the nation's second-ranked team and promptly blanked fourth-ranked Texas 21-0. Then they rode into the hailstorm of 19th-ranked Purdue and quarterback Len Dawson, who threw four touchdown passes as the Boilermakers romped, 27-14, in Notre Dame Stadium. Brennan's Irish righted what was wrong from there and ran through the rest of the schedule, dropping Pitt, Michigan State, Navy, Penn, North Carolina, Iowa, Southern Cal and SMU, in order to finish 9-1 as the nation's fourth-ranked team. In the 23-17 win over 17th-ranked Southern Cal, Jim Morse had rushed 19 times for 179 yards and a touchdown. With his performance on the season, Guglielmi was the consensus choice as All-American quarterback and finished fourth in the Heisman voting, won by Wisconsin's Alan Ameche.

After a frustrating freshman season on the scout squad in 1953, during which he considered transferring, Hornung had seen playing time as both a quarterback and fullback on the 1954 varsity. For 1955, he moved into the starting slot at quarterback. Jim Morse returned at right half and Don Schaefer at fullback, while Pat Bisceglia was

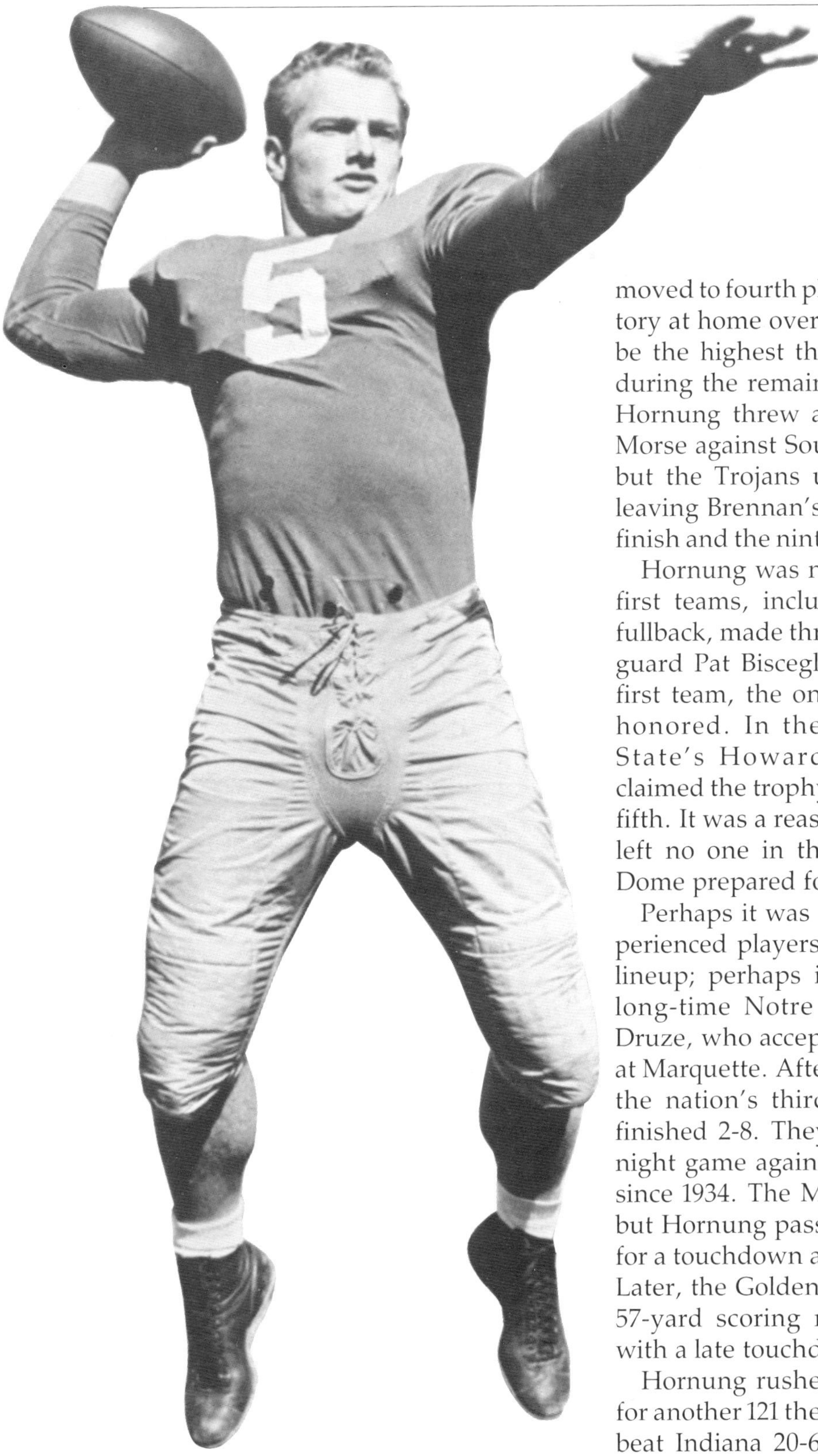

the veteran amid a rebuilding job on the line.

They opened like schedule-busters, shutting out SMU, Indiana and 15th-ranked Miami to move from 11th to fourth in the polls. But then 14th-ranked Michigan State whipped them soundly 21-7, just as enthusiasm was building. Restarting their drive after dropping to 11th in the polls, the Irish beat Purdue, Penn and fourth-ranked Navy to work their way back up to number five. The next week, against North Carolina, Lou Loncaric returned an interception 75 yards for a score that led them to a 27-7 win. They moved to fourth place and took a narrow victory at home over unranked Iowa. It would be the highest they would go in the polls during the remainder of Brennan's tenure. Hornung threw a 78-yard TD pass to Jim Morse against Southern Cal the next week, but the Trojans upset Notre Dame 42-20, leaving Brennan's second team with an 8-2 finish and the ninth spot in the final AP poll.

Hornung was named to five All-America first teams, including UPI. Schaeffer, the fullback, made three first-team squads. And guard Pat Bisceglia was voted to the AP's first team, the only Notre Dame player so honored. In the Heisman voting Ohio State's Howard 'Hopalong' Cassady claimed the trophy, with Hornung finishing fifth. It was a reasonably good finish, and it left no one in the domain of the Golden Dome prepared for the disaster of 1956.

Perhaps it was the large number of inexperienced players moving into the starting lineup; perhaps it was the resignation of long-time Notre Dame assistant Johnny Druze, who accepted the job as head coach at Marquette. After beginning the season as the nation's third-ranked team, the Irish finished 2-8. They lost a season opener, a night game against SMU, for the first time since 1934. The Mustangs took a 13-0 lead, but Hornung passed 55 yards to Jim Morse for a touchdown and kicked the extra point. Later, the Golden Boy tied the score with a 57-yard scoring run. But SMU answered with a late touchdown to win, 19-13.

Hornung rushed for 81 yards and threw for another 121 the next week as Notre Dame beat Indiana 20-6. But things turned sour from there. Purdue won next 28-14, despite two touchdown passes from Hornung. The next week they were tied with second-ranked Michigan State 7-7 at the half, but the Spartans exploded from there, winning 47-14 in Notre Dame Stadium. Even worse, Hornung was injured. Top-ranked Oklahoma took its turn next at wiping its feet on the Irish home turf, winning 40-0. That was followed by road losses to Navy and Pitt. Against the Panthers, Hornung started at fullback and ran 56 yards for a touchdown, but Notre Dame still lost 26-13. In his last home game Hornung scored three touch-

Left: *Paul Hornung was the starting quarterback for the Irish in 1955, and by 1956 his brilliant play earned him the Heisman Trophy. He went on to pro fame with Green Bay.*

Above: *Dean Studer (22) returns a Navy punt to the Navy 44 after taking the ball on the ND six-yard line in the first quarter of the game in South Bend in 1955. Notre Dame outscored Navy 21-7.*

Right: *Quarterback Paul Hornung (5) carries the ball during the 17-14 squeaker over Iowa in 1955.*

63
58

12
13
55
72
5
32

downs, as the Irish downed North Carolina 21-14. His winning score came with less than two minutes left in the game and led to a ride off the field on the shoulders of his teammates. Due to injuries, he played little against Iowa, and the third-ranked Hawkeyes won big, 48-8. It seemed the payback for the Leahy years would never end. In the final game against Southern Cal, Hornung returned a kickoff 96 yards for a touchdown, but the Trojans escaped 28-20.

As might be expected, the 1956 team set a record for kickoff returns – 49 in the season, for 1174 yards. Hornung himself set a record by returning 20 for 556 yards, a 28-yard per carry average. He was named to the AP All-America second team and the UPI first team. But the real surprise of the season came with the Heisman voting. He narrowly outpolled Johnny Majors of Tennessee to win the trophy. "I couldn't believe it when they told me I'd won it," he told a reporter the next day between classes at Notre Dame. "I did not think I was even up for consideration."

Asked about his plans for the future, Hornung replied, "I'm now involved in recuperation. It's been a rough season. Now I have free afternoons – no football drill – and it seems strange. I plan to devote all this additional time to the books." The Golden Boy of course would go on to fame with the Green Bay Packers.

Meanwhile, Notre Dame tried to regroup

Opposite top: *Paul Hornung holds the Heisman Trophy awarded him in 1956 as the nation's outstanding football player. With him is Coach Terry Brennan (right).*

Opposite bottom: *Monty Stickles (80) kicks the winning field goal for the Irish to give them a 23-21 victory over Army in 1957.*

Above: *Dick Lynch (25) sweeps into the end zone for a touchdown that gave the Irish the upset victory of the 1957 season, over the second-ranked Oklahoma Sooners 7-0. The game ended Oklahoma's 47-game winning streak, the longest in college football history.*

Right: *Notre Dame guard Allan Ecuyer (60) drives past an SMU blocker in action in 1957. The Irish slashed SMU 54-21.*

Opposite top: *Starting quarterback Daryle Lamonica (3) and backup Frank Budka (2) work with Coach Joe Kuharich at the opening of fall practice in 1961.*

Below: *Quarterback George Izo threw for 1067 yards and nine touchdowns, completing 68 of 118, in the 1958 season.*

its battered football program, and in fact Brennan did return the team to winning ways in 1957. The season brought a renewal of the Army rivalry, and after opening with shutout wins over Purdue and Indiana, the 12th ranked Irish met the 10th-ranked Cadets in Philadelphia. Army took a 12-0 lead and stretched it to 21-7 early in the fourth quarter. Brennan's team rushed back with two touchdowns, only to lag behind at 21-20 when Monty Stickles missed an extra point. The sophomore end redeemed himself in the final moments with a 39-yard field goal for an Irish win, 23-21. After that they whipped Pitt, but then flopped against 16th-ranked Navy. Notre Dame's Nick Pietrosante returned a punt 72 yards for the only Irish score, and the Middies won 20-6. Then fourth-rank Michigan State ran over the Irish 34-6, and the picture looked even worse as the 4-2 Irish headed to Oklahoma to play the second-ranked Sooners, who were sporting a national record 47-game winning streak.

The last time Oklahoma had lost was in September 1953 in Notre Dame Stadium. This time the Irish did them in at Owen Field. The Sooners had scored in 123 straight games, but Notre Dame ended that streak as well. The Notre Dame defense stopped an early Oklahoma drive at their 13, then battled even the rest of the way. In the fourth quarter, facing a fourth and goal at the Oklahoma three, Notre Dame quarterback Bob Williams pitched out to Dick Lynch, who ran it over for the game's only score. Brennan called the 7-0 upset "the greatest game of my life." On the day, the vaunted Sooner rushing game had managed but 98 yards.

From there, the Irish lost the next week to eighth-ranked Iowa, but finished the year 7-3 with big wins over SMU and Southern Cal. Guard Al Ecuyer was named to UPI's All-America first team, and to the casual observer it might have seemed that Brennan had turned the corner. But it was not to be.

Notre Dame faced a schedule with six teams ranked in the top 20 for 1958. They beat three of them and finished 6-4. For the season quarterback George Izo, despite missing some games with injury, threw for 1067 yards and nine touchdowns by completing 68 of 118 attempts. In a last-second loss to Pitt, Izo had struck with a 72-yard pass to Red Mack. The post-season All-America mentions went to Ecuyer and end Monty Stickles.

And the pink slip went to Brennan, who confirmed to reporters after the season that he had been fired. In his statement on the matter Father Hesburgh said, "It is with great reluctance that I accept this recommendation. In the five years that you have been head coach of the university, you have impressed all of us as the kind of young man that Notre Dame aspires to produce." The firing, following a winning season and the big upset of Oklahoma, brought a storm of protest from the media, which charged that Notre Dame had its priorities misplaced.

From there the program descended into a deep abyss of mediocrity. Joe Kuharich, a veteran college and professional coach, was hired to replace Brennan. In four years, he produced a dismal 17-23 record. His first team (1959) finished 5-5. His second, with Daryle Lamonica at quarterback and Nick Buoniconti on the line, won its opener, then lost eight straight, to finish 2-8. With Lamonica and Buoniconti returning for 1961, the Irish climbed to 5-5. Then Kuharich's 1962 team performed at the same level, giving him three 5-5 teams in four years. Believing that his firing was imminent, Kuharich resigned in March 1962 and was replaced by old Notre Dame hand Hugh Devore as interim coach for 1963. Kuharich became director of officials for the National Football League. "We appreciate Notre Dame's understanding in releasing Joe Kuharich from his contract," NFL Commissioner Pete Rozelle said. "With his 28 years of football experience, both college and pro, we feel he will be a valuable addition to the National Football League."

The 1963 season was one of few highlights. The 23 November Iowa game was cancelled due to the death of President John Kennedy. The Irish might well have wished to cancel the others. Notre Dame finished 2-7, although one of the two wins was an upset of seventh-ranked Southern Cal. Again, Notre Dame officials found themselves with the unenviable task of looking for another Rockne.

Below: *Former head coach Joe Kuharich turns over the reins to Hugh Devore in 1963. Devore had filled in as head coach during Frank Leahy's 1945 absence and had a 7-2-1 season.*

35
35

PARSEGHIAN

1964-74

Notre Dame picked Ara Parseghian, the son of an Armenian immigrant, as its next coach, and he quickly won his way into Irish hearts by turning the program around on a dime. Over the course of six short months the team went from being 2-7 losers to storybook challengers for the national championship.

In becoming an overnight sensation, Parseghian stopped the chorus of Notre Dame critics dead. Those who knew Parseghian weren't surprised at his success; he had a football background steeped in excellent coaching. Raised in a cultured family in Akron, Ohio, he came late to the athletic life. As a junior, he went out for his high school

Previous pages: *Halfback Bill Wolski (35) sweeps past Navy attackers in action from the 40-0 shutout of Navy in 1964.*

Above: *John Huarte developed into a fine quarterback in 1964, setting school records for passing yardage (2062) and touchdowns (16) in one season. He also won the Heisman Trophy that year.*

Above right: *This photo of Ara Parseghian was taken in 1957, when he was head football coach at Northwestern University.*

Right: *Parseghian in action on the sidelines during his first season as head coach for Notre Dame, in 1964.*

Above: *Fullback Jack Snow (85) grabs a pass from quarterback John Huarte for an 11-yard gain and sets a new Notre Dame season record for yards gained receiving in one season (1964), breaking Jim Kelly's record of 523 yards set in 1962.*

team and promptly won a starting position at guard. After high school and a brief stint at Akron University, he entered the Navy during World War II and again moved in as a starter, this time on the Great Lakes Naval Station team coached by the legendary Paul Brown. After the service, he enrolled at Miami (Ohio) University, where he earned little All-America honors. Just short of graduation in 1947 the 24-year-old Parseghian took up the offer of Paul Brown and the Cleveland Browns to turn professional. He played one year before a hip injury ended his career, then returned to Miami as an assistant to another legend, Woody Hayes. When Hayes left for Ohio State in 1951, Parseghian assumed the head coaching dutues at Miami.

In five years at Miami he won 39 games and lost just six, a good enough record to earn him the top job at Northwestern, where football fortunes had sagged in the post-war era. Parseghian reversed those after struggling through a dismal first season. In fact, his Northwestern teams won four straight games over Notre Dame, a factor that led to his hiring in South Bend. "I've known Ara Parseghian for many years and know he is one of the best," Athletic Director Moose Krause said of the hiring. "We are sure he will get the job done here at Notre Dame."

Appearing at first not be be impressed by the Notre Dame tradition, Parseghian made sweeping changes that spring of 1964, discarding the old split-T offense and picking up variations of the slot-T and I formations used by the pros. Parseghian had his mind set on the passing game. For the fall, he purchased new uniforms, with helmets that exactly matched the gold in the Golden Dome, blue jerseys and gold pants.

His first real task was to find a quarterback, and amid the scrapheap of talent on campus he discovered one, a forgotten senior, John Huarte, who had failed to letter in 1963 as a third-string junior. A 6-foot, 180-pounder out of Santa Ana, California, Huarte had attempted but 50 passes in two varsity seasons. But Parseghian found him to be just the athlete he needed to run the offense. He could move and throw, and the only ingredient missing seemed to be confidence. That of course would have to come with playing time in 1964.

Over the spring, the Notre Dame staff worked intensively to school Huarte in the offense, to refine his skills, and to assure him that he would be the starter that fall. His primary receiver for 1964 would be another Californian, Jack Snow, who would catch 60 passes in the season for 1114 yards. The others in the Notre Dame backfield were speedy sophomore Nick Eddy at right half, Bill Wolski at left half and Joe Farrell at fullback. Linebacker Jim Carroll was the heart of the defense, along with defensive back Tony Carey, end Alan Page and tackle Kevin Hardy.

The one negative looming in Notre Dame's preparation for the season was a shoulder injury suffered by Huarte in spring practice. Doctors contemplated surgery, but it would mean he would miss the season. So Huarte instead worked at strengthening the shoulder. Parseghian's attempts to turn the team around would hinge on how quickly Huarte started and how much his shoulder affected his passing. He answered those questions and more by throwing for 270 yards in the rain as the Irish opened the season by whipping Wisconsin 31-7 in a road game. Snow alone caught nine passes for 217 yards, setting a new school record. The defense did its part as well, holding the Badgers to a minus 51 yards rushing, a Notre Dame record.

From there, the confidence grew steadily as they defeated Purdue and Bob Griese (Hardy blocked a punt and Page grabbed the loose ball and ran 57 yards for a score), Air Force, UCLA, Stanford and Navy by big scores. Against the Middies, Huarte completed 10 passes for 274 yards, including a 74-yard scoring pass to Eddy.

The 40-0 win over Navy propelled them to number one in the polls, and Parseghian had converted his doubters. As so often is the case, that elevation to the top ranking was followed by a close game the next week, a 17-15 squeaker over Pitt, aided by Huarte's 91-yard scoring pass to Eddy and a late stand by the defense. From there, they blew out

Above: *Halfback Bill Wolski (35) goes around his right end for a short gain in the first quarter of the 1964 Notre Dame-Wisconsin game played in Madison, Wisconsin. The Irish won the season opener 31-7.*

Opposite top: *Quarterback John Huarte (7) keeps the ball and leaps past Michigan State defenders on his way to a fourth-quarter touchdown before a packed house in South Bend on 14 November 1964. The home crowd saw the Irish win 34-7.*

Opposite center: *Ace passer John Huarte in action against Pitt in 1964.*

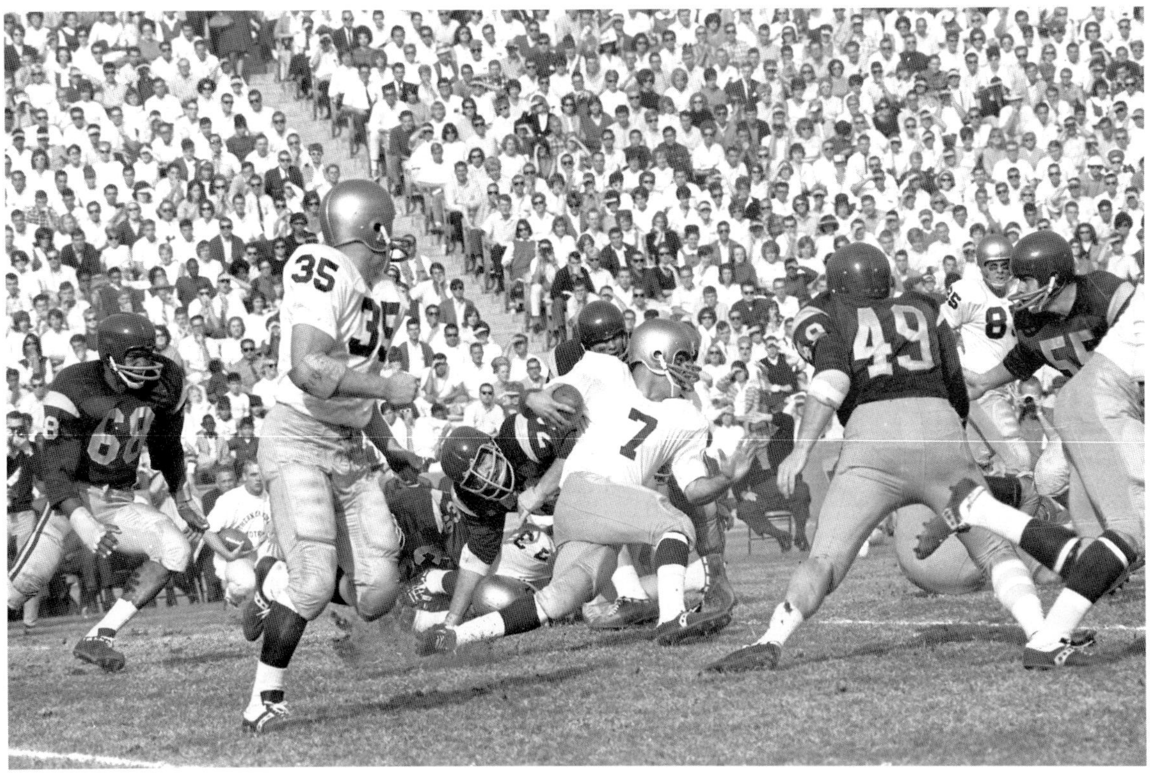

Opposite bottom: *Coach Ara Parseghian is carried off the field by his team after their eighth straight victory of the season, over Michigan State, 34-7.*

Left: *John Huarte cuts in for a four-yard gain against the University of Southern California in Los Angeles on 28 November 1964. Thirteen-point favorites, the Irish went down in the last game of the season, 20-17, spoiling their perfect record and costing them the national championship.*

Iowa and Michigan State to stand 9-0 heading into their final game on the road against Southern Cal and fleet back Mike Garrett. The Trojans fumbled the opening kickoff, and Notre Dame recovered, converting the turnover into a 3-0 lead minutes later on a Ken Ivan field goal. A short time later Huarte drove the Irish to a touchdown and a 10-0 lead by alternating his passes between Snow and receiver Phil Sheridan. As soon as USC's defense loosened to stop his passing, Huarte struck back hard with the ground game, and Notre Dame added another score, this time on a run by Wolski, to take the halftime lead 17-0.

The avenue seemed open for the Irish to coast from that point on to a storybook national championship. It seemed hard to believe they could traverse the distance from 2-7 to 10-0 so quickly. But their glimpse of glory vanished quickly in the third quarter, as Garrett returned a kickoff deep into Notre Dame territory, then scored a touchdown moments later after a short drive. Notre Dame drove to another score, but the play was brought back on a holding call, and they got nothing. A short time later, USC quarterback Craig Fertig tossed a short scoring pass to pull within four at 17-13, with just under five minutes left. Now the Notre Dame offense that had worked so well all season stumbled and failed to get the needed first down. The Trojans regained possession at their own 40 with two minutes left. Fertig used up the clock expertly, lancing a scoring pass into Irish hearts as the last few seconds

Far right: *Linebacker Jim Lynch was voted All-America in 1966 and also won the Maxwell Award that year.*

Below: *QB Terry Hanratty (right) and end Jim Seymour made a spectacular passing combination that brought the Irish the national championship in 1966, they couldn't bring back the magic in 1967 and 1968.*

bled from the scoreboard. There was time for the ensuing kickoff and no more. Notre Dame's dream had died, 20-17.

The consolations were nice and numerous, but somehow they couldn't replace a lost national championship. The Irish finished third in the final polls behind Alabama and Arkansas. The big surprise came when Huarte edged Jerry Rhone of Tulsa in the Heisman voting, one of the greatest surprises in the history of the trophy. Jack Snow finished fifth. On the year, Huarte had completed 114 of 205 attempts, for 2062 yards and 16 touchdowns (both yardage and touchdowns set new Notre Dame records). In addition, he rushed for three scores.

The news spread quickly across the football world. Joseph Huarte, his father, was interviewed shortly after the announcement. "His character is fixed," the father said of the son. "He hasn't changed since high school. These honors bring new responsibilities, and I just hope he retains what he has." At South Bend, Huarte offered reporters a modesty borne of three years on the bench when they asked about his incredible victory. "I was lucky, I had good receivers, great blocking and a great effort

from everybody," he said. Parseghian could only think of what would have happened had Huarte's shoulder injury proved more serious. "They almost operated on him," the coach told reporters. "Without Huarte we would have been a three yards and a cloud of dust type of team. We built our whole offense around him, and I've lived in constant dread of what we would do if something happened to him."

For the year, he ranked third nationally in total offense, with 2069 yards. He was named back of the year and player of the year by UPI. Snow was named to UPI's All-America first team and AP's second. Jim Carroll was a UPI second teamer, while Tony Carey and Kevin Hardy received mention on other teams. The Football Writers Association named Parseghian Coach of the Year, and the American Football Coaches Association decided he should share its Coach of the Year honor with Arkansas' Frank Broyles.

Matching the 1964 showing would prove impossible the next year. Huarte had been graduated to the New York Jets and was replaced by Bill Zloch, who was limited as a passer but full of heart and grit as a competitor. Wolski and Eddy remained the fixtures in the backfield, with Larry Conjar moving in at fullback. Dick Arrington and Tom Regner would lead a veteran offensive line. But the defense received a blow when Kevin Hardy was injured early on and missed most of the season. Going two ways, Arrington replaced him in the defensive lineup. Alan

Below: *Back Nick Eddy (47) is caught in mid-air by Purdue's Jim Long as he hurdles teammate Tom Regner (76) during action at Lafayette in 1965. The Irish fell victim to the sixth-ranked Boilermakers, 25-21.*

Above: *Bill Wolski (35) goes over the top for a short gain against USC in 1965. The Irish redeemed themselves after the 1964 heartbreaker by beating the Trojans in South Bend 28-7*

Page returned at defensive end, and Carey again was the man in the secondary.

All in all, it wasn't a bad year. They opened by blowing out California to move to number one in the polls, then lost the second game to Bob Griese and sixth-ranked Purdue 25-21. From there, they ripped through six victories, only to lose their ninth game 12-3 to top-ranked Michigan State. They closed out a 7-2-1 season with a scoreless tie with Miami (Florida) and a ninth-place finish in the polls.

Wolski, who had scored eight touchdowns, finished 11th in the Heisman voting, while Arrington and safety Nick Rassas both made UPI and AP All-America first teams, with Jim Lynch and Tom Regner being named to second teams.

Left: *John Huarte holds his Heisman Trophy while his mother and father congratulate him in a 1964 publicity photo.*

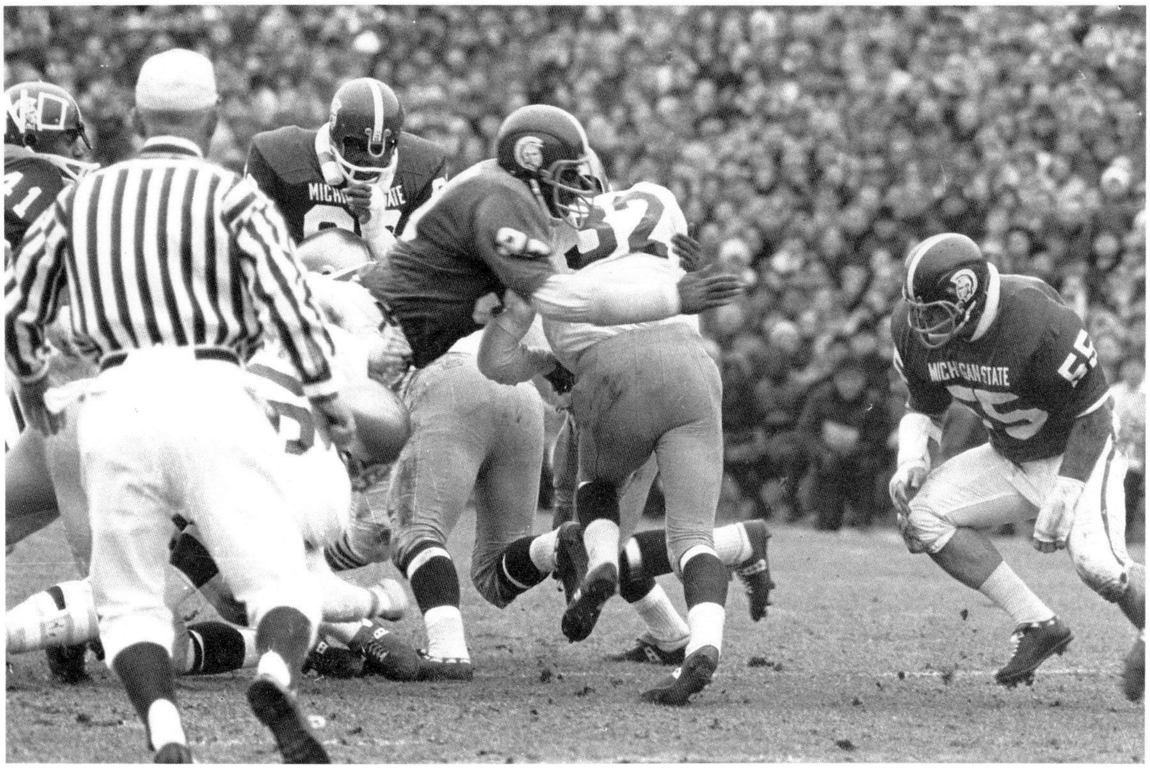

The coaching challenge for 1966 was to find a passer, and find one in a hurry, for the Irish would open the season against Purdue and senior Bob Griese. Their top candidates, Terry Hanratty and Coley O'Brien, both sophomores, had no varsity experience. After evaluating both, the coaches went with Hanratty, a 6-foot-1, 190 pounder from Pennsylvania. He was matched with another sophomore, 6-foot-4, 210-pound Jim Seymour, to give the Irish a passing combination equal to Huarte-Snow. Nick Eddy returned to left half as a senior, and Rocky Bleier moved in at right half. Kevin Hardy and Alan Page returned to the defensive line, and Notre Dame featured an excellent pair of linebackers in Jim Lynch and John Pergine.

There was hope that Hanratty and Seymour would be good, and in the days preceding the Purdue game those hopes spiralled. Seymour seemed to catch everything. Primed as they were, they exploded against eighth-ranked Purdue in Notre Dame Stadium. Bleier fumbled a pass toward the close of an opening drive, and Purdue's LeRoy Keyes picked up the ball and raced 95 yards to give the Boilermakers a 7-0 lead. That edge lasted only as long as it took Nick Eddy to return the kickoff 97 yards for a Notre Dame score. From there, Hanratty and Seymour did the rest. The young quarterback completed 16 of 24 passes for 304 yards and three touchdowns. Seymour caught 13 of those balls for a school-record 276 yards receiving and three touchdowns, as Notre Dame won 26-14.

Northwestern, Army and North Carolina all fell by big numbers, with the victories propelling Notre Dame to the top of the polls. Then the Irish did the same to 10th-ranked Oklahoma, 38-0, the worst loss the Sooners had suffered in more than two decades. The pace continued as Navy, Pitt and Duke collapsed by a combined score of 135-7. Each pounding provided more fuel for the Notre Dame steamroller, building enthusiasm and intensity across the campus. Students, fans, alumni all jumped on board, leaving the excitable Parseghian as engineer of a frenzied locomotive.

Their excitement was focused on the 19 November meeting with Duffy Daugherty's Michigan State team, also undefeated, also rolling on the hopes of a national championship. Like two freight trains they collided in East Lansing, Michigan, that Saturday afternoon, with a nationwide television audience looking on. It was, perhaps, the biggest college football game of the decade. The Spartans were led by their 6-foot-7 defensive end, Bubba Smith; the Irish by Seymour and Hanratty. Nick Eddy had an injured shoulder and was unable to play.

The Notre Dame team pulled up in their buses at the stadium to find a frenzied crowd of students from South Bend. "Goooo Irish, beeaaat Spartans," the students were chanting. Then they broke into "Win, win, win, win, win, win," and then, "Kill Bubba, kill Bubba, kill Bubba." One of the last players off the buses, Seymour turned to a reporter,

Opposite top: *Game action from the 1966 Notre Dame-Michigan State game played in East Lansing. The big game between the first-ranked Irish and second-ranked Spartans ended in a tie.*

Left: *End Jim Seymour (85) jumps to snag a pass in the 1966 Notre Dame-Purdue game.*

Above: *Backup QB Coley O'Brien is rushed by the Spartans' Bubba Smith, 1966.*

grinned and remarked, "We have a very passive group of students."

The second-ranked Spartans were primed for the showdown, particularly Bubba Smith. He knocked both Hanratty and starting center George Goeddeke out in the first quarter. Hanratty's shoulder injury finished him for the rest of the season. O'Brien, his replacement, had recently been diagnosed as having diabetes, placing a limitation on his stamina.

Michigan State ran out to a 10-point lead with a four-yard run by Regis Cavender and a 47-yard field goal by Dick Kenney. But O'Brien pushed the Irish downfield with a 54-yard drive capped by a 34-yard scoring pass to Bob Gladieux, Eddy's replacement. He again drove them into scoring position at the opening of the fourth quarter, but their progress died on the Spartan 10. From there, Joe Azzaro kicked a 28-yard field goal to tie the game at 10. With five minutes left, Tom Schoen intercepted a Michigan State pass

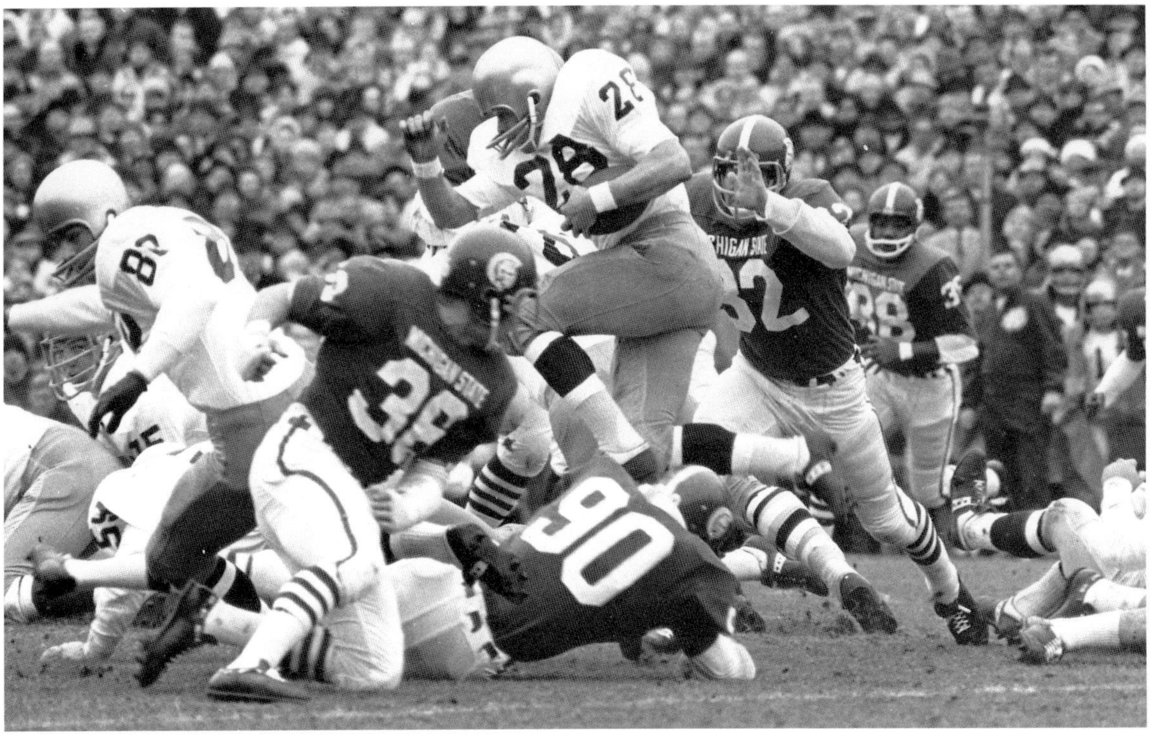

Left: *ND halfback Rocky Bleier (28) goes over the top for a short gain in the Notre Dame-Michigan State game in 1966.*

Opposite top: *The offense for the 1968 Fighting Irish.*

Opposite bottom: *Quarterback Terry Hanratty (5) looks to make the handoff in action from the 1967 game against top-ranked Southern Cal. The Irish were defeated 24-7.*

Below: *All-America end Jim Seymour placed third in the Heisman voting in 1968.*

and returned it to the Spartan 18. But State's defense threw back the Notre Dame offense, and Azzaro's field goal attempt from 42 yards was wide right. Late in the game the Irish got the ball back at their own 30 with time for several passing plays. But rather than risk an interception, Parseghian was conservative, a decision that brought rounds of criticism. The game ended tied.

The Notre Dame coach explained his decision to reporters afterward: "Interceptions almost cost Michigan State the game; we weren't going to give it away cheaply. It had to do with (Dick) Kenney's ability as a field-goal kicker. If it was early in the fourth quarter it would have been different, but we weren't going to give up the ball deep in our own territory and take a risk on losing the game after battling like we did."

On fourth and short in their own territory with the clock ticking down, Notre Dame had gone for and gotten a first down. Reporters wanted to know why Parseghian took that gamble. "We wanted to maintain possession." he said. "At that time, the lesser risk was the quarterback sneak. If we had punted, we might have had a bad snap, or the punt blocked, or a long punt return. The sneak was the lesser of the evils. And so was the possibility of Kenny being able to make a field-goal from that range."

Smith and the Michigan State players were irate "It was too obvious," Smith said. "They were playing like they really didn't want to come on and play." Another Spartan player was even more pointed. "I was hoping I could say that Notre Dame was a great team," he said, "but after the last few plays, I can't say that. We played to win. I respect 'em, but I resent 'em for what happened. We should be Number One now, because we played to win. Champions play to win and they weren't playing to win."

The game settled little for college football, as the polls were mixed in their judgment. But the decision was made easier when O'Brien and the Irish hammered Southern Cal 51-0 to close their season at 9-0-1. They were almost unanimously acclaimed national champions: Only the Helms Foundation and the National Football Foundation Hall of Fame selected Michigan State. Nick Eddy, who had closed out a college career with 1615 yards rushing (a 5.5 average gain), finished third in the Heisman voting, and Hanratty sixth. The sophomore quarterback had thrown for 1247 yards and eight touchdowns, enough for mention on the AP's All-American third team. Seymour had 862 yards in receptions. Nick Eddy and linebacker Jim Lynch were unanimous selections to the All-America first teams. Guard Tom Regner was also a consensus All-American. Eight other Irish players, including Alan Page, were named to second or third teams. Lynch, meanwhile, was voted the Maxwell Award as the outstanding player in college football.

With two more varsity seasons ahead of them, the football world seemed to be Terry Hanratty's and Jim Seymour's oyster. They had been featured on the cover of *Time* magazine and publicized far and wide by the sports media. Yet they never quite realized

Above: *End Tom Gatewood teamed with quarterback Jim Theismann in 1969 to produce a passing duo to rival Hanratty and Seymour, who had preceded them. By 1970 they were setting records.*

Top right: *Theismann (7) shows his passing form during a 1969 game against Northwestern as the Wildcats' Ray Forsthoffer (52) puts the rush on him.*

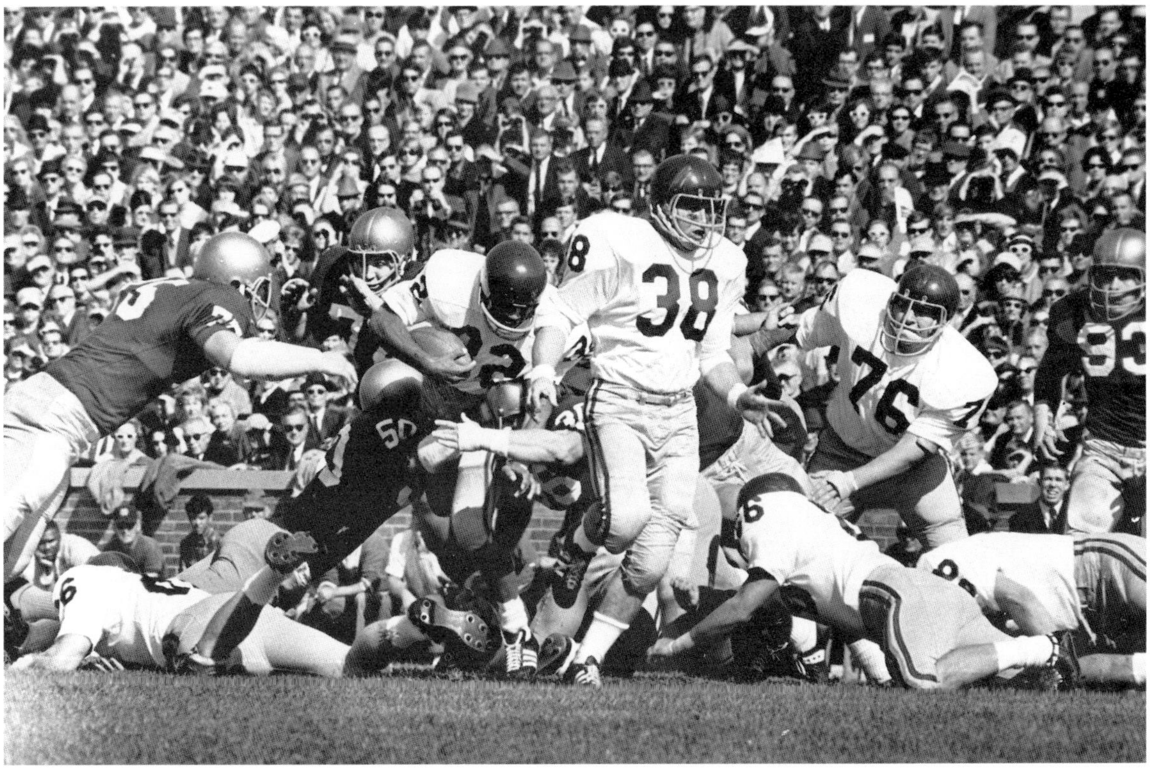

Above: *ND lineman John Pergine (50) tackles Southern Cal's O J Simpson during the first quarter of the 1967 matchup.*

their promise. The Irish opened the 1967 season as the nation's top-ranked team but lost to Purdue and Mike Phipps 28-21 in the second game: Hanratty's 366 yards passing wasn't enough to pull it out. After a 24-7 defeat by top-ranked Southern Cal and O J Simpson in the fourth game of the season they stood 2-2. Hanratty had begun throwing interceptions, and their confidence seemed rattled. They regrouped and went on to earn the school's 500th victory in the ninth game of the season against Georgia Tech. They finished the year 8-2 with a close victory over Miami, enough to earn them a fifth-place ranking in the final polls.

Tom Schoen, defensive back, and defensive end Kevin Hardy were consensus choices to the AP and UPI All-America first teams. Seymour made the UPI first team. But the potential of another championship had gone unfulfilled.

The same would happen in 1968, the senior season for Seymour and Hanratty. They opened third-ranked and full of steam, bashing fifth-ranked Oklahoma 45-21 in Notre Dame Stadium. But then Mike

Above: *Quarterback Joe Theismann jumps over teammate Ron Dushney (38) for a touchdown in the first quarter of the 1968 game against Pitt. Theismann, who started the game for the injured starting QB Terry Hanratty, went eight yards for the touchdown. He threw another touchdown in that game to lead the Irish to a 56-7 pasting of the Panthers.*

Phipps, Leroy Keyes and top-ranked Purdue ended their dreams again, 37-22. They pounded Iowa, Northwestern and Illinois in frustration, but then lost again to Michigan State 21-17. A victory over Navy gave them some hope, but Hanratty's college career was ended prematurely by injury the next week in practice.

He was replaced by a wiry little 6-foot sophomore, Joe Theismann, a nervy player who wanted fame so badly he would change the pronunciation of his last name from "Theesman" to rhyme with the trophy he coveted. The coaches figured Joe as a pretty good runner, but they also got a better look at his arm when he started against Pitt and threw two touchdown passes to lead Notre Dame in a 56-7 romp. The era of Joe Theismann had come in with a flickering of the scoreboard lights. The flashing continued the next week with a 34-6 win over Georgia Tech, as Theismann again showed his promise. The season ended, however, on another frustrating note, a 21-21 tie with Southern Cal in O J Simpson's final college game. The Irish had led 21-7, but Simpson brought the Trojans back.

Hanratty's career closed with his naming to the UPI and AP All-America first teams. Tackle George Kunz and Seymour made the UPI first team and the AP second. In the Heisman voting, Hanratty finished third behind Simpson.

With Seymour and Hanratty graduated, Theisman and 6-foot-2 sophomore Tom Gatewood became the Notre Dame passing combination for 1969. Around them, Parseghian rebuilt his team. Moving into the defensive picture were two super sophomores, end Walt Patulski and back Clarence Ellis. If nothing else, the '69 Irish got their problems out of the way early, losing to Purdue in the second game and tying third-ranked Southern Cal in the fifth. From there, they rushed to an 8-1-1 close and eighth place in the polls, as Theismann passed for 1531

Opposite: *All-American Joe Theismann holds the Notre Dame school record as single-season all-time passing leader, with 155 completions in 268 attempts for a total of 2429 yards and 16 touchdowns. He went on to star for Washington's Redskins.*

Above: *Game action from the 1968 meeting of Purdue and Notre Dame. The second game of the season, the Irish were defeated.*

Right: *Defensive end Walt Patulski arrived on the Notre Dame sports scene in 1969 and by his senior year, 1971, he was voted All-American.*

yards and 13 touchdowns.

The season marked the first time in 45 years that Notre Dame had agreed to go to a bowl game since Knute Rockne took the Four Horsemen to the 1925 Rose Bowl and whipped Stanford. For the grand coming out the '69 Irish were matched against top-ranked Texas in the Cotton Bowl. The Irish struck in the first quarter on a 26-yard field goal by Scott Hempel, then increased that lead to 10-0 in the second period when Theismann whipped Gatewood the ball for a 54-yard touchdown. Jim Bertelsen scored on a one-yard plunge for the Longhorns, to pull them within three, at 10-7, just before the half.

The third quarter developed as a grand defensive faceoff, but Texas drove 77 yards early in the fourth to take a 14-10 lead on a short run by Ted Koy. Running and passing, Theismann took Notre Dame back to paydirt just three minutes later, finishing off the drive with a 24-yard scoring pass to Jim Yoder for a 17-14 lead. The Longhorns responded with another drive, this time 76 yards, capped by yet another plunge, a one-yarder by Billy Dale for a 21-17 lead. On the drive, Texas had converted two critical

fourth down plays to keep moving. With a minute left, Theismann had just time enough to run his Irish back downfield. With 28 seconds left he had Notre Dame at the 39, but his next pass was intercepted, ending the threat. "I forced the pass," Theismann said afterward in the Notre Dame dressing room. "I had plenty of time, but I threw it high."

Still, the junior quarterback had broken two Cotton Bowl records. He completed 17 of 27 passes for 231 yards, moving past the 228 set by Roger Staubach in 1964, and his total offense of 279 yards bettered the 267 set by Duke Carlisle, also in 1964. "It was a tremendous football game," said Parseghian "They came up with two clutch plays on fourth down," the coach said. "I thought the pass to Speyrer was a poor pass, too low, and favorable for us. But it was a great catch." Defensive tackle Mike McCoy was a unanimous selection as All-American, with four other Irish receiving mention on second teams.

Notre Dame's 1969 frustration burst into an offensive explosion in 1970, as Theismann set passing records, Gatewood set receiving records and the team set total offense marks. Better yet, they all got to ring up another legendary season in the Irish annals. For the season, Theismann completed 155 of 268 passes for a school record 2429 yards and 16 touchdowns. Gatewood,

Top: *The Texas Longhorns take it over for a touchdown against Notre Dame in the 1970 Cotton Bowl.*

Above: *Coach Ara Parseghian has a word with quarterback Joe Theismann during the 1971 Cotton Bowl.*

meanwhile, caught 77 of those passes for 1123 yards and seven touchdowns Theismann's season totals would bring him 5432 yards of total offense, then a Notre Dame record later to be broken by Steve Beuerlein in 1986. Against Southern Cal alone Theismann completed 33 of 58 passes for 526 yards. In the second game of the season, against Purdue, Gatewood had 192 yards in receptions.

The great numbers, however, didn't always translate into big things on the scoreboard. The Irish zipped past opponents for seven big wins to move to the top spot in the polls. There, they struggled with lowly Georgia Tech before winning 10-7, then grazed seventh-ranked LSU 3-0 to stand 9-0 heading into their final regular-season game with none other than Southern Cal and coach John McKay. But as it had in the past, it rained on the Irish in Southern California. The Trojans raced out to a good lead, then held on for a 38-28 upset. The Irish saw their national championship washed away in a California storm drain.

Their redemption came with an invitation

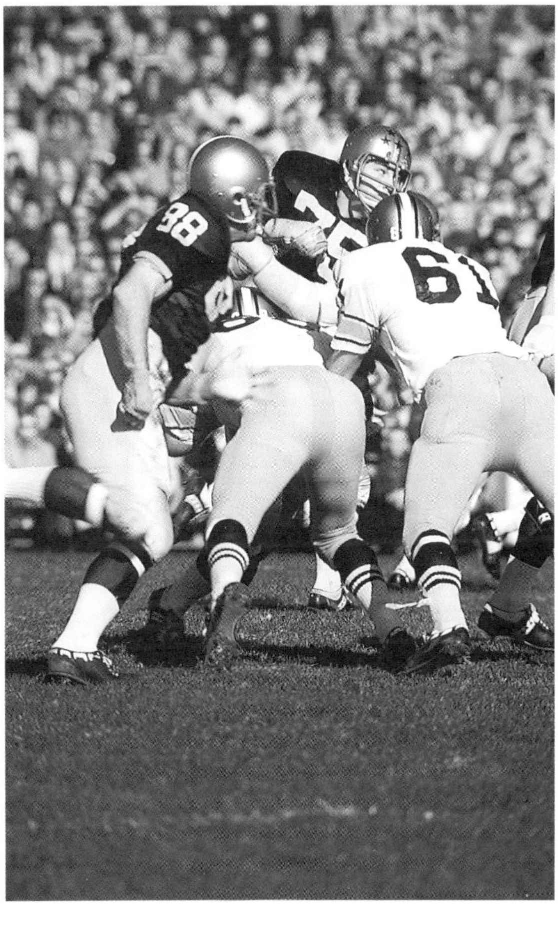

Above: *Theismann scrambles for a four-yard gain in the 1970 Notre Dame-USC game. The Trojans upset the Irish 38-28.*

Left: *Game action as the Fighting Irish meet the Pitt Panthers in 1970.*

Above: *Tom Gatewood (44) keeps an eye on the action during the Notre Dame-Northwestern game in 1971. Gatewood holds the school record for single-season top receivers, with 77 receptions for 1123 yards and 7 touchdowns in 1970.*

Right: *Big Walt Patulski (85) is all over the Wildcats' quarterback in this photo from the 1971 Notre Dame-Northwestern game.*

Opposite: *Six Notre Dame defensemen bring down a Wildcat ball-carrier during the 1971 game.*

to meet top-ranked Texas in the Cotton Bowl. Coach Darrel Royal's Longhorns came into the game with a 30-game winning streak and seeking another national championship. They left with the Irish brand still smoking on their rumps, as Theismann ran for two touchdowns and passed for another in the first two quarters. On that momentum, Notre Dame ran up 24 first-half points, taking a 21-3 lead. The Longhorns answered with a touchdown and two-point conversion late in the second quarter. But the Irish closed down all scoring in the second half and carried off a 24-11 upset. On the day, Notre Dame had forced nine Texas fumbles.

Theismann was ecstatic to close his career with a major victory. "I haven't been so happy since I was married," he said with a wide grin, "and that was only three weeks ago. . . . We really started getting mentally ready yesterday. It started in practice and you could just feel it. We had a good week of practice, and it all reached a peak today."

Theismann finished second in the Heisman voting to Stanford's Jim Plunkett and

was named to the AP All-America first team. He was voted second on the UPI team. Guard Larry DiNardo made both the AP and UPI first teams, while Clarence Ellis and Gatewood were UPI first teamers.

Turmoil came like a whirlwind in the 1971 season. On paper, at the opening of practice, it looked as if it could be a great year. Of 1970's 22 starters, 16 were returning, including receiver Tom Gatewood, defensive end Walt Patulski and defensive back Clarence Ellis. The big problem, however, was quarterback, where a group of newcomers were fighting to start. Parseghian opened the season with Pat Steenberge, Theismann's backup, but everyone got to play in a 50-7 wipeout of Northwestern. The offense bogged down the next week against Purdue, and Notre Dame escaped 8-7 only by virtue of a blocked punt for a touchdown late in the

game and a two-point conversion.

Steenberge was injured in the Purdue game, and Bill Etter started the following week against Michigan State, a 14-2 victory. Etter performed well but injured his knee late in the game. That set of circumstances brought the emergence of Cliff Brown, the first quarterback for the Irish. He led Notre Dame to a pair of shutouts over Miami and North Carolina, yet there was an uneasy feeling that he wasn't accepted. When the six-ranked Irish were upset by Southern Cal the next week, 28-14, those feelings increased. Navy, Pitt and Tulane were vanquished in order, giving Notre Dame the opportunity to play in the Gator Bowl after the season. The players were left to decide if they wanted to accept the bowl invitation, and after a heated dispute, the team voted not to accept. Apparently their dissension over the bowl led to their flat play in the final game of the season, a 28-8 loss to LSU. With their decision, the Irish ended their season 8-2 and ranked 13th in the final AP poll, the first time a Parseghian team at Notre Dame had finished out of the Top 10. Ellis and Patulski were both voted consensus All-Americans. And Gatewood finished his fine career with 157 receptions for 2283 yards and 19 touchdowns, an average of 112 yards per game.

For the 1972 season, Tom Clements, a fine sophomore, moved in at quarterback, with Brown as the backup. And Dave Casper,

Opposite top: *Defenseman Mike Townsend (80) is taken down by a Michigan State Spartan with one of his school-record ten season interceptions in 1972.*

Opposite bottom: *ND halfback Eric Penick (44) dashes 12 yards into the end zone for a third-quarter TD that put the Irish ahead of top-ranked Alabama, 21-17, in the 1973 Sugar Bowl. The Irish came up with the victory, 24-23.*

Top left: *ND quarterback Pat Steenberge looks for a receiver.*

Left: *Quarterback Tom Clements (2) tries to loft a pass over the arms of Nebraska's John Dutton in the 1973 Orange Bowl. The Cornhuskers crushed the Irish 40-6.*

who would go on to fame as a tight end, played left offensive tackle. On defense, 6-foot-5, 265-pound Greg Marx, a co-captain, would earn consensus All-America honors.

The Irish won their first four before being upset by Missouri 30-26 in the rain at Notre Dame Stadium. They won their next four after that, but top-ranked Southern Cal and Anthony Davis overpowered them 45-23 in the last game of the season, for another 8-2 finish. But this time, when the Orange Bowl offered, Notre Dame accepted.

Unfortunately, the Irish might have wished they hadn't. Johnny Rodgers ran wild in a Cornhusker romp, 40-6. Notre Dame finished the year 14th in the polls. The big note of the year was Mike Townsend's 10 interceptions, a season record at Notre Dame. Clements had finished his first season with 1163 yards throwing and eight touchdowns, a confidence-builder that would give the offense a good base for the next two seasons.

Art Best at left half and Eric Penick at right gave the Irish excellent speed. And fullback Wayne Bullock provided the power. Yet even with this balance of talent and experience, no one quite expected what the Irish accomplished in 1973. Unrelated to football, the early season brought the death of Clements' 13-year-old sister, who had been struck by an automobile. Clements was told of the accident just after Notre Dame's opening win over Northwestern. From there, they rolled through a string of blowouts, struggling with Michigan State 14-10 but defeating sixth-ranked USC and Anthony Davis 23-14. Pitt and Tony Dorsett fell 31-10. They closed out a perfect 10-0 regular season with a 44-0 thrashing of Miami.

On New Year's Eve, third-ranked Notre Dame would meet top-ranked Alabama in the Sugar Bowl. The Crimson Tide of Coach Bear Bryant was also undefeated. Quarterback Jeff Rutledge led Alabama's Wishbone offense, and oddsmakers considered it powerful enough to rate 'Bama a seven-point favorite.

The two teams gave New Orleans and the football world a classic to remember that

Above: *Tom Clements (2) is rushed by a SoCal Trojan in action from the 1973 game. Notre Dame defeated the sixth-ranked Trojans 23-14.*

Opposite top: *The Notre Dame defense takes down Purdue's QB in 1973. The Boilermakers were one of the 10 teams the Irish defeated for a perfect regular season.*

Opposite bottom: *The 1973 Notre Dame squad enters the stadium. They would go on to win the national championship.*

50

49
42
33
52
95
60
82

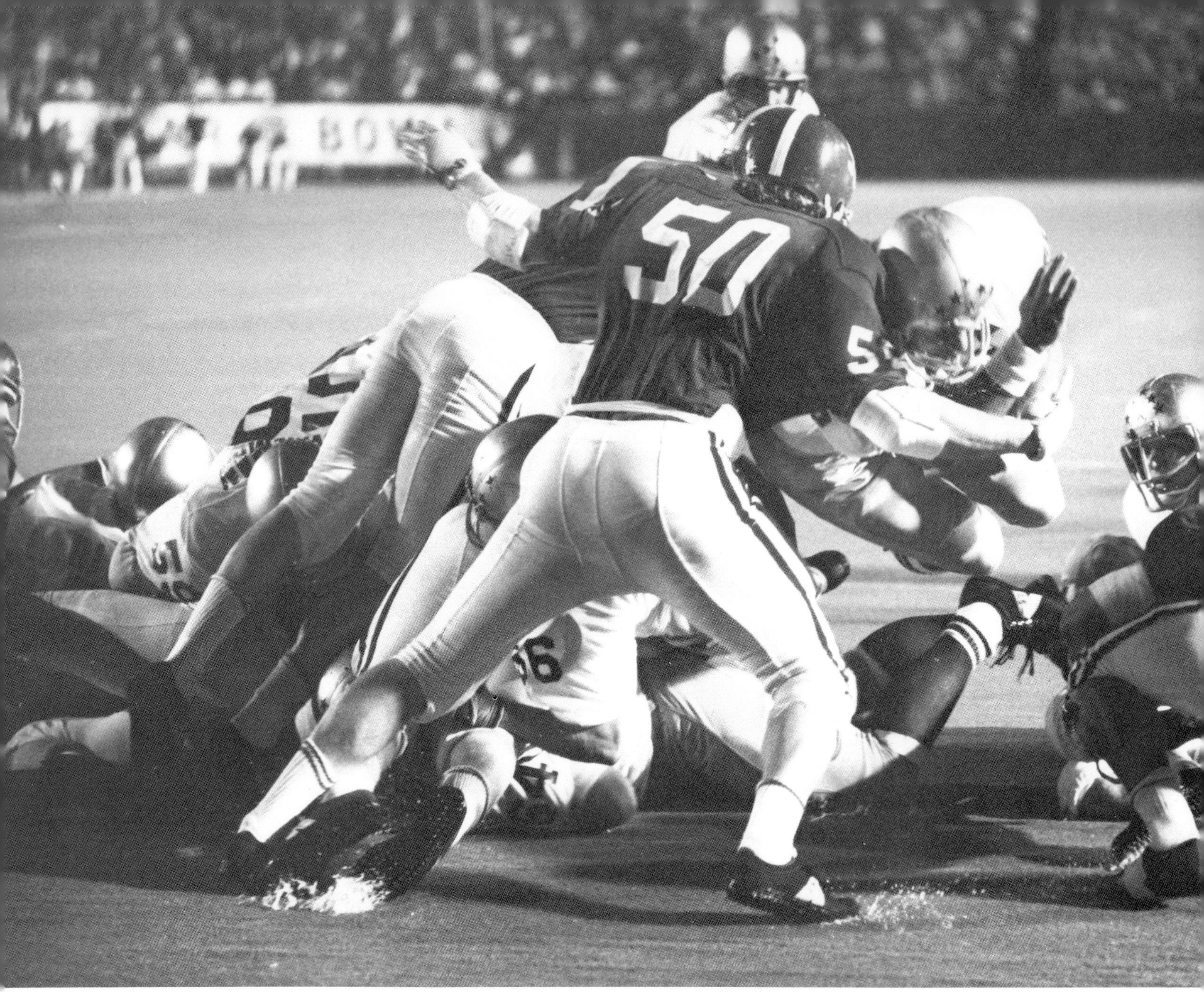

Above: *Fullback Wayne Bullock can't be stopped by Alabama's Wayne Hall (50) or the 'Bama line as he slashes into the end zone for the Irish's first touchdown in the 21-17 victory over the Crimson Tide.*

Right: *Ara Parseghian (right) symbolically hands the ball to Dan Devine, who would succeed him as head coach in 1975.*

night. Notre Dame struck first with a 64-yard drive fueled by Clements' passing. Bullock scored from the six, but the conversion kick failed because of a high snap from the center. Alabama took a 7-6 lead midway through the second period on a 52-yard drive. Notre Dame's special teams lashed right back, as Al Hunter returned the ensuing kickoff 93 yards for a touchdown. Clements threw for the two-point conversion and a 14-7 lead. Then, just before the half, the Tide drove to a field goal and trailed 14-10. Alabama took the lead, 17-14, early in the third quarter with a 93-yard drive. Notre Dame got it back toward the close of the period by converting an Alabama fumble into a short drive for a score. Penick ran 12 yards for a 21-17 lead. But the Irish stumbled early in the fourth, when Bullock's fumble set up a short Alabama drive for a 23-21 lead. This time, however, the Alabama conversion went awry in the winds of the Sugar Bowl.

Clements then drove the Irish to the winning points. A key play in the effort was a 19-yard pass to Dave Casper, who had moved from tackle to tight end before the season. Bob Thomas booted a 19-yard field goal for a 24-23 lead. The climax came with Notre Dame facing a third and eight from its own two. Clements threw for the first down to sophomore tight end Robin Weber. With another first down moments later, they successfully ran out the clock.

Parseghian was aglow. "I definitely feel we're the national champion," he said. "We beat the leading scoring team in the nation and the team that was leading in offensive yardage. They are an excellently disciplined football team. We beat a great football team, and they lost to a great football team."

The Associated Press voters bought Parseghian's pitch and voted the Irish National Champions. UPI however, voted the Tide tops. Townsend was a consensus All-American for the Irish. Casper made UPI's first team.

There was speculation that Parseghian

Above: *Wayne Bullock drops over the goal line for the first TD of the Orange Bowl game against Alabama in 1975. The 13-11 win over the nine-point favorite Tide was a perfect ending to a great career for Coach Parseghian.*

might leave Notre Dame for some other plum coaching assignment. But as one of the modern game's greatest, Parseghian had reached the pinnacle. When he left, it would be for good. Unfortunately for Notre Dame, that would be after only one more season.

Clements was back for 1974, as were Best and Bullock in the backfield. The Irish began the year second-ranked but couldn't maintain their sheen. They were upset by Purdue in the third game but held a 9-1 record going into their final regular season game on the road with sixth-ranked USC.

With Clements throwing crisply, the Irish took a 24-6 halftime lead, but then came one of the stranger moments in the school's history. Anthony Davis ran the second-half kickoff back 100 yards, starting the Trojans on a 49-point scoring binge over the next 17 minutes. When quarterback Pat Haden and Anthony Davis were through, Notre Dame had been demolished, 55-24, one of the most incredible comebacks in college football history.

Two weeks later Parseghian announced his resignation, saying he wanted a sabbatical from football. Twenty four hours later, Notre Dame officials announced Dan Devine, a former head coach of the Green Bay Packers and the University of Missouri, would be the next coach.

The ninth-ranked Irish met second-ranked Alabama, led by quarterback Richard Todd, in the Orange Bowl. The Tide was a nine-point favorite, but after the Southern Cal debacle the Irish were determined to give their coach an upset victory to close his career.

With drives in the first and second quarters, the Irish took a 13-3 lead at half, then held off the Tide in the second half to give Parseghian a 13-11 victory in his last game. Defensive back Reggie Barnett intercepted an Alabama pass in the closing seconds to kill the Tide's final effort.

"This game ranks right up there among the greats in my career," Parseghian said afterward. "I know the percentages were against us, but I had a lot of confidence the kids could get up." In 11 seasons, Parseghian had won 95 games, lost 17 and tied 4 for an .836 winning percentage, with two national championships.

Above: *Coach Parseghian is carried off the field after the 13-11 Orange Bowl victory in 1975.*

Opposite: *Ara Parseghian earned a place in Notre Dame football history with 95 victories, 17 losses and 4 ties in 11 seasons for an .836 winning percentage.*

Below: *The Notre Dame Band takes the field before a full house at Notre Dame Stadium.*

THE DEVINE DAYS

1975-80

The Dan Devine years of Notre Dame football are perhaps most remarkable for the emergence of quarterback Joe Montana, another golden boy quarterback for the Golden Dome, a comeback artist who played his way to fame despite coaches who underestimated him. But more about Joe in a minute. The changing of coaches was the focus of public attention in 1975. A 45-year-old father of seven, Dan Devine came to Notre Dame with a reputation for building college football programs from the basement up. That was a contrast of sorts, in that Notre Dame of course had a different blueprint, requiring not major construction but minor renovation.

In the early 1950s Devine had taken lowly Arizona State to the first undefeated season in its history, then moved to Missouri, where he coached the Tigers to the school's first football prominence. Compiling a 93-37-7 mark, his Missouri teams appeared in several bowls. But then Devine shifted in 1970 to the Green Bay Packers to take a turn at following the legend of Vince Lombardi. He experienced mixed results there (25-28-4 in four seasons), winning a divisional championship in 1972, but toward the end of his coaching tenure the rumbling of demanding Packer fans had grown ever louder.

Previous pages: *The ND defense takes down the Longhorn quarterback during the 38-10 bruising by the Irish at the 1978 Cotton Bowl.*

Above: *Head coach Dan Devine.*

Below: *The powerful 1975 Irish defense swamps the USC Trojans.*

Devine knew that Notre Dame's fans would be every bit as demanding, if not more. Yet the Notre Dame job offers any coach the opportunity to grasp a celebrity beyond football. For Devine the promise of that celebrity proved irresistible. "I'm delighted to be here at Notre Dame," he said warily but nevertheless genuinely. The season, however, was marked by problems of adjustment, as seniors shifted from Parseghian's unbridled enthusiasm to Devine's quiet, businesslike ways.

Fortunately, Ara Parseghian had left the program well-stocked with material for 1975, including defensive end Ross Browner, halfback Al Hunter and defensive back Luther Bradley, all of whom had been suspended a season for university rules infractions. Other

Above: *Joe Montana arrived on the Irish scene in 1975 and promptly established himself as a tough, unflappable quarterback.*

Above: *Big defensive tackle Steve Niehaus takes a breather between plays. An All-American in 1975, he had a whopping 112 tackles to his credit for the season.*

veterans from the Parseghian years included tight end Ken MacAfee (whose play would earn him a spot on UPI's All-America first team), tackle Ed Bauer, guard Al Wujciak and quarterback Rick Slager. The chief returnee was defensive tackle Steve Niehaus, a 6-foot-5, 265-pounder who would be named a unanimous consensus All-American for 1975 and finish 12th in the Heisman voting, a fine showing for a lineman. In the season, he would lead the team with 112 tackles.

The incoming recruits weren't bad either, including among them a solid fullback, Jerome Heavens. Then, of course, there was this matter of the young quarterback from Pennsylvania, Joe Montana, who had spent 1974 as a sub on the freshman team. Devine frowned at his practice habits, but there was plenty of athletic ability (Montana had turned down a basketball scholarship to NC State to come to Notre Dame). And there was a void at quarterback. None of the veterans had emerged in spring ball. Finally, Slager was slated to start the first game, and Montana remained the backup waiting for a chance.

They began the season, ranked ninth, with a rare road game at Boston College and sputtered a bit before winning 17-3. The next week, Purdue was Devine's second win, 17-0, as Luther Bradley returned an interception 99 yards for a touchdown. Then North-

Right: *Coach Dan Devine leads his team onto the field for the opening of fall practice in 1977.*

Left: *Halfback Vagas Ferguson displays some of the fancy footwork that earned him both the individual single-game rushing record (30 carries for 255 yards against Georgia Tech in 1978) and the career individual rushing record (673 carries for 3472 yards and 32 touchdowns from 1976 to 1979) at Notre Dame.*

western came to town and created Montana's moment. With the score tied at 7, Slager was injured. In came Joe, who whipped the ball around the field on the way to a 31-7 win. His effort paired nicely with the ground game of freshman fullback Heavens, who rushed for 106 yards. The next week they were tied at 3 with Michigan State late in the game when the Spartans' Tyrone Wilson made a freak touchdown for a 10-3 win. The doldrums continued the next week as the Irish fell behind North Carolina 14-0 going into the fourth quarter. Given just a minute of playing time late in the game, with his team trailing 14-6, Montana triggered an incredible 21-14 win, the clincher a pass to Ted Burgmeier, who ran 50 yards for the score (in all the play covered 80 yards). That game set the foundation of Montana's reputation as the comeback kid.

That salvage operation was followed by another Irish miracle, a 31-30 win over Air Force after trailing 30-10. With Slager as the team's leading passer (just under 700 yards) Notre Dame finished Devine's first season 8-3. Southern Cal whipped them 24-17 in Notre Dame Stadium as Ricky Bell rushed for 165 yards. But it was Pitt's Tony Dorsett who had the field day against the 1975 Irish, gaining 300 yards in the next to last game, won by the Panthers 34-20. From there, they closed things out with a 32-9 win over Miami, and Devine told reporters, "It was good to finish with a victory, and it makes for a good start for next season."

Yet the next season had anything but a good start. Montana separated his shoulder in the opening hame, as Tony Dorsett and Pittsburgh romped over the Irish 31-10. (The only bright footnote of the game was Dave Reeve's 53-yard field goal, a school record.) As dismal as the 1976 opening seemed, Notre Dame had the wherewithal to rebound. Ross Browner would have an incredible year leading the defense. And Rick Slager got the job done at quarterback,

Above: *Game action during the 1975 Irish defeat at the hands of the Southern Cal Trojans in South Bend, 24-17.*

Far left: Game action from the 1977 meeting of Notre Dame and USC. The Irish laid waste to the Trojans 49-19.

Left: *Quarterback Joe Montana sweats it out during the 1978 Cotton Bowl versus the Texas Longhorns.*

Opposite: *Ross Browner (89) led the tough defense that brought the 1978 Cotton Bowl victory to the Irish.*

Below: *Game action from the 1978 Cotton Bowl.*

throwing for 1281 yards and 11 touchdowns. Yet the real offensive wonders would be created on the ground, where halfback Al Hunter became the first 1000-yard rusher in Notre Dame history, with 1058 yards and 13 touchdowns. Boosting that backfield power was freshman Vagas Ferguson.

The schedule brought the first visit of Bear Bryant's Alabama Crimson Tide to South Bend: The Irish won 21-18. Again they finished the year 8-3, this time ranked 15th in the polls. They closed the season with a 17-13 loss to third-ranked Southern Cal. The answer to their postseason prayers was an invitation to the Gator Bowl to meet Joe Paterno's young Penn State team, with Matt Suhey, Jimmy Cefalo and Chuck Fusina. Hunter keyed the Irish by rushing for 102 yards and two touchdowns, and Slager turned in solid day, throwing 10 of 19 for 141 yards. Meanwhile, the defense intercepted two of Fusina's passes, and the Irish won 20-9.

Junior defensive end Ross Browner was a unanimous consensus All-American and won the Outland Trophy as college football's best lineman. Tight end Ken MacAfee repeated as a UPI first-team All-America selection, while defensive back Luther Bradley and defensive end Willie Fry received limited mention on other teams.

The 1977 season offered plenty of good reason for high expectations. Devine had all 11 defensive starters returning from 1976's all-star cast, including Ross Browner, Fry and noseguard Bob Golic. With Vagas Ferguson at left half and Jerome Heavens at fullback (Al Hunter had been suspended for violating university regulations), the Irish rushed into the season ranked third. The only surprise came as quarterback Rusty Lisch, starter of one game in 1976, got the nod over Joe Montana at quarterback.

Things seemed stable enough, however, as the Irish promptly dumped the defending national champions, seventh-ranked Pitt, 19-9. But they were upset by lowly Mississippi the next week and seemed headed for the same fate against Purdue in the third game of the season. Devine tried three other quarterbacks before finally resorting to Comeback Joe Montana with Notre Dame trailing 24-14. In six minutes of play Montana threw for an amazing 154 yards, propelling the Irish to 17 points and an exciting 31-24 comeback.

From that point on, the job was Joe's. With Montana working the air game with tight end Ken MacAfee and split receiver Kris Haines, Notre Dame rolled to eight straight wins, including a 49-19 emasculation of fifth-ranked Southern Cal. For the season, Heavens rushed for 994 yards, and Montana threw for 1604 and 11 touchdowns. In a blowout of Navy, Jerome Heavens became the first back in Notre Dame history to rush for 200 yards in a game, reaching just that number with 34 carries.

In 11 games the Irish had racked up 382 points in offense, and the reward was a date

with top-ranked Texas and Earl Campbell in the Cotton Bowl. Under first-year coach Fred Akers, the Longhorns had won 11 straight and were favored heavily over Notre Dame. But Devine used the odds-makers' snubbing in his pre-game talk, and the Irish brought the Texas joyride to a halt. It would be easy to write off the game as another highlight in the Joe Montana clip file, yet this one belonged to Browner and the defense, for the most part. They forced six Texas turnovers in driving the Longhorns down 38-10. Ferguson and Heavens each rushed for 100 yards, and Ferguson and Irish halfback Terry Eurick each ran for two touchdowns. Ferguson also caught a 17-yard scoring pass from Montana, who threw for 111 yards. "This was not like us," Akers told reporters. "You just can't keep turning it over like we did."

Devine on the other hand had silenced his doubters and was ebullient. Asked about the national rankings, Devine said: "This game puts us where Texas was. We played the team that was rated Number One and beat them. Are we Number One? I leave that to the voters. Yes, I think we ought to be Number One." The voters, it seemed, agreed. The Texas loss wiped out college football's last unbeaten team and propelled the fifth-ranked Irish to a unanimous national championship.

Likewise, Browner and MacAfee were unanimous All-America selections, with the tight end finishing third and Browner fifth in

Left: *Defensive end Ross Browner was selected All-American in 1976 and 1977 and finished fifth in the Heisman voting in 1977.*

the Heisman voting. Bradley, guard Ernie Hughes, noseguard Bob Golic, Fry and Ted Burgmeier all received mention on one All-America team or another. MacAfee became the only lineman ever voted the Walter Camp Award as the nation's most valuable football player, and Browner won the Lombardi Award as college football's best lineman, as well as the Maxwell Award as college football's outstanding player.

The sad part of the story, at least for Devine, was that just about all of them were graduated. Devine rebuilt his team for 1978. Golic, Heavens and Montana were the captains, but most of the other familiar names had disappeared.

Missouri upset them 3-0 at Notre Dame Stadium the first week of the season, the first time the Irish had been shutout in 131 games. They continued to reach back into the past the next week by playing old rival Michigan for the first time since 1943. The Wolverines fell behind 14-0, but the comeback magic was theirs, not Montana's. They finished with a four-touchdown flurry for a 28-14 win. At 0-2, the Irish dropped from the Top 20. The Notre Dame fans were of course by now complaining loudly, but the team finally subdued Purdue 10-6. Then, finding the right footing, Montana pushed them to seven more wins, including a 26-17 whipping of ninth-ranked Pitt, where Heavens' 120 yards rushing pushed him ahead of

Below: *Noseguard Bob Golic (55) was one of the star defensemen for the Irish from 1976 to 1978.*

Top left: *Notre Dame celebrates a touchdown during the 1978 duel with Purdue, which ended in a 10-6 Irish victory.*

Above: *Quarterback Joe Montana takes the snap in action from the 1978 Cotton Bowl. Top-ranked Texas was defeated by the fifth-ranked Irish, who collected the national championship.*

George Gipp as the school's all-time career yardage leader. In a 38-21 whipping of Georgia Tech, Vagas Ferguson carried 30 times for a school record 255 yards. Earlier he had rushed for 211 yards on 33 carries against Navy. By the end of the streak the Irish had an 8-2 record and a ranking of eighth in the polls. Now they headed into their final regular game with Southern Cal.

The Trojans charged out to a 24-6 fourth-quarter lead, just the setting Montana needed to get his competitive juices flowing. First, he struck long to Kris Haines, and with a missed conversion, Notre Dame trailed, 24-12. Montana followed that with a 97-yard drive for another score, featuring a play where he broke out of the pocket and ran 46 yards to the Southern Cal three. The Irish scored on the next play to move to 24-19. With three minutes left, the Trojans couldn't get a first down. But Joe and his boys sure could. They rushed downfield with another drive, capped by a two-yard scoring pass to fullback Pete Holohan for a 25-24 lead. The two-point conversion failed, and with it, so did the Irish hopes. Awakening from their punch drunkeness, the Trojans picked their way back into Irish territory, where Frank Jordan won it, 27-25, with a 37-yard field goal. The loss left Notre Dame 8-3 and headed to yet another Cotton Bowl, this time against ninth-ranked Houston.

It was a 17-degree day in Dallas, and the Cougars battered the Irish and their quarterback. Suffering from hypothermia and 96-degree body temperature, Montana was out much of the second quarter and all of the third, while doctors nursed him back to health with chicken soup. The Cougars held a 34-12 lead and the celebration had already begun on the sidelines when Montana returned to the game with about seven minutes left. The Irish defense quickly blocked a punt, which Steve Cichy picked up and ran into the end zone. A two-point conversion cut the Cougar lead to 34-20. After a short Houston possession, Montana whipped the offense right back into scoring position and did the damage himself with a bootleg from the two. That and his two-

but the storybook ending gave him something to savor. "These players have done it for four years," he told reporters. "It's amazing the number of comebacks they've had in winning games. Of all the comebacks I've been associated with in coaching, this had to be the greatest."

For the season, Ferguson rushed for 1192 yards and seven touchdowns. Montana finished off a 4121-yard passing career by throwing for 2010 yards and 10 touchdowns for '78. Bob Golic, with 152 tackles, was voted unanimously to the UPI and AP All-America first teams. Center Dave Huffman made the UPI first team and the AP second.

Unfortunately for Devine, 1979 was the kind of season to harrow the soul of Irish football. Notre Dame finished the season 7-4 and out of the Top 20 altogether. Vagas Ferguson set a single-season rushing record with 1437 yards. He also set the school scoring record with 17 touchdowns for 102 points. On defense, middle linebacker Bob Crable set a school record with 187 tackles. But the Irish lost games to 17th-ranked Purdue, fourth-ranked USC (Charles White

Opposite: *Halfback Vagas Ferguson rams through the Wolverine defense in 1978. Michigan won 28-14.*

Left: *Coach Dan Devine monitors his team's performance in the 1978 Navy game. His six-season record of 53-16-1 won him a place in the National Football Foundation Hall of Fame.*

Below: *Joe Montana calls his signals during the Notre Dame-Navy game. The Irish subdued the Middies 27-7.*

point conversion pass moments later narrowed the margin to 34-28. Suddenly the Cotton Bowl was on edge.

Houston coach Bill Yeoman gambled then, and with less than 40 seconds left went for a fourth and one at his own 29. The Notre Dame defense showed Yeoman nothing but snakeyes and stuffed the Cougar offense for no gain. With 28 seconds left, Montana and the offense had a chance to win it. Joe ran for 11 yards and a first down at the 18, then threw to Haines for 10. With eight seconds left, he missed on another pass to Haines, then another seconds later. Finally, with two seconds left, he completed the game-tying pass to Haines in the end zone.

The score set up the extra point kick by Joe Unis. It was good, but Notre Dame was offsides, so the ball was moved back five yards and Unis knocked it up again, giving Notre Dame a 35-34 victory and Montana another chapter in his book of comebacks.

"I didn't have time to think about being nervous," said Unis, a 5-foot-8-inch junior form Dallas. "Every kicker fantasizes about winning games like this." Asked about his decision to go for first down rather than punt, Yeoman said, "We were kicking the ball only 10 or 12 yards into the wind, and Chuck Brown had a bad wrist and couldn't snap the ball."

It hadn't been a great season for Devine,

Top: *Game action in 1980, versus the University of Michigan Wolverines. Notre Dame rang up an exciting late-game victory, 29-27.*

Left: *Center John Scully (center in photo) fights off Purdue attackers.*

Above: *Joe Montana.*

rushed for 262 yards and four touchdowns in Notre Dame Stadium) and 14th-ranked Clemson. Even worse, Notre Dame was blown out 40-18 by unranked Tennessee in the eighth game of the season.

It was bad enough to drive Devine to announce his resignation heading into the 1980 season, effective at the end of the schedule. He cited "family considerations and personal reasons" in his statements to the press. "It's something my wife and I have been thinking about," he said. "Naturally you confide in a few people, but usually when you tell somebody a secret, it's no longer a secret. So I didn't want the squad and the staff to hear about it from somebody else."

In preparing his team for his final season Devine faced another choice at quarterback – between freshman Blair Kiel and senior Mike Courey. He resolved the question by using both, depending upon field position. With the graduation of Ferguson and Heavens, Devine had a new round of faces in the backfield. Substitute Jim Stone emerged to lead the team in rushing, with 908 yards. But kicker Harry Oliver was the big scorer, with 18 field goals. Linebacker Bob Crable again led the defense, with 154 tackles.

Considering the circumstances, it was a fine year, and the Irish started it off right with a 31-10 dumping of ninth-ranked Purdue. The high point of the season came the next week with a late-game 29-27 win over Michigan, the big points coming on a 51-yard field goal by Oliver with no time on the clock. It was a heartbreaker for the Wolverines, and Michigan Coach Bo Schembechler would talk about it for years to come.

Then running back Phil Carter carried a school-record 40 times for 254 yards to lead the Irish over Michigan State 26-21. From there they dropped Miami, Army, Arizona and Navy to move to the top spot in the polls with a 7-0 record. Strangely, they then stumbled against lowly Georgia Tech (with a 1-7 record) and needed a late field goal to escape with a 3-3 tie. They whipped fifth-ranked Alabama in a road game 7-0 and downed Air Force, but fell in an upset to Southern Cal in the last game of the season, 20-3.

The loss dropped them from second to seventh in the polls. Still, the Irish had a shot at the limelight. At 9-1-1, they were matched against top-ranked Georgia and Herschel Walker in the Sugar Bowl. They might have won the game if they hadn't given away two first-half touchdowns with turnovers deep in their own territory, including a fumbled kickoff. The Irish outgained the Bulldogs in net yards, 328 to 127, but Georgia's 17 first-half points did the trick. Devine's final team went down 17-10. "We have not been a team that turned over the ball deep inside our territory," Devine told reporters. "That got us today."

A decidedly bittersweet chapter in Notre Dame's history closed with the final gun of the game. Once again school officials found themselves in the familiar guessing game: Where will we find our next legend, and what credentials should he bring with him?

Above: *Running back Phil Carter (22) carries the ball during the 29-27 subjugation of Michigan in 1980. In the next game of the season, against Michigan State, Carter carried for a school-record 40 times for 254 yards to lead the Irish to a 26-21 victory.*

36

GERRY FAUST'S UNHAPPY TENURE

1981-85

Previous pages: *The Notre Dame defense closes in on Michigan's Thomas Wilcher in the 1985 season opener.*

Opposite: *Tight end Tony Hunter was the key receiver for the Irish, 1980 to 1982. He was All-America in 1982.*

Right: *Coach Gerry Faust shouts instructions from the sidelines in 1981. He had a 29-25-1 record over five seasons (1981-85).*

Bottom: *Linebacker Bob Crable (43) was All-America in 1981.*

Gerry Faust, Jr, rolled up a phenomenal record as coach of Moeller High School in Cincinnati. In 18 years he won 174 games, lost just 17 and tied two, for a Rockne-like winning percentage of .907, plus 12 city, five state and four national championships. Of his 174 victories, 90 were shutouts. Roughly 250 athletes who played for him earned college football scholarships to NCAA Division I schools. Of that number, 20 had gone to Notre Dame, including such standouts as defensive tackle Steve Niehaus, kicker Harry Oliver, linebacker Bob Crable and receiver Tony Hunter. At the time of his hiring, the only question about him seemed to be his lack of college coaching experience. In retrospect, it seems to have been a pretty good question.

Faust had played quarterback for his father, Gerry Faust, Sr, at Chaminade High School in Dayton, Ohio, and by his senior year he had earned a spot in the state All-Star game, playing opposite another young quarterback, Len Dawson. Faust's big hope in high school had been to go on to play at Notre Dame, but when he realized the Irish would be offering no scholarship, he went to the University of Dayton in his hometown, where he lettered three years at quarterback.

He was a man of tremendous optimism and enthusiasm, with substantial gifts as a motivating speaker. He would need all these qualities and more. He inherited a solid array of good players, many of them starters for Dan Devine: Phil Carter at running back; sophomore Blair Kiel at quarterback; receiver Tony Hunter; kicker Harry Oliver;

Above: *Wide receiver Alvin Miller (17) in 1983.*

Opposite: *Blair Kiel called the signals for the Irish full-time in 1981 and 1982.*

linebackers Mark Zavagnin, Joe Rudzinski and Bob Crable; strong safety Dave Duerson; cornerbacks Stacey Toran and John Krimm; and right offensive tackle Phil Pozderac. With such talent, Faust had the framework of a fine team.

When they opened the season ranked fourth in the nation and played like it, whipping LSU 27-9, the uneasiness among Notre Dame fans settled substantially. There was still that hum of excitement the following week when the Irish moved to the top spot in the polls. Yet whatever Gerry Faust had going for him as Notre Dame's coach expired that next week, as 11th-ranked Michigan knocked the Irish from their perch 25-7. It could be argued that Gerry Faust never fully recovered from that game. Purdue followed the Michigan insult by scoring late to beat them 15-14 the following week. Along the rest of the way they would fall victim to Florida State, Southern Cal, Penn State and Miami. It was a tough schedule, and most of the losses were close against tough programs. But Faust finished 5-6.

Wasn't it better, the critics asked as the season progressed, to jettison this guy Faust now? The Notre Dame administration, however, was not about to welsh on its committment to Gerry Faust. The single high note was linebacker Bob Crable's selection as a consensus All-American.

Faust warmed the fans again the next season, 1982, by starting off with four impressive victories, over 10th-ranked Michigan, Purdue, Michigan State and seventh-ranked Miami. Carter, Kiel and Hunter were all back at the skill positions, and with the wins hopes soared a bit as they moved to ninth in the polls. Then came a late loss to Arizona, a late tie with Oregon and a victory over Navy. At 5-1-1 and having fallen out of the Top 20, they faced top-ranked Pitt in a road game. Their 31-16 upset seemed to be the turning point for a program hanging in the balance. Then they lost their final three games to finish 6-4-1. It would be Faust's best record. If Irish supporters singed Dan Devine over 7-4, their irritation with Faust is easy to imagine.

Freshman Steve Beuerlein replaced senior Kiel at quarterback for 1983, and Notre Dame rode through another roller-coaster season to finish 6-5. Bud Dudley, the executive director of the Liberty Bowl and a Notre Dame alumnus, realized a lifelong dream when he was able to attract the Irish to his bowl. It was an interesting little match, with Faust's team pitted against Boston College and Doug Flutie. Yet in a sense, the invitation to a lesser bowl only increased the irritation in South Bend. The criticism grew, and Faust answered it with his seemingly boundless optimism. "I honestly think we're on the verge of some awfully good things at Notre Dame," he said.

Coach Jack Bicknell's Boston College team had compiled a 9-2 record behind Flutie's passing. His players were more than a bit puzzled by the matchup. "We've got to be playing the legend of Notre Dame," said Brian Waldron, the punter. "They didn't make it here on their record." The 5-foot-9 Flutie, however, saw a special significance in playing Notre Dame. "I grew up idolizing them," he said. "It just feels like we're the underdog. We came in here with the better record and ranking but we're still Boston College and we get excited when we play big teams. It's no upset if they win."

Flutie did his best to prevent that from

Above: *Running back Greg Bell (28) in 1983.*

Opposite top: *Tailback Allen Pinkett (20) holds second place in career rushing at Notre Dame: 634 carries for 3031 and 38 TDs from 1982 to 1984. He is also a two-time single-season scoring leader, with 110 total points for 1983 and 108 for 1984. He was All-America in 1983.*

Opposite bottom: *The Notre Dame band takes the field in 1983.*

happening. He threw for 287 yards and almost pulled off a last-second comeback. But Kiel started and passed for 151 yards and a touchdown, and Allen Pinkett rushed for 111 yards and two scores, as the Irish won 19-18. It was a strange game, with the Eagles failing on three extra point attempts and Notre Dame flubbing two of three.

For 1984, Faust's fourth Irish team offered a repeat performance, another 6-5 record and another invitation to a secondary bowl, this time the Aloha Bowl against Southern Methodist. The Mustangs ran out to an early 14-0 lead, but Notre Dame battled back to tie the game at 17 in the third quarter. SMU pushed back to a 27-17 lead, only to watch the Irish pull up to 27-20. Beuerlein moved them into scoring position for a chance to win in the closing seconds. But on fourth down, on the SMU 17, Beuerlein missed receiver Milt Jackson wide open in the end zone, and SMU won 27-20.

"We thought we had one of the best bowl matchups," SMU coach Bobby Collins told reporters. "That's four years in a row for 10 wins. Maybe now people will say SMU is for real." But SMU football would be dead in two more seasons, killed by NCAA sanctions against repeated recruiting violations.

As for Faust, he returned to South Bend to face incredible pressure heading into 1985. Still, he had a large number of lettermen returning, and there was hope. "I was so used to winning all the time," he said in an interview for the school's press guide heading into the season. "In the beginning, it was very difficult for me to rebound from a loss. . . . It's probably been the four roughest years for me in wins and losses. But it's probably been the four best years I've ever had coaching. Everything has worked out well, except the wins. I think we really turned things around the way we played the last month of the season in '84. The attitude

now is really great because of that. I really love this place. I really wanted to be here, in this job. I have no desire to coach anywhere else."

But the fans and the alumni saw things differently: They wanted him out. Finally, with a 5-5 record heading into his last game against the University of Miami, his optimism had burned out. He resigned in order to give the school time to hire a new coach in time for recruiting. For some reason, the image of the United States leaving Saigon in 1975 comes to mind. The Irish didn't escape their fate clinging to a helicopter pod that day, but they might have wished they could. The Hurricane humiliated Faust and Notre Dame 58-7 on national television. It wasn't a pretty picture. Lou Holtz, Notre Dame's new coach, watched the debacle on television and for the first time realized just how far he had to go. There was no doubt that he had his work cut out for him.

THE COMING OF LOU HOLTZ

1986-87

Charged with waking up the echoes, Lou Holtz used the tool that had served him well at William and Mary, NC State, Arkansas, Minnesota and just about everywhere else he had coached: He tickled them with his sense of humor. In his career Holtz had been accused of many things, but pomposity wasn't one of them. He was a man of non-stop humor, generating a stream of one-liners to break the heavy air that always seems to hang around losing football programs. Everywhere, it seemed, Holtz was teaching losers how to win. He had just performed that task for the University of Minnesota when Notre Dame came calling. He had always wanted to coach in South Bend. That was evidenced by the fact that his Minnesota contract had an escape clause allowing him to leave for a Notre Dame offer. He knew that once there, he would have to tone down his fun a bit. Yet he also knew that if Notre Dame ever needed its sense of humor it was in 1986.

Still, the school hired Holtz for far more than his comedy routine. Gene Corrigan, Notre Dame's athletic director at the time, explained to reporters: "When we hired Lou, we wanted an experienced head coach. We wanted someone who wouldn't be intimidated by pressure. We wanted a winner, someone who had worked with college kids and had a proven record at that level.

Holtz enjoyed the early honeymoon, but his first battle was to downplay expectations. "Many people who identify with Notre Dame believe in miracles," he told reporters. "I believe in miracles. But I believe they are not created by coaches." Still, he performed one of sorts, taking a team that had been thoroughly defeated at the close of the '85 season and preparing it to scare third-ranked Michigan within an inch of its life opening the 1986 season. Holtz achieved this competitiveness by selecting the team's best athlete and building around his talents. That athlete was Tim Brown, a talented junior receiver from Dallas, Texas.

Fittingly, Holtz's first challenge, Michigan, was Notre Dame's rival in the all-time college standings. In this game the Irish gained the edge statistically and outplayed the Wolverines. But they couldn't convert their statistics and early Michigan mistakes into scores. As a result, Michigan led 24-20 going into the game's late moments. Senior quarterback Steve Beuerlein, who had had a strong day passing, with 263 yards and a touchdown, moved the Irish into scoring position at the Michigan eight. From there he hit tight end Joel Williams with what appeared to be a touchdown pass. But the officials ruled that Williams' foot had grazed the out-of-bounds line.

"I felt my heart would come up all the way through my throat on that call," said Beuerlein. "The way I saw it, Joel had his left foot in and his right foot close to the line. Michigan's ballboy was right there and told our ballboy that Williams clearly had both feet in the end zone."

Previous pages: *Wide receiver Ray Dumas (82) in action in 1986.*

Opposite: *Tailback Mark Green (24) puts the moves on the Wolverines in 1986 game action.*

Top left: *Lou Holtz took over coaching duties from Gerry Faust in 1986.*

Above: *Tailback Tim Brown (81) was a rushing sensation in 1986. His performance earned him the Heisman Trophy and an All-America selection that year.*

Above: *The 1986 Notre Dame squad takes the field. They had a 5-6-0 record for the season.*

Without the touchdown, John Carney kicked a field goal to bring Notre Dame to 24-23. They got the ball back again in the dying seconds and put Carney in position to kick the game winner from 45 yards out. He had made 15 of 16 attempts from that range during his Notre Dame career, yet his effort that day was short and wide left. The game ended Michigan 24, Notre Dame 23. "What can I say but that it was a heck of a game," Holtz said afterward. "There are an awful lot of sad young men in our lockerroom right now. Our kids never quit, although they had every reason to. I think 10 years from now they'll remember the fun they had in the nine months it took to get here."

Yet the adversity wasn't finished for the Irish. They would struggle to a 5-6 record for the 1986 season. The year would establish Tim Brown's credentials as a legitimate superstar: In another moral victory, he would return a punt 53 yards against Southern Cal late in the game to set up a winning field goal for Notre Dame. And Beuerlein would set career records in passing (473 completions for 6527 yards) and total offense (6459 yards).

But for Notre Dame, a 5-6 record is far from palatable. Heading into 1987, Holtz felt the weight of tradition upon him. When reporters asked about pressure in the preseason, he was ready with an answer. "I don't

Above: *The Notre Dame defense takes out a Wolverine runner in 1986 game action.*

think there's pressure at Notre Dame," he said. "What I feel is an awesome responsibility because of what has gone on in the past. Because of what the Rocknes, the Leahys, the Parseghians have accomplished, you feel a responsibility to keep up that great tradition."

Holtz may not have liked to talk about "pressure," but when he described the expectations of the Notre Dame fans it was difficult to think of any better word: "Fans don't think the Notre Dame football team has any problems. They think if we go out and put on the helmets and the uniforms that everything is going to change and any problems we have are going to dissipate. That isn't going to be true. But I understand alumni. They aren't interested in how rocky the sea is. They are interested in seeing the ship come in. Our fans expect a minor miracle every Saturday and a major one every now and then."

They brought the ship in for 1987, or at least within sight of shore. They finished 8-3 and received an invitation to the Cotton Bowl, reward enough in a year where team expectations were relatively modest. The real pressure was on Tim Brown, who was listed as the preseason favorite for the Heisman Trophy. He had broken Notre Dame's record for all-purpose yardage – returning kicks and receiving – as a junior. As a senior,

JACKSON
1

Opposite: *Split end Pat Terrell (15) comes up with the pass as Purdue's Steve Jackson moves in to make the tackle in the first half of the 1987 game played in West Lafayette, Indiana.*

Above: *Tight end Dan Tanczos (86) brings in a touchdown against Southern Cal in 1986.*

Next page: *Tim Brown.*

he was determined to keep his focus, despite substantial media attention and high expectations. His detractors felt that the Heisman was more suited to a running back or quarterback, someone who controlled the ball regularly, not a mere receiver. Yet ultimately he won it because he had reminded the football world that broken-field running is an art form.

In fact he won the Heisman early in the season by returning two punts for touchdowns to kill Michigan State before a nationwide ESPN TV audience. Syracuse quarterback Don McPherson had driven his team to an undefeated regular season record, and there was some late debate about whether McPherson should receive the award (he was later voted the Maxwell Award). But when the vote was taken Tim Brown was the runaway winner, and Notre Dame had another chapter in its book of legends.

Their losses were to Pittsburgh, Penn State and top-ranked Miami. And then the close to the season was anything but storybook. They were thoroughly outclassed by Texas A&M in the Cotton Bowl. Even worse, the game was marred by an incident. The Aggies' 12th man, a player from the student body who is allowed to participate on kickoff teams, tackled Brown on a late-game kickoff, and seeing the opportunity to seize a souvenir, ripped the small towel from Brown's pants and attempted to leave the field with it. Enraged by the thievery, Brown chased him down and retrieved his towel. Hardly suitable behavior for a Heisman winner, many of the opinion-mongers tut-tutted the next day in newspaper columns.

Would they have been so censorious if Brown had played for any team other than Notre Dame? Maybe, but it's not likely. People seem to judge Notre Dame by a special set of standards, and perhaps rightly so. Lou Holtz has an explanation for this that could be as good as any ever offered: "Notre Dame is one of the few places that is perceived from the outside as being great and actually is even better than that . . . Let me tell you something about the kind of people who come here and the kind of leadership they receive. Four years ago, Notre Dame enrolled 1804 freshmen. Three of them flunked out, and three of them dropped out. A total of 1798 returned as sophomores. We were the only school in America that lost as many football games as we did students."

IRISH
81
81

APPENDIX:

100 YEARS OF NOTRE DAME FOOTBALL

1887

Coach: None Captain: Henry Luhn

November	23	L	Michigan	0-8
			(0-1-0)	

1888

Coach: None Captain: Edward Prudhomme

April	20	L	Michigan	6-26
April	21	L	Michigan	4-10
December	6	W	Harvard School (Chi.)	20-0
			(1-2-0)	30-36

1889

Coach: None Captain: Edward Prudhomme

November	14	W	Northwestern	9-0
			(1-0-0)	

1890-1891–No team

1892

Coach: None Captain: Pat Coady

October	19	W	South Bend H.S.	56-0
November	24	T	Hillsdale	10-10
			(1-0-1)	66-10

Above: ND *vs Michigan, 1986.*

1893

Coach: None Captain: Frank Keough

October	25	W	Kalamazoo	34-0
November	11	W	Albion	8-6
November	23	W	DeLaSalle	28-0
November	30	W	Hillside	22-10
January	1'94	L	Chicago	0-8
			(4-1-0)	92-24

1894

Coach: James L. Morison Captain: Frank Keough

October	13	W	Hillside	14-0
October	20	T	Albion	6-6
November	15	W	Wabash	30-0
November	22	W	Rush Medical	18-6
November	29	L	Albion	12-19
			(3-1-1)	80-31

1895

Coach: H. G. Hadden Captain: Dan Casey

October	19	W	Northwestern Law	20-0
November	7	W	Illinois Cycling Club	18-2
November	22	L	Indpls. Artillery (S)	0-18
November	28	W	Chicago Phys. & Surg	32-0
			(3-1-0)	70-20

1896

Coach: Frank E. Hering Captain: Frank E. Hering

October	8	L	Chicago Phys. & Surg	0-4
October	14	L	Chicago	0-18
October	27	W	S.B. Commerical A.C.	46-0
October	31	W	Albion	24-0
November	14	L	Purdue	22-28
November	20	W	Highland Views	82-0
November	26	W	Beloit	8-0
			(4-3-0)	182-50

1897

Coach: Frank E. Hering Captain: Jack Mullen

October	13	T	Rush Medical	0-0
October	23	W	DePauw	4-0
October	28	W	Chicago Dental Surg	62-0
November	6	L	Chicago	5-34
November	13	W	St. Viator	60-0
November	25	W	Michigan State	34-6
			(4-1-1)	165-40

1898

Coach: Frank E. Hering Captain: Jack Mullen

October	8	W	Illinois	5-0
October	15	W	Michigan State	53-0
October	23	L	Michigan	0-23
October	29	W	DePauw	32-0
November	11	L	Indiana	5-11
November	19	W	Albion	60-0
			(4-2-0)	155-34

1899

Coach: James McWeeney **Captain**: Jack Mullen

September	27	W	Engelwood H.S.	29-5
September	30	W	Michigan State	40-0
October	4	L	Chicago	6-23
October	14	W	Lake Forest	38-0
October	18	L	Michigan	0-12
October	23	W	Indian	17-0
October	27	W	Northwestern	12-0
November	4	W	Rush Medical	17-0
November	18	T	Purdue	10-10
November	30	L	Chicago Phys. & Surg.	0-5
			(6-3-1)	169-55

1900

Coach: Pat O'Dea **Captain**: John Farley

September	29	W	Goshen	55-0
October	6	W	Engelwood H.S.	68-0
October	13	W	S.B. Howard Park	64-0
October	20	W	Cincinnati	58-0
October	25	L	Indiana	0-6
November	3	T	Beloit	6-6
November	10	L	Wisconsin	0-54
November	17	L	Michigan	0-7
November	24	W	Rush Medical	5-0
November	29	W	Chicago Phys. & Surg.	5-0
			(6-3-1)	261-73

1901

Coach: Pat O'Dea **Captain**: Al Fortin

September	28	T	South Bend A.C.	0-0
October	5	W	Ohio Medical U.	6-0
October	12	L	Northwestern	0-2
October	19	W	Chicago Medical Col.	32-0
October	26	W	Beloit	5-0
November	2	W	Lake Forest	16-0
November	9	W	Purdue	12-6
November	16	W	Indiana	18-5
November	23	W	Chicago Phys. & Surg.	34-0
November	28	W	South Bend A.C.	22-6
			(8-1-1)	145-19

1902

Coach: James F. Faragher **Captain**: Louis (Red) Salmon

September	27	W	Michigan State	33-0
October	11	W	Lake Forest	28-0
October	18	L	Michigan	0-23
October	25	W	Indiana	11-5
November	1	W	Ohio Medical U.	6-5
November	8	L	Knox	5-12
November	15	W	American Medical	92-0
November	22	W	DePauw	22-0
November	27	T	Purdue	6-6
			(6-2-1)	203-51

1903

Coach: James F. Faragher **Captain**: Louis (Red) Salmon

October	3	W	Michigan State	12-0
October	10	W	Lake Forest	28-0
October	17	W	DePauw	56-0
October	24	W	American Medical	52-0
October	29	W	Chicago Phys. & Surg.	46-0
November	7	W	Missouri Osteopaths	28-0
November	14	T	Northwestern	0-0
November	21	W	Ohio Medical U.	35-0
Novemberf	26	W	Wabash	35-0
			(8-0-1)	292-0

1904

Coach: Louis (Red) Salmon **Captain**: Frank Shaughnessy

October	1	W	Wabash	12-4
October	8	W	American Medical	44-0
October	15	L	Wisconsin	0-58
Octgober	22	W	Ohio Medical U.	17-5
October	27	W	Toledo A.A.	6-0
November	5	L	Kansas	5-24
November	19	W	DePauw	10-0
November	24	L	Purdue	0-36
			(5-3-0)	94-127

1905

Coach: Henry J. McGlew **Captain**: Pat Beacom

September	30	W	N. Davison H.S. (Chi.)	44-0
October	7	W	Michigan State	28-0
October	14	L	Wisconsin	0-21
October	21	L	Wbash	0-5
October	28	W	American Medical	142-0
November	4	W	DePauw	71-0
November	11	L	Indiana	5-22
November	18	W	Bennett Med. Col. (Chi.)	22-0
November	24	L	Purdue	0-32
			(5-4-0)	312-80

1906

Coach: Thomas A. Barry **Captain**: Bob Bracken

October	6	W	Franklin	26-0
October	13	W	Hillsdale	17-0
October	20	W	Chi. Phys. & Surg.	28-0
October	27	W	Michigan State	5-0
November	3	W	Purdue	2-0
November	10	L	Indiana	0-12
November	14	W	Beloit	29-0
			(6-1-0)	107-12

Left: *Pat O'Dea, Notre Dame's fifth head football coach (1900-03).*

Opposite top: *A view of Notre Dame's first homecoming. A crowd of 10,000 watched the Irish blank Purdue 28-0.*

1907

Coach: Thomas A. Barry **Captain**: Dom Callicrate

October	12	W	Chi. Phys. & Surg.	32-0
October	19	W	Franklin	23-0
October	26	W	Olivet	22-4
November	2	T	Indfiana	0-0
November	9	W	Knox	22-4
November	23	W	Purdue	17-0
November	28	W	St. Vincent's (Chi.)	21-12
			(6-0-1)	137-20

1908

Coach: Victor M. Place **Captain**: Harry Miller

October	3	W	Hillsdale	39-0
October	10	W	Franklin	64-0
October	17	L	Michigan	6-12
October	24	W	Chicago Phys. & Surg.	88-0
October	29	W	Ohio Northern	58-4
November	7	W	Indiana	11-0
November	13	W	Wabash	8-4
November	18	W	St. Viator	46-0
November	26	W	Marquette	6-0
			(8-1-0)	326-20

1909

Coach: Frank C. Longman **Captain**: Howard Edwards

October	9	W	Olivet	58-0
October	16	W	Rose Ply	60-11
October	23	W	Michigan State	17-0
October	30	W	Pittsburgh	6-0
November	6	W	Michigan	11-3
November	13	W	Miami (Ohio)	46-0
November	20	W	Wabash	38-0
November	25	T	Marquette	0-0
			(7-0-1)	236-14

1910

Coach: Frank C. Longman **Captain**: Ralph Dimmick

October	8	W	Olivet	48-0
October	22	W	Butchel (Akron)	51-0
November	5	L	Michigan State	0-17
November	12	W	Rose Poly	41-3
Noember	19	W	Ohio Northern	47-0
November	24	T	Marquette	5-5
			(4-1-1)	192-25

1911

Coach: John L. Marks **Captain**: Luke Kelly

October	7	W	Ohio Northern	32-6
October	14	W	St. Viator	43-0
October	21	W	Butler	27-0
October	28	W	Loyola (Chi.)	80-0
November	4	T	Pittsburgh	0-0
November	11	W	St. Bonaventure	34-0
November	20	W	Wabash	6-3
November	30	T	Marquette	0-0
			(6-0-2)	222-9

1912

Coach: John L. Marks **Captain**: Charles (Gus) Dorais

October	5	W	St. Viator	116-7
October	12	W	Adrian	74-7
October	19	W	Morris Harvey	39-0
October	26	W	Wabash	41-6
November	2	W	Pittsburgh	3-0
November	9	W	St. Louis	47-7
November	28	W	Marquette	69-0
			(7-0-0)	389-27

1913

Coach: Jesse Harper **Captain**: Knute Rockne

October	4	W	Ohio Northern	87-0
October	18	W	South Dakota	20-7
October	25	W	Alma	62-0
November	1	W	Army	35-13
November	7	W	Penn State	14-7
November	22	W	Christian Bros. (St. Louis)	20-7
November	27	W	Texas	30-7
			(7-0-0)	268-41

1914

Coach: Jesse Harper **Captain**: Keith Jones

October	3	W	Alma	56-0
October	10	W	Rose Poly	103-0
October	17	L	Yale	0-28
October	24	W	South Dakota	33-0
October	31	W	Haskell	20-7
November	7	L	Army	7-20
November	14	W	Carlisle	48-6
November	26	W	Syracuse	20-0
			(6-2-0)	287-61

1915

Coach: Jesse Harper **Captain**: Freeman Fitzgerald

October	2	W	Alma	32-0
October	9	W	Haskell	34-0
Octgober	23	L	Nebraska	19-20
October	30	W	South Dakota	6-0
November	6	W	Army	7-9
November	13	W	Creighton	41-0
November	25	W	Texas	36-7
November	27	W	Rice	55-2
			(7-1-0)	230-29

1916

Coach: Jesse Harper **Captain**: Stan Cofall

September	30	W	Case Tech	48-0
October	7	W	Western Reserve	48-0
October	14	W	Haskell	26-0
October	28	W	Wabash	60-0
November	4	L	Army	10-30
November	11	W	South Dakota	21-0
November	18	W	Michigan State	14-0
November	25	W	Alma	46-0
November	30	W	Nebraska	20-0
			(8-1-0)	293-30

1917

Coach: Jesse Harper **Captain**: Jim Phelan

October	6	W	Kalamazoo	55-0
October	13	T	Wisconsin	0-0
October	20	L	Nebraska	0-7
October	27	W	South Dakota	40-0
November	3	W	Army	7-2
November	10	W	Morningside	13-0
November	17	W	Michigan State	23-0
November	24	W	Wash. & Jefferson	3-0
			(6-1-1)	141-9

Right: *Knute Rockne.* Opposite top: *Jim Crowley.*

1918

Coach: Knute Rockne **Captain**: Leonard Bahan

September	28	W	Case Tech	26-6
November	2	W	Wabash	67-7
November	9	T	Great Lakes	7-7
November	16	L	Michigan State	7-13
November	23	W	Purdue	26-6
November	28	T	Nebraska	0-0
			(3-1-2)	133-39

1919

Coach: Knute Rockne **Captain**: Leonard Bahan

October	4	W	Kalamazoo	14-0
October	11	W	Mount Union	60-7
October	18	W	Nebraska	14-9
October	25	W	Western Michigan	53-0
November	1	W	Indiana	16-3
November	8	W	Army	12-9
November	15	W	Michigan State	13-0
November	22	W	Purdue	33-13
November	27	W	Morningside	14-6
			(9-0-0)	229-47

1920

Coach: Knute Rockne **Captain**: Frank Coughlin

Month	Day	Result	Opponent	Score
October	2	W	Kalamazoo	39-0
October	9	W	Western Michigan	42-0
October	16	W	Nebraska	16-7
October	23	W	Valparaiso	28-3
October	30	W	Army	27-17
November	6	W	Purdue	28-0
November	13	W	Indiana	13-10
November	20	W	Northwestern	33-7
November	25	W	Michigan State	25-0
			(9-0-0)	251-44

1921

Coach: Knute Rockne **Captain**: Eddie Anderson

Month	Day	Result	Opponent	Score
September	24	W	Kalamazoo	56-0
October	1	W	DePauw	57-10
October	8	L	Iowa	7-10
October	15	W	Purdue	33-0
October	22	W	Nebraska	7-0
October	29	W	Indiana	28-7
November	5	W	Army	28-0
November	8	W	Rutgers	48-0
November	12	W	Haskell	42-7
November	19	W	Marquette	21-7
November	24	W	Michigan State	48-0
			(10-1-0)	375-41

1922

Coach: Knute Rockne **Captain**: Glen Carberry

Month	Day	Result	Opponent	Score
September	20	W	Kalamazoo	46-0
October	7	W	St. Louis	26-0
October	14	W	Purdue	20-0
October	21	W	DePauw	34-7
October	28	W	Georgia Tech	13-3
November	4	W	Indiana	27-0
November	11	T	Army	0-0
November	18	W	Butler	31-3
November	25	W	Carnegie Tech	19-0
November	30	L	Nebraska	6-14
			(8-1-1)	222-27

1923

Coach: Knute Rockne **Captain**: Harvey Brown

Month	Day	Result	Opponent	Score
September	29	W	Kalamazoo	74-0
October	6	W	Lombard	14-0
October	13	W	Army	13-0
October	20	W	Princeton	25-2
October	27	W	Georgia Tech	35-7
November	3	W	Purdue	34-7
November	10	L	Nebraska	7-14
November	17	W	Butler	34-7
November	24	W	Carnegie Tech	26-0
November	29	W	St. Louis	130
			(9-1-0)	275-37

1924

Coach: Knute Rockne **Captain**: Adam Walsh

Month	Day	Result	Opponent	Score
October	4	W	Lombard	40-0
October	11	W	Wabash	34-0
October	18	W	Army	13-7
October	25	W	Princeton	12-0
November	1	W	Georgia Tech	34-3
November	8	W	Wisconsin	38-3
November	15	W	Nebraska	34-6
November	22	W	Northwestern	13-6
November	29	W	Carnegie Tech	40-19
			(9-0-0)	258-44
			ROSE BOWL	
January	1	W	Stanford	27-10

1925

Coach: Knute Rockne **Captain**: Clem Crowe

Month	Day	Result	Opponent	Score
September	26	W	Baylor	41-0
October	3	W	Lombard	69-0
October	10	W	Beloit	19-3
October	17	L	Army	0-27
October	24	W	Minnesota	19-7
October	31	W	Georgia Tech	13-0
November	7	T	Penn State	0-0
November	14	W	Carnegie Tech	26-0
November	21	W	Northwestern	1310
November	26	L	Nebraska	0-17
			(7-2-1)	200-64

1926

Coach: Knute Rockne **Co-Captains**: Gene Edwards and Tom Hearden

Month	Day	Result	Opponent	Score
October	2	W	Beloit	77-0
October	9	W	Minnesota	20-7
October	16	W	Penn State	28-0
October	23	W	Northwestern	6-0
October	30	W	Georgia Tech	12-0
November	6	W	Indiana	26-0
November	13	W	Army	7-0
November	20	W	Drake	21-0
November	27	L	Carnegie Tech	0-19
December	4	W	USC	13-12
			(9-1-0)	210-38

1927

Coach: Knute Rockne **Captain**: John Smith

Month	Day	Result	Opponent	Score
October	1	W	Coe	28-7
October	8	W	Detroit	20-0
October	15	W	Navy	19-6
October	22	W	Indiana	19-6
October	29	W	Georgia Tech	26-7
November	5	T	Minnesota	7-7
November	12	L	Army	0-18
November	19	W	Drake	32-0
November	26	W	USC	7-6
			(7-1-1)	158-57

1928

Coach: Knute Rockne **Captain**: Fred Miller

September	29	W	Loyola	12-6
October	6	L	Wisconsin	6-22
October	13	W	Navy	7-0
October	20	L	Geogia Tech	0-13
October	27	W	Drake	32-6
November	3	W	Penn State	9-0
November	10	W	Army	12-6
November	17	L	Carnegie Tech	7-27
December	1	L	USC	14-27
			(5-4-0)	99-107

1929

Coach: Knute Rockne **Captain**: John Law

October	5	W	Indiana	14-0
October	12	W	Navy	14-7
October	19	W	Wisconsin	19-0
October	26	W	Carnegie Tech	7-0
November	2	W	Georgia Tech	26-6
November	9	W	Drake	19-7
November	16	W	USC	13-12
November	23	W	Northwestern	26-6
November	30	W	Army	7-0
			(9-0-0)	145-38

1930

Coach: Knute Rockne **Captain**: Tom Conely

October	4	W	SMU	20-14
October	11	W	Navy	26-2
October	18	W	Carnegie Tech	21-6
October	25	W	Pittsburgh	35-19
November	1	W	Indiana	27-0
November	8	W	Pennsylvania	60-20
November	15	W	Drake	28-7
November	22	W	Northwestern	14-0
November	29	W	Army	7-6
December	6	W	USC	27-0
			(10-0-0)	265-74

1931

Coach: Heartley (Hunk) Anderson **Captain**: Tommy Yarr

October	3	W	Indiana	25-0
October	10	T	Northwestern	0-0
October	17	W	Drake	63-0
October	24	W	Pittsburgh	25-12
October	31	W	Carnegie Tech	19-0
November	7	W	Pennsylvania	49-0
November	14	W	Navy	20-0
November	21	L	USC	14-16
November	28	L	Army	0-12
			(6-2-1)	215-40

1932

Coach: Heartley (Hunk) Anderson **Captain**: Paul Host

October	8	W	Haskell	73-0
October	15	W	Drake	62-0
October	22	W	Carnegie Tech	42-0
October	29	L	Pittsburgh	0-12
November	5	W	Kansas	24-6
November	12	W	Northwestern	21-0
November	19	W	Navy	12-0
November	26	W	Army	21-0
December	10	L	USC	0-13
			(7-2-0)	255-31

1933

Coach: Heartley (Hunk) Anderson **Co-Captains**: Hugh Devore and Tom Gorman

October	7	T	Kansas	0-0
October	14	W	Indiana	12-2
October	21	L	Carnegie Tech	0-7
October	28	L	Pittsburgh	0-14
November	4	L	Navy	0-7
November	11	L	Purdue	0-19
November	18	W	Northwestern	7-0
November	25	L	USC	0-19
December	2	W	Army	13-12
			(3-5-1)	32-80

Left: *Halfback Marchy Schwartz in 1929.*

1934

Coach: Elmer Layden **Captain**: Dom Vairo

Month	Day	Result	Opponent	Score
October	5	L	Texas	66-7
October	13	W	Purdue	18-7
October	20	W	Carnegie Tech	13-0
October	27	W	Wisconsin	19-0
November	3	L	Pittsburgh	0-19
November	10	L	Navy	6-10
November	17	W	Northwestern	20-7
November	24	W	Army	12-6
December	8	W	USC	14-0
			(6-3-0)	108-56

1935

Coach: Elmer Layden **Captain**: Joe Sullivan

Month	Day	Result	Opponent	Score
September	28	W	Kansas	28-7
October	5	W	Carnegie Tech	14-3
October	12	W	Wisconsin	27-0
October	19	W	Pittsburgh	9-6
October	26	W	Navy	14-0
November	2	W	Ohio State	18-13
November	9	L	Northwestern	7-14
November	16	T	Army	6-6
November	23	W	USC	20-13
			(7-1-1)	143-62

1936

Coach: Elmer Layden **Captain**: Bill Smith – John Lautar

Month	Day	Result	Opponent	Score
October	3	W	Carnegie Tech	21-7
October	10	W	Washington (St. Louis)	14-6
October	17	W	Wisconsin	27-0
October	24	L	Pittsburgh	0-26
October	31	W	Ohio State	7-2
November	7	L	Navy	0-3
November	14	W	Army	20-6
November	21	W	Northwestern	26-6
December	5	T	USC	13-13
			(6-2-1)	128-69

1937

Coach: Elmer Layden **Captain**: Joe Zwers

Month	Day	Result	Opponent	Score
October	2	W	Drake	21-0
October	9	T	Illinois	0-0
October	16	L	Carnegie Tech	7-9
October	23	W	Navy	9-7
October	30	W	Minnesota	7-6
November	6	L	Pittsburgh	6-21
November	13	W	Army	7-0
November	20	W	Northwestern	7-0
November	27	W	USC	13-6
			(6-2-1)	77-49

1938

Coach: Elmer Layden **Captain**: Jim McGoldrick

Month	Day	Result	Opponent	Score
October	1	W	Kansas	52-0
October	8	W	Georgia Tech	14-6
October	15	W	Illinois	14-6
October	22	W	Carnegie Tech	7-0
October	29	W	Army	19-7
November	5	W	Navy	15-0
November	12	W	Minnesota	19-0
November	15	W	Northwestern	9-7
December	3	L	USC	0-13
			(8-1-0)	149-39

Right: *Tackle Ziggy Czarobski in 1946.*

1939

Coach: Elmer Layden **Captain**: Johnny Kelly

Month	Day	Result	Opponent	Score
September	30	W	Purdue	3-0
October	7	W	Georgia Tech	17-14
October	14	W	SMU	20-19
October	21	W	Navy	14-7
October	28	W	Carnegie Tech	7-6
November	4	W	Army	14-0
November	11	L	Iowa	6-7
November	18	W	Northwestern	7-0
November	25	L	USC	12-20
			(7-2-0)	100-73

1940

Coach: Elmer Layden **Captain**: Milt Piepul

Month	Day	Result	Opponent	Score
October	5	W	Col. of Pacific	25-7
October	12	W	Georgia Tech	26-20
October	19	W	Carnegie Tech	61-0
October	26	W	Illinois	26-0
November	2	W	Army	7-0
November	9	W	Navy	13-7
November	16	L	Iowa	0-7
November	23	L	Northwestern	0-20
December	7	W	USC	10-6
			(7-2-0)	168-67

1941

Coach: Frank Leahy **Captain**: Paul Lillis

Month	Day	Result	Opponent	Score
September	27	W	Arizona	38-7
October	4	W	Indiana	19-6
October	11	W	Georgia Tech	20-0
October	18	W	Carnegie Tech	16-0
October	25	W	Illinois	49-14
November	1	T	Army	0-0
November	8	W	Navy	20-13
November	15	T	Northwestern	7-6
November	22	W	USC	20-18
			(8-0-1)	189-64

1942

Coach: Frank Leahy **Captain**: George Murphy

Month	Day	Result	Opponent	Score
September	26	T	Wisconsin	7-7
October	3	L	Georgia Tech	6-13
October	10	W	Stanford	27-0
October	17	W	Iowa Pre-Flight	28-0
October	24	W	Illinois	21-14
October	31	W	Navy	9-0
November	7	W	Army	13-0
November	14	L	Michigan	20-32
November	21	W	Northwestern	27-20
November	28	W	USC	13-0
December	5	T	Great Lakes	13-13
		(7-2-2)		184-99

Right: *Emil Sitko.*

Opposite: *Frank Leahy.*

1943

Coach: Frank Leahy **Captain**: Pat Filley

Month	Day	Result	Opponent	Score
September	25	W	Pittsburgh	41-0
October	2	W	Georgia Tech	55-13
October	9	W	Michigan	35-12
October	16	W	Wisconsin	50-0
October	23	W	Illinois	47-0
October	30	W	Navy	33-6
November	6	W	Army	26-0
November	13	W	Northwestern	25-6
November	20	W	Iowa Pre-flight	14-13
November	27	L	Great Lakes	14-19
		(9-1-0)		340-69

1944

Coach: Ed McKeever **Captain**: Pat Filley

Month	Day	Result	Opponent	Score
September	30	W	Pittsburgh	58-0
October	7	W	Tulane	26-0
October	14	W	Dartmouth	64-0
October	21	W	Wisconsin	28-13
October	28	W	Illinois	13-7
October	4	L	Navy	13-32
November	11	L	Army	0-59
November	18	W	Northwestern	21-0
November	25	W	Georgia Tech	21-0
December	2	W	Great Lakes	28-7
		(8-2-0)		272-118

1945

Coach: Hugh Devore **Captain**: Frank Dancewicz

Month	Day	Result	Opponent	Score
September	29	W	Illinois	7-0
October	6	W	Georgia Tech	40-7
October	13	W	Dartmouth	34-0
October	20	W	Pittsburgh	39-9
October	27	W	Iowa	56-0
November	3	T	Navy	6-6
November	10	L	Army	0-48
November	17	W	Northwestern	34-7
November	24	W	Tulane	32-6
December	1	L	Great Lakes	7-39
		(7-2-1)		255-122

1946

Coach: Frank Leahy **Captain**: Game Captains

Month	Day	Result	Opponent	Score
September	28	W	Illinois	26-6
October	5	W	Pittsburgh	33-0
October	12	W	Purdue	49-6
October	26	W	Iowa	41-6
November	2	W	Navy	28-0
November	9	T	Army	0-0
November	16	W	Northwestern	27-0
November	23	W	Tulane	41-0
November	30	W	USC	26-6
		(8-0-1)		271-24

1947

Coach: Frank Leahy **Captain**: George Connor

Month	Day	Result	Opponent	Score
October	4	W	Pittsburgh	40-6
October	11	W	Purdue	22-7
October	18	W	Nebraska	31-0
October	25	W	Iowa	21-0
November	1	W	Navy	27-0
November	8	W	Army	27-7
November	15	W	Northwestern	26-19
November	22	W	Tulane	59-6
December	6	W	USC	38-7
		(9-0-0)		291-52

1948

Coach: Frank Leahy **Captain**: Bill Fischer

Month	Day	Result	Opponent	Score
September	25	W	Purdue	28-27
October	2	W	Pittsburgh	40-0
October	9	W	Michigan State	26-7
October	16	W	Nebraska	44-13
October	23	W	Iowa	27-12
October	30	W	Navy	41-7
November	6	W	Indiana	42-6
November	13	W	Northwestern	12-7
November	27	W	Washington	46-0
December	4	T	USC	14-14
		(9-0-1)		320-93

1949

Coach: Frank Leahy **Co-Captains**: Leon Hart and Jim Martin

Month	Day	Result	Opponent	Score
September	24	W	Indiana	49-6
October	1	W	Washington	27-7
October	8	W	Purdue	35-12
October	15	W	Tulane	46-7
October	29	W	Navy	40-0
November	5	W	Michigan State	34-21
November	12	W	North Carolina	42-6
November	19	W	Iowa	28-7
November	26	W	USC	32-0
December	3	W	SMU	27-20
		(10-0-0)		360-86

1950

Coach: Frank Leahy **Captain**: Jerry Groom

September	30	W	No. Carolina	14-7
October	7	L	Purdue	14-28
October	14	W	Tulane	13-9
October	21	L	Indiana	7-20
October	28	L	Michigan State	33-36
November	4	W	Navy	19-10
November	11	W	Pittsburgh	18-7
November	18	T	Iowa	14-14
December	2	L	USC	7-9
			(4-4-1)	139-140

1951

Coach: Frank Leahy **Captain**: Jim Mutscheller

September	29	W	Indiana	48-6
October	5	W	Detroit	40-6
October	13	L	SMU	20-27
October	20	W	Pittsburgh	33-0
October	27	W	Purdue	30-9
November	3	W	Navy	19-0
November	10	L	Michigan State	0-35
November	17	W	North Carolina	12-7
November	24	T	Iowa	20-20
December	1	W	USC	19-12
			(7-2-1)	241-122

1952

Coach: Frank Leahy **Captain**: Jack Alessandrini

September	27	T	Pennsylvania	7-7
October	4	W	Texas	14-3
October	11	L	Pittsburgh	19-22
October	18	W	Purdue	26-14
October	25	W	North Carolina	34-14
November	1	W	Navy	17-6
November	8	W	Oklahoma	27-21
November	15	L	Michigan State	3-21
November	22	W	Iowa	27-0
November	29	W	USC	9-0
			(7-2-1)	183-108

1953

Coach: Frank Leahy **Captain**: Don Penza

September	26	W	Oklahoma	28-21
October	3	W	Purdue	37-7
October	17	W	Pittsburgh	23-14
October	24	W	Georgia Tech	27-14
October	31	W	Navy	38-7
November	7	W	Pennsylvania	28-20
November	14	W	North Carolina	34-14
November	21	T	Iowa	14-14
November	28	W	USC	48-14
December	5	W	SMU	40-14
			(9-0-1)	317-139

1954

Coach: Terry Brennan **Co-Captains**: Paul Matz and Dan Shannon

September	25	W	Texas	21-0
October	2	L	Purdue	14-27
October	9	W	Pittsburgh	33-0
October	16	W	Michigan State	20-19
October	30	W	Navy	6-0
November	6	W	Pennsylvania	42-7
November	13	W	North Carolina	42-13
November	20	W	Iowa	34-18
November	27	W	USC	23-17
December	4	W	SMU	26-14
			(9-1-0)	261-115

1955

Coach: Terry Brennan **Captain**: Ray Lemek

September	24	W	SMU	17-0
October	1	W	Indiana	19-0
October	7	W	Miami (Fla.)	14-0
October	15	L	Michigan State	7-21
October	22	W	Purdue	22-7
October	29	W	Navy	21-7
November	5	W	Pennsylvania	46-14
November	12	W	North Carolina	27-7
November	19	W	Iowa	17-14
November	26	L	USC	20-42
			(8-2-0)	210-112

1956

Coach: Terry Brennan **Captain**: Jim Morse

September	22	L	SMU	13-19
October	6	W	Indiana	20-6
October	13	L	Purdue	14-28
October	20	L	Michigan State	14-47
October	27	L	Oklahoma	0-40
November	3	L	Navy	7-33
November	10	L	Pittsburgh	13-26
November	17	W	No. Carolina	21-14
November	24	L	Iowa	8-48
December	1	L	USC	20-28
			(2-8-0)	130-289

Above: *Terry Hanratty (5).* Opposite: *Ara Parseghian (left).*

1957

Coach: Terry Brennan **Captain**: Dick Prendergast and Ed Sullivan

September	28	W	Purdue	12-0
October	5	W	Indiana	26-0
October	12	W	Army	23-21
October	26	W	Pittsburgh	13-7
November	2	L	Navy	6-20
November	9	L	Michigan State	6-34
November	16	W	Oklahoma	7-0
November	23	L	Iowa	13-21
November	30	W	USC	40-12
December	7	W	SMU	54-21
			(7-3-0)	200-136

1958

Coach: Terry Brennan **Co-Captains**: Al Ecuyer and Churck Puntillo

September	27	W	Indiana	18-0
October	4	W	SMU	14-6
October	11	L	Army	2-14
October	18	W	Duke	9-7
October	25	L	Purdue	22-29
November	1	W	Navy	40-20
November	8	L	Pittsburgh	26-29
November	15	W	North Carolina	34-24
November	22	L	Iowa	21-31
November	29	W	USC	20-13
			(6-4-0)	206-173

1959

Coach: Joe Kuharich **Captain**: Ken Adamson

September	26	W	North Carolina	28-8
October	3	L	Purdue	7-28
October	10	W	California	28-6
October	17	L	Michigan State	0-19
October	24	L	Northwestern	24-30
October	31	W	Navy	25-22
November	7	L	Georgia Tech	10-14
November	14	L	Pittsburgh	13-28
November	21	W	Iowa	20-19
November	28	W	USC	16-6
			(5-5-0)	171-180

1960

Coach: Joe Kuharich **Captain**: Myron Pottios

September	24	W	California	21-7
October	1	L	Purdue	19-51
October	8	L	North Carolina	7-12
October	15	L	Michigan State	0-21
October	22	L	Northwestern	6-7
October	29	L	Navy	7-14
November	5	L	Pittsburgh	13-20
November	12	L	Miami (Fla.)	21-28
November	19	L	Iowa	0-28
November	26	W	USC	17-0
			(2-8-0)	111-188

1961

Coach: Joe Kuharich **Co-Captains**: Norb Roy and Nick Buoniconti

September	30	W	Oklahoma	19-6
October	7	W	Purdue	22-20
October	14	W	USC	30-0
October	21	L	Michigan State	7-17
October	28	L	Northwestern	10-12
November	4	L	Navy	10-13
November	11	W	Pittsburgh	26-20
November	18	W	Syracuse	17-15
November	25	L	Iowa	21-42
December	2	L	Duke	13-37
			(5-5-0)	175-182

1962

Coach: Joe Kuharich **Captain**: Mike Lind

September	29	W	Oklahoma	13-7
October	6	L	Purdue	6-24
October	13	L	Wisconsin	8-17
October	20	L	Michigan State	7-31
October	27	L	Northwestern	6-35
November	3	W	Navy	20-12
November	10	W	Pittsburgh	43-22
November	17	W	North Carolina	21-7
November	24	W	Iowa	35-12
December	1	L	USC	0-25
			(5-5-0)	159-192

1963

Coach: Hugh Devore **Captain**: Bob Lehmann

September	28	L	Wisconsin	9-14
October	5	L	Purdue	6-7
October	12	W	USC	17-14
October	19	W	UCLA	27-12
October	26	L	Stanford	14-24
November	2	L	Navy	14-35
November	9	L	Pittsburgh	7-27
November	16	L	Michigan State	7-12
November	23		Iowa*	
November	28	L	Syracuse	7-14
			(2-7-0)	108-159

*Game cancelled because of the assassination of President Kennedy

1964

Coach: Ara Parseghian **Captain**: Jim Carroll

September	26	W	Wisconsin	31-7
October	3	W	Purdue	34-15
October	10	W	Air Force	34-7
October	17	W	UCLA	24-0
October	24	W	Stanford	28-6
October	31	W	Navy	40-0
November	7	W	Pittsburgh	17-15
November	14	W	Michigan State	34-7
November	21	W	Iowa	28-0
November	28	L	USC	17-20
			(9-1-0)	287-77

1965

Coach: Ara Parseghian **Captain**: Phil Sheridan

September	18	W	California	48-6
September	25	L	Purdue	21-25
October	2	W	Northwestern	38-7
October	9	W	Army	17-0
October	23	W	USC	28-7
October	30	W	Navy	29-3
November	6	W	Pittsburgh	69-13
November	13	W	North Carolina	17-0
November	20	L	Michigan State	3-12
November	27	T	Miami (Fla.)	0-0
			(7-2-1)	270-73

1966

Coach: Ara Parseghian **Captain**: Jim Lynch

September	24	W	Purdue	26-14
October	1	W	Northwestern	35-7
October	8	W	Army	35-0
October	15	W	North Carolina	32-0
October	22	W	Oklahoma	38-0
October	29	W	Navy	31-7
November	5	W	Pittsburgh	40-0
November	12	W	Duke	64-0
November	19	T	Michigan State	10-10
November	26	W	USC	51-0
			(9-0-1)	362-38

1967

Coach: Ara Parseghian **Captain**: Bob (Rocky) Bleier

September	23	W	California	41-8
September	30	L	Purdue	21-28
October	7	W	Iowa	56-6
October	14	L	USC	7-24
October	21	W	Illinois	47-7
October	28	W	Michigan State	24-12
November	4	W	Navy	43-14
November	11	W	Pittsburgh	38-0
November	18	W	Georgia Tech	36-3
November	24	W	Miami (Fla.)	24-22
			(8-2-0)	337-124

1968

Coach: Ara Parseghian **Co-Captains**: George Kunz and Bob Olson

September	21	W	Oklahoma	45-21
September	28	L	Purdue	22-37
October	5	W	Iowa	51-28
October	12	W	Northwestern	27-7
October	19	W	Illinois	58-8
October	26	L	Michigan State	17-21
November	2	W	Mavy	45-14
November	9	W	Pittsburgh	56-7
November	16	W	Georgia Tech	34-6
November	30	T	USC	21-21
			(7-2-1)	376-170

1969

Coach: Ara Parseghian **Co-Captains**: Bob Olson and Mike Oriard

Month	Day	Result	Opponent	Score
September	20	W	Northwestern	35-10
September	27	L	Purdue	14-28
October	4	W	Michigan State	42-28
October	14	W	Army	45-0
October	18	T	USC	14-14
October	25	W	Tulane	37-0
November	1	W	Navy	47-0
November	8	W	Pittsburgh	49-7
November	15	W	Georgia Tech	38-20
November	22	W	Air Force	13-6
			(8-1-1)	334-113
			COTTON BOWL	
January	1	L	Texas	17-21

1970

Coach: Ara Parseghian **Co-Captains**: Larry DiNardo and Tim Kelly

Month	Day	Result	Opponent	Score
September	19	W	Northwestern	35-14
September	26	W	Purdue	48-0
October	3	W	Michigan State	29-0
October	10	W	Army	51-10
October	17	W	Missouri	24-7
October	31	W	Navy	56-7
November	7	W	Pittsburgh	46-14
November	14	W	Georgia Tech	10-7
November	21	W	Louisiana State	3-0
November	28	L	USC	28-38
			(9-1-0)	330-97
			COTTON BOWL	
January	1	W	Texas	24-11

1971

Coach: Ara Parseghian **Co-Captains**: Walt Patulski and Tom Gatewood

Month	Day	Result	Opponent	Score
September	18	W	Northwestern	50-7
September	25	W	Purdue	8-7
October	2	W	Michigan State	14-2
October	9	W	Miami (Fla.)	17-0
Octgober	16	W	North Carolina	16-0
October	23	L	USC	14-28
October	30	W	Navy	21-0
November	6	W	Pittsburgh	56-7
November	13	W	Tulane	21-7
November	20	L	Louisiana State	8-28
			(8-2-0)	225-86

1972

Coach: Ara Parseghian **Co-Captains**: John Dampeer and Greg Marx

Month	Day	Result	Opponent	Score
September	23	W	Northwestern	37-0
September	30	W	Purdue	35-14
October	7	W	Michigan State	16-0
October	14	W	Pittsburgh	42-16
October	21	L	Missouri	26-30
October	28	W	TCU	21-0
November	4	W	Navy	42-23
November	11	W	Air Force	21-7
November	18	W	Miami (Fla.)	20-17
December	2	L	USC	23-45
			(8-2-0)	283-152
			ORANGE BOWL	
January	1	L	Nebraska	6-40

1973

Coach: Ara Parseghian **Tri-Captains**: Dave Casper, Frank Pomarico and Mike Townsend

Month	Day	Result	Opponent	Score
September	22	W	Northwestern	44-0
September	29	W	Purdue	20-7
October	6	W	Michigan State	14-10
October	13	W	Rice	28-0
October	20	W	Army	62-3
October	27	W	USC	23-14
November	3	W	Navy	44-7
November	10	W	Pittsburgh	31-10
November	22	W	Air Force	48-15
December	1	W	Miami (Fla.)	44-0
			(10-0-0)	358-66
			SUGAR BOWL	
December	31	W	Alabama	24-23

1974

Coach: Ara Parseghian **Co-Captains**: Tom Clements and Greg Collins

Month	Day	Result	Opponent	Score
September	9	W	Georgia Tech	31-7
September	21	W	Northwestern	49-3
September	28	L	Purdue	20-31
October	5	W	Michigan State	19-14
October	12	W	Rice	10-3
October	19	W	Army	48-0
October	26	W	Miami	38-7
November	2	W	Navy	14-6
November	16	W	Pittsburgh	14-10
November	23	W	Air Force	38-0
November	30	L	USC	24-55
			(9-2-0)	305-136
			ORANGE BOWL	
January	1	W	Alabama	13-11

Left: *Joe Theismann.*

Opposite: *Tom Gatewood.*

1975

Coach: Dan Devine **Captain**: Ed Bauer and Jim Stock

September	15	W	Boston College	17-3
September	20	W	Purdue	17-0
September	27	W	Northwestern	31-7
October	4	L	Michigan State	3-10
October	11	W	North Carolina	21-14
October	18	W	Air Force	31-30
October	25	L	USC	17-24
November	1	W	Navy	31-10
November	8	W	Georgia Tech	24-3
November	15	L	Pittsburgh	20-34
November	22	W	Miami (Fla.)	32-9
			(8-3-0)	244-144

1976

Coach: Dan Devine **Co-Captains**: Mark McLane and Willie Fry

September	11	L	Pittsburgh	10-31
September	18	W	Purdue	23-0
September	25	W	Northwestern	48-0
October	2	W	Michigan State	24-6
October	16	W	Oregon	41-0
October	23	W	South Carolina	13-6
October	30	W	Navy	27-21
November	6	L	Georgia Tech	14-23
November	13	W	Alabama	21-18
November	20	W	Miami (Fla.)	40-27
November	27	L	USC	13-17
			(8-3-0)	274-149
			GATOR BOWL	
December	27	W	Penn State	20-9

1977

Coach: Dan Devine **Tri-Captains**: Ross Browner, Terry Eurick and Willie Fry

September	10	W	Pittsburgh	19-9
September	17	L	Mississippi	13-20
September	24	W	Purdue	31-24
October	1	W	Michigan State	16-6
October	15	W	Army	24-0
October	22	W	USC	49-19
October	29	W	Navy	43-10
November	5	W	Georgia Tech	69-14
November	12	W	Clemson	21-17
November	19	W	Air Force	49-0
December	3	W	Miami (Fla.)	48-10
			(10-1-0)	382-129
			COTTON BOWL	
January	2	W	Texas	38-10

1978

Coach: Dan Devine **Tri-Captains**: Bob Golic, Jerome Heavens and Joe Montana

September	9	L	Missouri	0-3
September	23	L	Michigan	14-28
September	30	W	Purdue	10-6
October	7	W	Michigan State	29-25
October	14	W	Pittsburgh	26-17
October	21	W	Air Force	38-15
October	28	W	Miami (Fla.)	20-0
November	4	W	Navy	27-7
November	11	W	Tennessee	31-14
November	18	W	Georgia Tech	38-21
November	25	L	USC	25-27
			(8-3-0)	258-163
			COTTON BOWL	
January	1	W	Houston	35-34

1979

Coach: Dan Devine **Tri-Captains**: Vagas Ferguson, Tim Foley and Dave Waymer

September	15	W	Michigan	12-10
September	22	L	Purdue	22-28
September	29	W	Michigan State	27-3
October	6	W	Georgia Tech	21-13
October	13	W	Air Force	38-13
October	20	L	USC	23-42
October	27	W	South Carolina	18-17
November	3	W	Navy	14-0
November	10	L	Tennessee	18-40
November	17	L	Clemson	10-16
November	24	W	Miami (Fla.)	40-15
			(7-4-0)	243-197

1980

Coach: Dan Devine **Tri-Captains**: Bob Golic, Tom gibbons and John Scully

September	6	W	Purdue	31-10
September	20	W	Michigan	29-27
October	4	W	Michigan State	26-21
October	11	W	Miami	32-14
October	18	W	Army	30-3
October	25	W	Arizona	20-3
November	1	W	Navy	33-0
November	8	T	Georgia Tech	3-3
November	15	W	Alabama	7-0
November	22	W	Air Force	24-10
December	6	L	USC	3-20
			(9-1-1)	238-111
			SUGAR BOWL	
January	1	L	Georgia	10-17

1981

Coach: Gerry Faust **Co-Captains**: Bob Crable and Phil Carter

Month	Day	Result	Opponent	Score
September	12	W	LSU	27-9
September	19	L	Michigan	7-25
September	26	L	Purdue	14-15
October	3	W	Michigan State	20-7
October	10	L	Florida State	13-19
October	24	L	USC	7-14
October	31	W	Navy	38-0
November	7	W	Georgia Tech	35-3
November	14	W	Air Force	35-7
November	21	L	Penn State	21-24
November	27	L	Miami	15-37
			(5-6-0)	232-160

1982

Coach: Gerry Faust **Co-Captains**: Phil Carter, Dave Duerson and Mark Zavagnin

Month	Day	Result	Opponent	Score
September	18	W	Michigan	23-17
September	25	W	Purdue	28-14
October	2	W	Michigan State	11-3
October	9	W	Miami	16-14
October	16	L	Arizona	13-16
October	26	T	Oregon	13-13
October	30	W	Navy	27-10
November	5	W	Pittsburgh	31-16
November	13	L	Penn State	14-24
November	20	L	Air Force	17-30
November	27	L	USC	13-17
			(6-4-1)	206-174

1983

Coach: Gerry Faust **Co-Captains**: Blair Kiel and Stacey Toran

Month	Day	Result	Opponent	Score
September	10	W	Purdue	52-6
September	17	L	Michigan State	23-28
September	24	L	Miami	0-20
October	1	W	Colorado	27-3
October	8	W	South Carolina	30-6
October	15	W	Army	42-0
October	22	W	USC	27-6
October	29	W	Navy	28-12
November	5	L	Pittsburgh	16-21
November	12	L	Penn State	30-34
November	19	L	Air Force	22-23
			(6-5-0)	297-159
			LIBERTY BOWL	
December	29	W	Boston College	19-18

1984

Coach: Gerry Faust **Co-Captains**: Mike Golic, Joe Johnson and Larry Williams

Month	Day	Result	Opponent	Score
September	8	L	Purdue	21-23
September	15	W	Michigan State	24-20
September	22	W	Colorado	55-14
September	29	W	Missouri	16-14
October	6	L	Miami	13-31
October	13	L	Air Force	7-21
October	20	L	South Carolina	32-36
October	27	W	LSU	30-22
November	3	W	Navy	18-17
November	17	W	Penn State	44-7
November	24	W	USC	19-7
			(7-4-0)	279-212
			ALOHA BOWL	
December	29	L	SMU	20-27

1985

Coach: Gerry Faust **Captain**: Tony Furjanic, Mike Larkin, Allen Pinkett, Tim Scannell

Month	Day	Result	Opponent	Score
September	14	L	Michigan	12-20
September	21	W	Michigan State	27-10
September	28	L	Purdue	17-35
October	5	L	Air Force	15-21
October	19	W	Army	24-10
October	26	W	USC	37-3
November	2	W	Navy	41-17
November	9	W	Mississippi	37-14
November	16	L	Penn State	6-36
November	23	L	LSU	7-10
November	30	L	Miami	7-58
			(5-6-0)	230-234

1986

Coach: Lou Holtz **Captain**: Mike Kovaleski

Month	Day	Result	Opponent	Score
September	13	L	Michigan	23-24
September	20	L	Michigan State	15-20
September	27	W	Purdue	41-9
October	4	L	Alabama	10-28
October	11	L	Pittsburgh	9-10
October	18	W	Air Force	31-3
November	1	W	Navy	33-14
November	8	W	SMU	61-29
November	15	L	Penn State	19-24
November	22	L	LSU	19-21
November	29	W	USC	38-37
			(5-6-0)	299-129

1987

Coach: Lou Holtz **Co-Captains**: Chuck Lanza, Byron Spruell

Month	Day	Result	Opponent	Score
September	12	W	Michigan	26-7
September	19	W	Michigan State	31-8
September	26	W	Purdue	44-20
October	10	L	Pittsburgh	22-30
October	17	W	Air Force	35-14
October	24	W	USC	26-15
October	31	W	Navy	56-13
November	7	W	Boston College	32-25
November	14	W	Alabama	37-6
November	21	L	Penn State	20-21
November	28	L	Miami	0-24
			(8-3-0)	329-183
			COTTON BOWL	
January	1	L	Texas A&M	10-35

Left: *Tim Brown (81).*

Page numbers in *italics* refer to illustrations; *n* indicates text in caption

Picture Credits

The Bettmann Archive, Inc.: pages 18, 19(bottom), 30, 36, 37(bottom), 52(bottom), 55(top two), 56(below), 62(bottom), 64(top), 70(bottom left), 71(center), 74, 74-5, 79(bottom).
Bison Picture Library: pages 12, 47, 48, 106(top), 112, 124(top), 149(left), 158(bottom right).
Chance Brockway: page 157(both).
Malcolm W. Emmons: pages 1, 2-3, 10(bottom), 14(all three), 15(all three), 118-19, 127, 128(bottom), 129(both), 130(top left), 132, 133(both), 135(bottom), 136(both), 137, 138(both), 139(top), 140, 141(both), 145, 146-7, 148(bottom), 149(right), 150(bottom), 151, 152(both), 152-3, 153, 154(both), 155(both), 156, 158(top & bottom left), 159, 162, 163(both), 164, 165, 166, 167(both), 168-9, 170, 171(both), 172-3, 173, 175, 176, 177, 189, 190.
Indiana Historical Society: page 7.
University of Iowa Photo Service: page 53(top).
Kevin Knepp Studio, Inc.: pages 11, 144(bottom).
Library of Congress: page 28.
Bill Mesler Collection: page 6.
University of Michigan Sports Information Dept.: pages 160-1.
National Baseball Library, Cooperstown, NY: pages 27, 29.
The National Football Foundation and Hall of Fame: pages 46(right), 50-1, 55(bottom), 178.
New York Public Library Picture Collection: page 19(top), 21.
Northern Indiana Historical Society: page 52(top).
University of Notre Dame Archives: pages 8(both), 16-17, 20, 22, 23, 24-5, 26(right), 31(both), 34-5, 35(both), 36, 37(both), 39(top), 40(both), 41, 44, 45(top left & bottom), 179.
Ohio State University Photo Archives: page 81(top).
Pro-Football Hall of Fame: page 45(top right).
UPI/Bettmann Newsphotos: pages 4-5, 9, 10(top), 13(both), 20-1, 33, 34, 42, 43, 46(left), 53(bottom), 54(both), 56(top), 56-7, 58(top two), 59(both), 60-1, 62(top), 63(top), 64(bottom), 65(center & bottom), 66-7, 67, 68(both), 69, 70(top & bottom right), 71(top & bottom), 72-3, 75(both), 76(both), 77(both), 78, 79(top), 80(both), 81(bottom), 82(both), 83, 84-5, 86(both), 87(both), 88(both), 89(both), 90(both), 92-3, 94, 95(all three), 96, 97(both), 98, 99(both), 100, 101(both), 102, 102-03, 103, 104, 105(both), 106(bottom), 107(both), 108-09, 110, 111(both), 113(both), 114(both), 115(both), 116, 117(both), 120(all three), 121, 122(both), 123(all three), 124(bottom), 125(all three), 126, 126-7, 128(top), 130(top right & bottom), 131, 134(both), 135(top), 138(bottom), 139(bottom), 142, 142-3, 143, 144(top), 150(top), 174, 180, 181, 184, 185, 186, 187, 188.
Yale University: page 26(left).

Acknowledgments
The author and publisher would like to thank the following people who helped in the preparation of this book: John Kirk and Jean Chiaramonte Martin, who edited it; Mike Rose, who designed it; Donna Cornell Muntz, who did the picture research; and Florence Norton, who prepared the index.